THE LIGHTHOUSE FIRE

Donald F. Averill

ISBN
978-1-956161-52-6 (Paperback)
978-1-956161-49-6 (eBook)

Acknowledgments

Thanks to the following group of readers for their
assistance with the preparation of the manuscript:

Bob Griswold
Jill Nicklos
Barbara Schroeder
Efren Sifuentes

And to Mary Stebbins
for creating the cover artwork

Other books by the author include:

The Kuiper Belt Deception
The Niffits
An Iceberg's Gift
Glacier Fires
Wolves' Hollow Murders
Detour in Oregon
The Antarctic Deception
Missing Notes, Hidden Talents, and Other Stories
The Lighthouse Library
The Kidnapping of Megan Isaacs
A Professor's Affair
The Bitterroot Diamonds
The Bitterroot Fire

Contents

Chapter 1

FIRST DAY HOME

There was break in the music flowing from the Chevrolet Fleetline radio speaker. An update to the 2:00 p.m. weather forecast lasted about two minutes. My driver, Ensign Wardel, and I laughed when the weatherman gave his name, Storm Swells. The forecaster stated a slight breeze was coming off the Atlantic, the water fairly calm. I looked out the window. The almost entirely blue sky didn't even suggest the approach of stormy weather. That was quite a difference from the weather brewing in the Sea of Japan, west of Hokkaido, where I had been a few days earlier. The music resumed with a song by Eddie Fisher. Since I had been out of the states and without knowledge of the pop culture, I didn't know much about him. I had been watching periodically as the wispy white clouds drifted high above us for the last hour after napping during the first part of my trip from Boston, where I had expected to find my family.

At Boston Logan Airport, my commercial flight from Chicago was met by Ensign Floyd Wardel. In naval uniform, he was holding a sign above his head that read CDR Linfield. I was wearing navy-blue trousers, a white dress shirt, and a light-brown sports jacket. I told him who I was, he saluted me, and we shook hands. He led me to a navy car and I gave him directions to my home, but I was unaware my family had moved to Crafton, Maine, a small coastal town where my wife's mother, Martha Makler, lived.

When I read the note on the front door in Framingham, all that came to mind was damn! The plan to surprise my family would have to be delayed for a few more hours. Talk about disappointment! I returned to the car waiting at the curb. I leaned down to the open passenger side window and said, "Ensign, we need to go to Crafton, Maine."

"Sir, do you know where that is?"

"You'd better consult a map. I was only there once—several years ago. My memory of the roads is pretty hazy."

The ensign popped open the glove box and extracted a handful of maps. After he consulted the highway map of coastal Maine, we continued our trip.

I was glad to get away from the metropolis and was enjoying the open expanses separating small communities as we drove farther into the Northeast. When we arrived at the Crafton lighthouse near dinner time, I thanked the ensign and told him he could return to base, or proceed to his next assignment. He gave a snappy salute, said, "Aye, aye, Sir. Good luck, Commander," and slowly drove the service car to the highway, stopped, turned onto the main road and accelerated. I watched the tail lights disappear over the hill that overlooked the small harbor. I felt a bit naked, standing there alone, somewhat apprehensive about what was to come in the next few minutes.

I had gotten out of the car without assistance, as I had in Boston; my left leg still weak. It was healing slowly, and I favored it, being careful not to twist or use it for leverage. I had passed up the offer of a wheelchair or a cane at the military hospital in Alaska. I wanted complete independence, exactly the opposite of the condition I had been in for the last eighteen months. The compound fracture had been set by a Manchurian village doctor eight months earlier in a mountainous region not far from the northeastern Chinese border with the Soviet Union. The medical doctor had done the best he could under the circumstances. A poor diet and physical stress had slowed the healing process.

My presence in Manchuria was kept secret from authoritarian figures, especially the foreign military. An American pilot found in Northeastern China during the Korean conflict would have suffered severe punishment and probably death, as would an entire Chinese family; perhaps even a whole village. China was supporting North Korea during the Korean conflict, afraid the Allies might venture into China. If I had been caught, I would have had to endure torture and deprivation, if not immediate execution.

The Navy physicians said exercise and good food should guarantee full recovery, but I should be careful for a while. They advised me that I might retain a slight limp.

I turned slowly and looked at the medium-sized, reddish-brown, two-story building, the residence of the lighthouse keeper. Actually, the building wasn't two-stories, it was more like one and a half. It appeared to have an attic, but with more head room than usual. What I could see of the dark-green roof shingles looked as if they needed some minor repairs. If I hadn't known where I was, I would have guessed the Northeastern coast of the USA.

I could hear a radio or television, the sounds escaping through the screen door. I had that uneasy feeling, kind of like I had experienced when in grade school, having to stand in front of the class to give a book report or show-and-tell. But I knew what I was going to say to Sandra. I had been saying it over and over in my mind for a year and a half, ever since I crashed in Northeastern China just a few miles across the Yalu River from North Korea.

I had a brown leather bag in my left hand and a novel, *Knights of the Devil*, in my right. I had finished reading the book by the time I reached Chicago, but I couldn't just throw or give it away. It was my only possession, except for some clean skivvies, since arriving back in the states from Tokyo. The bag was much more than a satchel; it carried some toiletries, underwear, my navy blues, and a letter Sandra had written to the War Department a year ago asking of my whereabouts. Seeing her signature on that paper brought back memories of the times we had when dating. When separated, we used to send each other notes, telling what we had been doing and how nice it was going to be to see each other again.

Sandra was in the FBI then, and I, a naval lieutenant, was being shuttled around the country, not knowing where, if ever, I would have at least a semi-stable station. Now, retired, as Commander Leland S. Linfield, I was able to have a permanent location.

A loose gravel path led to a small covered porch, almost the same color as the roof, not much to navigate, only one step up and two paces, about five feet, to the screen door. I rang the bell, heard a buzzing sound, somewhat like the sound from an old telephone switchboard, and a freckled, redheaded young girl appeared. She had to be Susan, my daughter, but I hadn't seen Susan in eighteen months and little kids change very fast as they're growing up. She was nearly a foot taller than the last time I saw her. I think she expected me to say something; she probably thought I was a salesman. I was dressed in a white shirt and khakis. I had changed my pants in the car. She waited with one hand pulling on her ponytail and the other holding on to the door knob. She had a faint smile, her eyes dancing.

"Can I help you?"

"May I talk to your mother, young lady?" I heard a familiar voice, that of Sandra, my wife. There was no doubt about that sound.

"Who is it? Does he have a Bible?"

Susan turned from me and skipped down the hallway. I heard her innocent voice say that I had a book, but she couldn't tell if it was a Bible. That's when I realized Sandra was worried someone had come to tell her I was dead. She wasn't aware that when a death notice was delivered, two officers conveyed the bad news. I wanted to call out to her, but our reunion would be over in a few minutes anyway. I kept silent. I heard Sandra tell Susan that she would be coming to the door. I didn't even hear what Susan said to me when she reappeared, because when I saw Sandra walking toward me, tears came to my eyes, and I was almost choking on the words I planned to say. Those simple words seemed to be lodged tightly in my throat. Sandra didn't recognize me immediately; I had lost more than fifteen pounds and the somewhat shaggy beard concealed my face, but when she was within about two feet of the screen door, I croaked, "Hi, beautiful."

She was still drying her hands in her apron when she froze in position like a marble museum statue. She frowned, then smiled, and said, "Oh, my God! Lee!" She pushed the screen door open, almost knocking me backwards, exclaiming, "Kids, your daddy is home!" We hugged each other and looked into each other's eyes, tears streaming down our cheeks. We kissed as if it was to be our last. I wanted to pick Sandra up and twirl her around, but I was afraid my weak leg might give way. She buried her face in my chest and we clutched each other with as much force as our arms could exert.

I could hear and feel her sobbing as we stood together on the porch, her body throbbing, almost uncontrollably. My face was buried in her hair. She smelled so good, something I hadn't forgotten. I couldn't talk at first, but I finally was able to say, "It's all right, Sandy, I'm home. I missed you so much. I missed you all so much."

I heard Susan's little voice ask, "Is that man my daddy?" Still holding Sandra tightly, I wiped my eyes with my sleeve and looked down at my red-headed little girl. She seemed confused, she was biting her lower lip and frowning.

Sandra released her hold on me, turned slightly and gathered Susan to us. "Yes, Susan, this is your daddy. Give him a big hug and kiss."

I bent down and picked her up. She threw her arms around my neck, kissed my cheek, and said, "Did you get the message I sent to Heaven?"

That was the most confusing thing I had heard since I arrived stateside, but I answered the best I could. "I wasn't in Heaven, Susan, I was in Manchuria." I made a mental note to ask Sandra about Susan's question.

I became aware of my son, Rocky, standing just inside the screen. He was watching me intently, probably trying to think of what to do. I called to him, "Rocky, come give your dad a big hug." He came from the house, slowly. I think he was trying to see through my beard to recognize my features from the last time I saw him. He raised his right hand, as if to shake hands, but I pulled him close and squeezed him tightly. "You've grown a foot since I last saw you, Son. It won't be long and you'll be a man."

He was smiling, but I saw tears begin to trickle down his cheeks. He made no attempt to hide them. "Were you a prisoner, Dad?"

"Not really, I was hidden by a man on a little farm in Manchuria until we could travel to Russia."

"Were you shot?"

"No. I fell and broke my leg when travelling. It's still weak. I have to be careful for a while." I noticed Rocky looking into the house. "Is something wrong in there?"

"I think Mom has forgotten about the carrots on the stove."

`Rocky had picked up my book and satchel and dropped them on the seat of the tan corduroy-covered, overstuffed chair, turned so the occupant could see TV without neck strain.

Susan was standing at the end of the sofa watching me as I looked around the living room. She gradually approached, until she stood in front of me, her fingers interlaced waist high. "Can I sit beside you?"

"I'd like that. Get up here so we can talk." I patted the cushion and she climbed next to me, wiggled into place, and let out a big sigh.

"I don't remember you. I thought I knew what you looked like. Did you have a beard before?"

"Nope. I'll shave it off tomorrow. Maybe you'll remember what I look like after the beard is gone."

"Maybe. I thought you were bigger."

"Well, Susan, you were much smaller when you last saw me."

"Susan, please set another place at the table for your father." Sandra had called out from the kitchen. "Ask him what he wants to drink."

Before Susan had a chance to ask, I volunteered, "Water will be fine."

Susan turned her head slightly and yelled back toward the kitchen, "He said water will be fine."

"Thank-you." Sandra's voice had a lilt to it.

Susan replied, "You're welcome," and laughed. I didn't know why she laughed. I would have to find out later. As I began to think of all the little things I would have to do now that I was home. I had to slow down my brain and prioritize so I would not make mistakes, at least try to minimize them. I knew I would have to renew my driver's license. I hadn't driven in two years.

Something took me back to when I was Rocky's age. I remembered coming out of a movie theater with my parents and walking into a parking meter. Mom grabbed me and pulled me toward her, but I walked into the next one also. I just couldn't get my legs working properly. Manchuria was eleven time zones away, half a world from Crafton, Maine. My biorhythm was going to be out of whack for a few days. I leaned back into the sofa, but I was afraid I was going to fall asleep and miss having the first dinner with my family in nearly two years. I looked around the room to keep my eyes and mind active so not to drowse off.

Rocky was in that big chair, leaning forward, elbows on his knees and head in his hands. "Will you tell us some war stories, Dad?"

"Sure, but they aren't too exciting. I'll tell you all about getting shot down over North Korea and how I got back home. It's a long story, though, it might take a week or so. After I get adjusted to being home, I'll tell you all about it."

"Okay. Maybe you can tell Jerry, too."

"Who's Jerry?"

"He's my best friend. His father and mother lived in Russia. His dad was killed by Germans, but his mom remarried and now his name is Jerry Morgan. I've got lots to tell you—about spies and the FBI."

MY FIRST LIGHTHOUSE DINNER

Sitting at the dinner table with my family was not a new experience, but it felt new, different. I felt like I was eating at a friend's house, just having met his family. My Chinese friends in Manchuria knew little of what was going on in their own backyard, and I even knew less about Northeastern China than they did about the Northeastern United States. Fortunately, the man who found me, Zhang Lanfu, was educated; he was a doctor who had studied in Beijing. One of his uncles had taken classes at Oregon State, so he knew some English, at least enough for basic communication.

I was cutting into the steak Sandra had so carefully broiled when Rocky said, "Tell us how you were shot down, Dad." I looked at Sandra for her approval and she smiled. She must have realized I wouldn't go into any morbid details. I wasn't too sure of that myself after seeing some of the horrors of modern warfare. But I considered, if I spoke slowly and thought ahead, I wouldn't make the story too bloody.

"Well, I was flying a Corsair on a bombing run to knock out the railroad bridge connecting China to North Korea. The bridge, a little over half-a-mile long, spanned the Yalu river. We couldn't bomb the Chinese end, so we had to be careful and only drop our bombs on the Korean part, the southern half of the bridge. But we had some major problems, there were strong crosswinds and lots of enemy antiaircraft fire filling the sky."

Susan was holding her fork near her mouth with a bite of potatoes on it, listening to every word I said. She stuck the potatoes in her mouth and asked, "Who was with you in your airplane?" I could see the un-chewed potatoes as she talked.

"Susan, don't talk with your mouth full. Talk when you don't have food in your mouth."

Susan looked at Sandra and said, "Okay, Mommy."

I smiled and answered Susan's question. "Just me. I was alone."

She frowned and said, "But you said we had problems."

"Oh, yes. There were four planes attacking the bridge: Buzz Nelson, Drew Santee, Joey Bynum, and me. Buzz went first and I followed. Buzz's bomb hit the top of the bridge and a big chunk of it fell into the water. My bomb hit one of the support columns, but as I began pulling out of my dive, my engine coughed and sputtered. Black smoke came pouring out of the engine, oil was streaming back on the windscreen making it difficult to see, and then a bullet hit somewhere in the cockpit and I felt a sting, like a bee, on my cheek."

"Was it a bee, Daddy?" She had swallowed the potatoes.

I took a bite of steak, chewed for a minute, swallowed, and continued, "A piece of bullet hit me in the face and blood got in my eye—kind of like smearing blood from a nose bleed all over your face. When I shave, I'll show you the scar; it's not very big."

I noticed that nobody was eating, so I said, "I'll tell you more after dinner, okay?"

We finished dinner, the first home-cooked American meal I'd had in almost two years. The food, the family, and not having to worry about being caught by the enemy, made eating dinner one of the most enjoyable times I could remember. After desert, Neapolitan ice cream, the kids did some homework, and got ready for bed. Tomorrow was Thursday and they had to go to school. I helped Sandra with the dishes. She washed and I dried.

Sandra had many questions about my stay in Manchuria, but I gave her short, concise answers. We would talk in more detail later, when the whole family could hear what I had experienced. I didn't want to go over the details many more times, I had already spent two days being debriefed by a Navy officer at Elmendorf Air Force Base. I knew Rocky was going to have many questions.

It seemed like after every dinner plate I dried, we embraced and kissed. Sandra giggled when my beard tickled her. I wished that we had had company for dinner, there would have been more dinner plates. As we finished the dishes, Rocky showed up in his blue-and-white striped pajamas.

"What's a Corsair, Dad? I thought you flew a Sabre jet."

"Well, when I got transferred to Korea, I hadn't finished training with F-86s; those are Sabres. The UN forces wanted to bomb the bridge over the Yalu River, where troops and equipment were crossing from China to North Korea, so Corsair pilots were needed. When jets tried to bomb the bridge, they had to come in from the side and it was difficult to knock out the bridge. Corsairs were slower prop jobs, but could bomb from above. When we dove at the bridge, we had our wheels down to slow us so we had better accuracy, and could still pull out of our dive, but then the enemy fire could hit us easier. That's what happened to me. They hit my engine and I had to glide into Manchuria to avoid going down in North Korea. That's where I crashed."

"But you got the bridge, right?"

"You bet. My bomb knocked out a concrete support column. The Navy told me a day ago that twenty-four hours after I went down, the bridge fell into the water. Unfortunately, in a few days the river froze over and the enemy crossed over the ice. They didn't need the bridge."

"Maybe you can show me a picture of a Corsair, I'd like to see what one looks like."

I thought for a moment and said, "Is there a hobby shop in Crafton?"

Rocky thought for a minute and answered, "Umm. I don't think so, but Elena bought a box kite once. I don't know where she got it."

"Elena? Is she your girlfriend?"

I saw Rocky's eyes light up, but he said, "No. I don't have one. She's an FBI agent. She's Lt. Nesbitt's girlfriend. She looked after us when Granma went to Boston one day. She took us kite flying and Suz sent a message up the string."

That answered my question about Susan sending a message to heaven. Things are beginning to make sense. I think I will be learning a lot about my family in the next few weeks. I wonder who this Lt. Nesbitt is.

Sandra, who was listening as she cleaned up around the kitchen sink, suddenly reacted, "Oh! Marty doesn't know you're home. I have to call her."

I heard Sandra talking to the operator and then I was distracted. Susan came into the kitchen in pink PJs carrying a stuffed monkey toy. I asked, "Is he your sleeping buddy?"

She nodded and asked me, "Do you know we have a dog?"

"We do? I haven't seen a dog around here." I looked around the room.

Susan smiled and said, "That's because we pick up his poop. He's at Granma's." Rocky added to what Susan had told me, "Surprise stays at Granma's during the week when we're going to school. We have him on the weekends, holidays, and stuff like that." Rocky seemed to be studying my beard. I was thinking he was imagining what I would look like without it. Then he asked, "Why did you want to know if there's a hobby shop in Crafton?"

"I was thinking of buying a model plane to build—one made from balsa wood. I'd like to see if we can get one of a Corsair. We could build it together."

"That sounds neat. With a gas engine in it?"

"Rubber bands. I'll bet you know where there's a flat area without any trees."

I watched Rocky think for a few seconds and then he replied, enthusiastically, "Sure, the school playground. We'd have to avoid the swings, a slide, and a small merry-go-round, that's all. I don't think there's a hobby store like that though, just a dime store. Maybe Edgewater has one."

"Where's Edgewater, Rocky?"

"It's about twenty miles up the coast. It's bigger than Crafton. We'd have to drive there. I'll ask Jerry tomorrow at school if he knows if Edgewater has a hobby store. He's been there. Jerry's dad might know. We can ask Granma, too. She's lived around here for a coon's age."

I laughed at Rocky's use of that expression. He must have heard it from his grandmother, Sandra's mom. She taught Sandra so much as a child, Sandra could have skipped going to school, at least for a few years. When I first met Sandra, I knew getting to know her was going to be a challenge, but I had fallen for her the first time I laid eyes on her, and I have always been a bit stubborn. Back then I had no idea she was already working as an FBI agent, but after a couple of dates, she told me about her assignment in Groton, Connecticut. I was there briefly, reviewing security at the submarine base. It was 1940 and the US wasn't in the war yet.

Sandra came into the living room and said, "You two have to get in bed; tomorrow's a school day."

Susan's eyes twinkled and a big grin appeared. "Mom, that means you and I can stay up."

"Funny girl. You and Rocky are the ones that have to go to bed. Give your dad a kiss and get in bed. We'll come and say good night in a few minutes."

Rocky said, "Is Granma coming over?"

"Yes, but she's not bringing Surprise with her. You'll see him Friday night. Now, off to bed. Your dad and I will take you to school in the morning; you won't have to ride the bus."

"How come?"

"I want your father to see where you go to school, and I want to show him the pier and the downtown stores."

"Oh. Good night."

"Good night, Son. See you in the morning."

"Oh, Dad, is it all right to tell kids you're back home?"

"Sure. You can tell them I was in Manchuria, Northeast China." Rocky walked down the hall into his bedroom and shut the door.

Susan grabbed Sandra's hand and said, "Come on, Mom, you can tuck me in. Granma knows where we live."

As soon as Sandra and Susan had disappeared down the hallway, there was a rap on the screen door. I got up to let Mrs. Makler in, but she was already in the house, closing, and locking the door. She turned toward me and stared for a moment.

I said, "Hi, Marty," and then she rushed to give me a hug. "I wasn't sure that you really were the Leland Linfield that married my daughter. That beard threw me for a moment. Sandra didn't tell me you needed a shave, but when I heard your voice, I knew it was you." We hugged for a few seconds, I put my arm around her waist and escorted her to the sofa.

"It's good to see you, Marty. I'm going to shave off this bush in the morning. Hopefully the kids will respond better then. They were a little hesitant when I first arrived. My beard and I have disrupted their world."

"Why didn't you phone ahead? You should have let us know you were alive and coming home."

"I was going to call Sandra from Alaska, but the Navy kept me busy for several days with reports and interviews, and I was so tired, I slept twelve or more hours each day. Then, I figured I would call when I reached the lower forty-eight, but I couldn't seem to adjust to the time zone changes, so I decided to wait a while longer. When I got to Chicago, I tried to call, but the number was out-of-order, so I waited. When I arrived in Boston, I found out Sandy and the kids had moved to Crafton, so I had my driver bring me here."

"How did you find out Sandra and the kids were here at the lighthouse?"

"My driver stopped for gas and I asked the attendant if he knew the Linfield family. He thought for a moment and then told me Mrs. Linfield had taken over the lighthouse and the library. I like it here, and you live a short distance away. You and the kids can walk to each other's homes. That's a nice arrangement."

Sandra came into the living room wearing her nightgown, and said, "Hi, Mom. What do you think of Lee's new look?"

Martha gave a kind of grunting laugh. "Well, if you don't mind kissing between the shrubberies, I guess it's all right. I like my man clean shaven."

"Don't worry, ladies, I'll shave it off in the morning. I'm getting tired of it anyway. I'm tired of combing out the lice and mice." I laughed and rubbed my overgrown hairy face. "I think I've scared the kids enough." I looked at Sandra and inquired, "You don't mind sleeping with a bearded man, do you?"

Sandra hesitated, grinned, and said, "The last man I slept with was clean shaven. He looked a lot like you, Lee." She winked at her mom. We all laughed and Sandra continued, "I'm going to make a chocolate drink. Anyone want some?"

I yawned and replied, "I think I'd better drink some coffee."

I made some navy coffee and the ladies had hot chocolate. We snacked on Graham crackers and talked for about an hour before Marty excused herself and left for home. Before Marty had driven away, Sandra had locked the door and turned out the lights. Sandra led the way to the bedroom after placing my hands on her hips. She helped me undress in the dark, slipped out of her robe, and our bodies got happily reacquainted beneath the covers.

Chapter 3

EDGEWATER

I had asked Sandra to set the alarm for a half-hour earlier than her normal school day morning so I would have time to shave without the hubbub of the morning interfering. When the alarm went off, I silenced it in a fraction of a second and reset it for a half-hour later. I learned to react rapidly with split second notice of the presence of Chinese military forces. My biological clock was always ready for rapid response. If my host family was getting up at 5:00, I would be ready, without the aid of an alarm, at 4:55. I don't remember planning to get up at certain times, it just happened.

I swung my legs out of bed and placed my feet right beside my slippers. God, Sandra thinks of everything. I slipped into my furry house shoes and divested myself of shorts and T-shirt. My dresser drawers were just as I had left them, so I found clean skivvies without any problems. My clean clothing smelled like it had just been washed. I'll bet she washed everything and dried it outside on the clothesline when they moved into the lighthouse facilities. Sandra and the kids had only been here for about three weeks. It was the end of September and the first month of school had just been completed.

My shaving brush and soap were just as I had left them in the medicine cabinet above the bathroom sink in Boston. There was a pair of scissors on top of the toilet tank. I went for them first and started cutting my reddish moustache. It took about five minutes to get down to stubble I could remove with a safety razor. I soaped up and started cutting but I ran into difficulty close to my nose and under my earlobes. A little pulling and stretching of the skin worked to my advantage. Just as I finished, I heard Sandra's alarm clock sound off. I went over to the bed, sat down, and watched her preparing to get up.

When she looked at me, she looked startled, but then smiled and said, "I like you better this way. Did all that hair plug the toilet?"

"No, but the two mice almost did. I had to hold the lid down so they couldn't get out. I think they'll find their way back to China, but it's a long swim."

"I almost forgot how funny you can be. Are you done in there?" Smiling, she pointed at the bathroom.

"Yes, ma'am."

She tossed back the covers, grabbed an armful of clothes from the bedside chair, and disappeared into the bathroom. I finished dressing and went in the kitchen to start coffee. I didn't know what the kids would eat for breakfast, but I set the table with the half-full Wheaties and Cheerios boxes, two bowls and spoons, and a bottle of milk. The toaster was on the counter near the sink. I made the coffee, but I realized, after it was ready to pour, that it was probably too strong for Sandra. Navy coffee I had experienced was just short of being a solid. I'll have to wait and see if she turns up her nose after the first sip.

Rocky and Susan arrived at the table a few seconds before Sandra appeared in a brightly colored floral-print dress and white flats. I had expected the kids to be in school uniforms, but I quickly realized they weren't going to a military- or church-affiliated school. I guess I was too used to nearly everyone wearing uniforms. Rocky wore white corduroy pants and a red, green, and yellow plaid shirt. Susan had on a pleated light-green skirt and white blouse. We looked like a family going to church or perhaps a birthday party. Everything was so colorful in the states.

The kids looked at me like I was someone that had come by the lighthouse to service the beacon, but they soon adjusted to the appearance of my old features. The noise from the toast popping up, almost becoming airborne, startled me. The kids didn't even notice. I gave Rocky one piece and I buttered the other one for Susan.

"You look like what I remember, Daddy. Show me your scar." Susan was scanning my face.

"Okay, but you'll have to come closer, it's not a very big one." I leaned down so Susan could see my cheek clearly and I put my index finger below the mark of the old injury.

"You're right. It's not a big scar. I bet it hurt though."

"Uh-huh."

Rocky was buttering his toast and said, "I'm glad it's Friday."

I asked, "Because it's the last day of the week?"

"Well, 'cause we get to spend the whole weekend with you, like a regular family—with a mom and a dad."

Sandra looked at me. I wondered if that comment hurt her feelings in any way; as if she hadn't been a good parent while I was out of the picture. I thought I should say something in her defense.

"Rocky, don't you think your mom deserves some credit for being both a mom and a dad while I was away?"

"Oh! I didn't mean Mom didn't do a good job. She took care of us and did her FBI job, too. She was great! I just wanted a dad like most of the other kids. I think I was a little jealous. I know one thing though, Mom is the best looking mom in the whole school." He smiled at Sandra and she smiled back. That was all there was to understanding what Rocky was thinking about, so Sandra and I didn't raise that subject again. I don't think she was as concerned as I was.

"Do you guys want some cereal?" I asked. Sandra was frying some eggs and bacon so I dropped two more slices of bread in the toaster. Both kids said no to the cereal and were washing toast down with milk. As the eggs and bacon cooked, Sandra poured us some orange juice and asked if the kids had done their homework. Susan said she didn't have any and Rocky had done some arithmetic. He told us it was easy—it was about money. I had to smile.

The eggs and bacon disappeared rapidly, and as I watched Sandra take a sip of coffee, I was amazed that she didn't run to the sink and spit it out. Her only reaction was, "Next time, put in a pinch of salt; it won't be so bitter. It's about the same strength as I had every day at the FBI. I suspect that whoever made it was formerly a navy man." She smiled and we both had a good laugh. I confessed that I hadn't made coffee for some time; in Manchuria, everyone drank tea.

We didn't bother with the dishes, it was time to get the kids off to school. I felt like a house guest, depending on Sandra for most everything. It was cool outside and the kids wore jackets. I got my long coat from the hall closet and Sandra wore a sweater. I held the car door for her as she climbed behind the wheel. The kids had scrambled into the back seat and I got in the front passenger side.

As we pulled away from the lighthouse, Sandra exclaimed, "Oh, I should have put up a sign telling library patrons we might be late opening today."

I pondered what Sandra had said. I thought we were going to take the kids to school and return to the lighthouse. What did she have in mind? Maybe she's going to take me to get a driver's license. I guess I'll wait and see; she's doing the driving. We avoided a small school bus and took a position in the parking area in front of the school, an older, two-story, beige brick building, probably constructed in the 1930s. The previous times I had been in Crafton, I had never had reason to go near the elementary school. Two kids were raising the flag on the pole near the main entrance.

Rocky and Susan slid out of the back seat. Rocky slammed the door and said, "See you after school, Dad." Susan yelled as she started running, "See you at home, Mom." We watched to make sure they got in the building safely.

Sandra glanced at me and smiled. "We've got several hours of free time. Let's drive to Edgewater and see about a hobby shop. Okay?"

Sandra had overheard Rocky's and my conversation, and last night I had forgotten to ask Marty if she knew whether Edgewater had a hobby shop. Obviously, Sandra had also forgotten to ask. "Okay, let's go. I'll tell you what I've been thinking."

She started to put the car in reverse when Rocky suddenly appeared at my window. He was with another boy, a little bigger. I rolled down the window and asked, "Is something wrong, Rocky?"

"Dad, this is Jerry Morgan. He wants to meet you. I told him you got home from Manchuria yesterday."

I opened the door and stepped out beside Rocky. The boy moved toward me, extended his hand, and said, "It's nice to meet you, Mr.

Linfield. I can tell you're Rocky's dad, you have the same reddish-brown hair. You'll have to meet my dad. He was in World War II. I bet you'll have some stories to tell."

I shook hands with Jerry and replied, "Glad to meet you, Jerry. Rocky told me you're his best friend. I'd like to meet your father. We'll have to get together some day—maybe for one of the holidays coming up."

We all heard the school bell ring. Rocky pulled at Jerry's arm and said, "Come on, Jerry. We don't want to be late. See you after school, Mom, Dad."

I waved as the boys turned away from the car and ran toward the main entrance. I shouted, "Maybe Thanksgiving."

Sandra backed the car, giving plenty of room to pull forward around the car in front of us. "That's the principal's car," Sandra pointed out.

"I guess principals don't get paid that much." The car was a Ford sedan with a bent rear fender and some scratches in the paint on the driver's door.

When we reached the highway, Route 32, I started to tell Sandra what I had been thinking about for a job and our family's future. But, I didn't know what her financial situation was. How much did she make as lighthouse caretaker and librarian? Her wages for running the lighthouse probably came from the state, and I wasn't sure if she got anything for being in charge of the library. We discussed our finances for about fifteen minutes. We'd need a budget.

By the time we were on the outskirts of Edgewater, a small town, but about twice the size of Crafton, I knew that a family of four could not make ends meet solely with Sandra's income. When my back pay was exhausted, we had to have another revenue source. We had stopped at a red light and I called to a gentleman holding a folded newspaper. He was standing on the corner waiting for the light to change.

"Sir! Is there a hobby store in town?"

He stepped off the sidewalk, came to my window, and said, "There sure is." He pointed, "Two blocks down and a block to the right. It's called Edgewater Crafts. You can't miss it."

"Thank-you!"

"You're welcome."

The light changed and he hustled to the corner and crossed the street as we continued down Jefferson Boulevard. Sandra drove right to the store, a light-blue two-story building with the store name painted in fancy red letters across the front windows. I wasn't impressed with the location. It was sandwiched between a large, secondhand furniture store and a corner tavern. The towering, distressed, tavern sign was, in my opinion, a big eyesore. I didn't think the tavern would offer much encouragement for children to shop near it; even their parents might find the environment a bit repugnant. Then I wondered if I was a too straight-laced.

We parked and I put a nickel in the meter, although I didn't think we would be there for an hour. The meter didn't take pennies. Sandra dropped the car keys into her black satin purse and we made our way across the battleship-gray cement entryway to the full-length glass door. The hours were displayed: OPEN 8:00 a.m.-4:00 p.m. My watch indicated it was 8:27. I opened the door and ushered Sandra into the store, looking at the well-worn floor that creaked when I stepped. A new covering of linoleum, something bright, would help. The lighting, enough to read a newspaper, but not enough to recognize details, was provided by fixtures high above our heads. One fixture had a spider web hanging from it. There was an odor of tobacco smoke.

Sandra looked at me, exhibiting a questioning frown, as if to say, "This is a hobby shop?" She undoubtedly noticed a similar expression on my face. Some balloons, constrained by strings, were clustered above a cash register, behind which stood a portly, nearly bald man about fifty years old. We separated and began looking at the display cases along the left and right walls. I gravitated to the model planes in the case next to the HO gauge model trains.

"Can I help you?" came from behind the cash register. I assumed the gentleman was the proprietor, wearing jeans and a white T-shirt, a little too small for his out-of-shape body. Some ashes fell from his cigarette as he put the self-made smoke between his lips.

I moved in front of the register and asked, "Would you have a balsa model of a Corsair?"

He replied with a definite, "Maybe, but I'm trying to get rid of all the models of warplanes. People are tired of war. Doesn't seem to be much interest in prop-driven fighters. All the new stuff is coming out in plastic—jet planes. Personally, I don't like all the plastic crap."

"I can understand that. What would you say to an offer to buy all your balsa wood kits and supplies?"

"Uh, I'd have to think about that. Do you mean, glue, paint, rubber, props, wood stock, everything?"

"That's right, catalogs, too." I could see the man's interest was suddenly intensified. He picked up a pad, walked to the cabinet containing the models and started writing. I eyed the trains and said, "Add in the trains, also, and the ships." It took him about ten minutes to generate a total. He returned to the register counter and said, "Twelve hundred dollars."

He watched me closely as I thought about his offer. I went over to Sandra and pretended to talk it over with her, but I was asking her if she knew of property in Crafton that would serve as a hobby shop. She said she thought so. I turned back to the owner and said, "I'll give you nine-hundred—cash, right now."

He didn't answer me, but looked at his pad containing a bunch of numbers. Before he could answer, I added, "Throw in the airplane engines and fuel and I'll make it an even thousand—cash." I hoped he would take the deal. Sandra's car would hold everything, nothing more. I thought he might, at least, take the $900 deal. I figured I could gross about $4,000 or make three times my investment.

Chapter 4

CRAFTON'S HOBBY STORE

"You said cash, right?" The smoker stuck out his hand and we shook. His grip was firm, but not overpowering like I had experienced from some young naval officers. "I'm Josh Reynolds. I've been meaning to get out of this business for the last year or so. My neighbor wants this place so he can expand and have room for a stage and dancing." He pointed his right thumb in the direction of the tavern. "They're going to have live music." He would probably frequent the expanded tavern to dance and meet women. He didn't seem to me to be a church-goer.

"I'm Lee Linfield, retired Navy. I just got back from Korea and need a new job. I figured a hobby store might be just the thing. This is my wife, Sandra. She runs the lighthouse in Crafton."

After the introductions, Josh went to the back room and brought out several empty boxes. I took out my wallet and counted out ten one-hundred dollar bills next to the cash register. Josh extracted a sales book from below the cash machine and wrote up the sale. Sandra started packing a box with the model trains and I started filling up another container with model airplanes. In all, when we had finished packing, nine full boxes were piled next to the shop's front door. No other customers had visited the store during our half-hour stay.

23

We were able to get four boxes in the trunk, two on the floor behind the front seat and the rest on the back seat. Sandra said she could still see out of the rearview mirror—barely. Josh shook hands with us again and I wished him good luck, as he did us. As we drove away, Sandra started laughing. I joined in her merriment and said, "I think I got what I wanted."

She continued with little fits of laughter as we were back on the highway driving south.

"What's so funny, dear?"

"Where did you get all that money? Did you rob a bank in Boston? I've been imagining different scenarios of you holding up a bank with a squirt-gun, limping out to get in a Navy car and speeding away. All my versions are funny."

"Do you think I paid too much?"

"No! I think you got a wonderful deal. I'd never seen you do any bartering before."

"I was afraid you might not approve of my plan to start a business, but the situation called for rapid action, so I offered good-old Josh some quick money. I figured it might help him make a decision to sell his stock. I'll call him in a few days and see if I can get some more things from him. But now, I need to find a building for our store, Crafton Crafts."

Sandra asked again, "Did that money come from back pay?"

"Uh-huh. I meant to answer you before, but I was drawn into your bank robbing scheme and got distracted," I chuckled. "Why did you say I was using a squirt gun?"

"Because I knew you wouldn't want to hurt anybody when holding up a bank."

"Hmm, thank-you for that. You know me pretty well. Your FBI training has paid off. Now, tell me about this location for our store."

Sandra drove for about a minute before she started the tale. I didn't want to prod her, but I wondered what she was thinking. What I thought was going to be a simple explanation turned out to be story of twists and turns involving, Russian spies, the FBI, Marty, Rocky, and Jerry. I was to learn a surprising number of facts about three weeks of my kids' summer vacation with their grandmother. When she was finished, we were back at the lighthouse. I was thinking the story she related could have been fictional, written for a Hollywood movie.

"So, this Mr. Sherner was in cahoots with the crew of the Elena?"

"Uh-huh. He's the one who shot Elena, the FBI agent. I'm sure you'll meet her. She's Lieutenant Nesbitt's fiancée."

"And he's Marty's neighbor's son?"

Sandra parked close to our front door. "Right again. I think you're going to know most of the citizens of Crafton in just a few days." We both smiled and climbed out of the car. We'd have to store the boxes of hobby materials in the house temporarily. I checked my watch. It was ten after eleven. I thought we should have the car emptied by eleven-thirty.

After lunch, Sandra put a note on the lighthouse door. The courthouse records showed we could assume possession of Mr. Sherner's store after paying some back taxes and insurance. The city owned the building which we could rent for a modest amount: $800 per year. We co-signed all the documents and Sandra wrote a check for the fees. It was just before two in the afternoon when we got to the bank. After I had made a deposit to Sandra's checking account so she wouldn't be overdrawn, we opened a joint account for Crafton Crafts, our new business. I deposited ten thousand dollars, by endorsing a government cashier's check. We left the bank hurriedly, the kids would be home from school in a few minutes. We had both gotten so caught up in financing, we had forgotten about opening the library, except for the note.

When we got to the lighthouse, there was a dark-green Ford pickup parked in the library lot. A state emblem decal was on the driver's door. I took a quick look at Sandra and she shook her head. We stepped out of the car and walked over to the pickup. I wondered if it was an official visit. The driver rolled down the window.

"Hi, folks. Are you in charge of the library?"

I answered, "Yes. Is there a problem of some kind?"

"Well, I don't really know. I'd like to inspect the lighthouse, if you would kindly unlock the door."

"One moment, I'll have to get the key from the house," Sandra stated.

The driver, dressed in black pants and shoes, white shirt, open at the neck so one could see his chest hair, and a black baseball cap, slid from the front seat and planted his feet in the gravel. "I'm Eugene Schapter, State Fire Marshal." He looked more like a linoleum salesman, able to estimate the area of a floor to the nearest square foot.

"I'm Lee Linfield, Retired Navy. How are you?"

"Fine, thanks. And you?"

"Just fine." I squinted and frowned, "Has someone reported a code violation of some sort?"

"I'm not at liberty to give out any names, but a member of the community contacted our office and asked if the lighthouse passed the fire safety regulations. Apparently there are books on the steps leading to the gallery—lots of books."

"I'm not aware of that. I just got home yesterday and haven't had a chance to look in the lighthouse."

"Well, I guess we'll see what's in there at the same time then."

I could hear Sandra's steps on the concrete and gravel. I watched as she approached the door, unlocked it, turned toward the inspector, and said, "Please come in, sir." She pushed hard on the door and it swung open, the hinges creaking, not much, but enough to make it a little creepy to a child. I couldn't see into the dark cylindrical tower and the inspector hesitated.

"I'll get the light." Sandra stepped into the darkness and suddenly light flooded the interior space. I followed the fire marshal and stopped just inside the lighthouse. There weren't any books on the steps circling up to the top of the structure, however, there were books in boxes, stacked along the floor against the circumferential wall of the tower. I figured there must be several hundred bound volumes.

The fire marshal walked slowly, inspecting the boxes of books as he circled the floor. When he had completed his stroll and rejoined us near the door, he said, "Highly unusual for a lighthouse, but since the books do not offer any hindrance to accessing the gallery, and no danger to anyone moving up the walkway, I see no reason to write a citation. However, for everyone's safety, I recommend you put up a no smoking sign on the door—outside, and another sign in here."

Sandra commented, "We'll do that. I wonder who would have reported any impropriety. Maybe someone who had never visited the lighthouse."

Mr. Schapter asked, "Do you have any plans for making the books more accessible?"

"Yes, sir. We have a storage building that will house the books, but currently the building is full of antique lighthouse parts we plan to have removed by a salvage company. They are supposed to pick up the materials next week. We'll put up shelves and lighting—make it into a regular library, including fiction, non-fiction, and reference volumes." She paused, "Oh, yes, I want to put in a children's section in one corner."

"Sounds like you have a good plan. Good luck. I'll let you get back to work now."

Sandra said, "It was nice meeting you, sir. Have a nice trip."

We watched the fire marshal back out of the parking area, turn, stop momentarily at the highway, turn left onto the paved road, and drive away.

"Whew! That was a close one!"

"What do you mean?"

She grinned, "Until last weekend, all those books were on the steps leading to the gallery. The kids and I put them in boxes, labeled them, and put them where they are now. What I told the marshal is true. I want to put the books on shelves in the storage building behind our quarters. Older people don't want to climb all those steps. You're going to help me get the shelves and bring the book list up-to-date."

"Geez, that's something I've always wanted to do. When do we start?"

"Tomorrow," she grinned. "I thought that project was on your to do list."

"Tomorrow sounds good. I feel a nap coming on."

We heard the squeak of breaks at the turnoff from the highway. The yellow school bus had stopped to let off Rocky and Susan, who waved to the driver and to the kids looking out the windows. They came running toward us, Susan dragging her jacket.

I asked, "How was school today?"

Susan was rocking back and forth like she had to go, so Sandra started walking her toward the house. Rocky replied, "We had a film strip about President Roosevelt. Did you know President Truman was his Vice President?"

"Sure did, Rocky. Do you know what your mom and I did today?"

"Uh, what?"

"We bought some things for a hobby store and we signed papers to take over Mr. Sherner's store on the pier. Now it's going to be called Crafton Crafts."

"Really? That's neat. Did you get a model of a Corsair?"

"No, we'll have to order one. There's a B-29 kit though."

"Where is it? Can I see?"

"Come with me, they're in the house in Susan's closet."

Sandra and I had put all the boxes in Susan's bedroom, under her bed, in the bottom drawer of her bureau, and in her closet. We reasoned that she wouldn't care to open the boxes since none of the materials interested her, but as Rocky and I walked toward the house, I suddenly thought that she was so inquisitive, she might go through the boxes like Christmas presents. Sandra and I had to talk to both kids. We had to stress that the models were for a business; they couldn't play with them.

Rocky and I went to Susan's bedroom and found the girls sitting on the bed. Sandra had already started the lecture. She had one hand on Susan's shoulder, apparently to keep the six-year old's attention. Susan was looking very intently into Sandra's eyes as her mother explained why she was not allowed to open the boxes.

Rocky and I stood at the door and listened. When Sandra finished the explanation, she asked, "Do you understand, Susan?"

"Yes. Are there any dolls in the boxes?"

Sandra replied, "No, just airplanes, boats, and trains."

"Okay. If there aren't any dolls, I won't open the boxes. I promise."

Sandra combed Susan's hair with her fingers and said, "Good girl."

I had both hands on Rocky's shoulders. I turned him around so we were facing each other and said, "The same goes for you, bud. You'll see the models when you help me put them in the display cases in the store. When we get the models ready for sale, we'll pick out one to work on, okay?"

"Uh, okay. I can't even show Jerry the boxes?"

Sandra responded quickly, "Rocky, did you hear what I told your sister?"

"Yeah. I promise not to mess with the boxes. When can I help Dad get the store ready?"

I could answer that, so I said, "Sunday, after we go the church. Tomorrow we'll work on the library." Sandra glanced at me and smiled.

Chapter 5

FIRE ALARMS

We heard two beeps of a car horn. Sandra and I both went to the front door and saw a white Cadillac parked in the lighthouse lot pointing toward our front door. The passenger side door swung open and a rather large, well-dressed woman stepped out. She might have just come from shopping at a high-end department store, but fancy stores don't exist in Crafton. She wasn't fat, she just had large bones—something Sandra would have mentioned, being more socially aware with her language than I am. I have to admit my social skills need some honing. She had a book in her left hand, evidently wanting to return it. Rocky stepped past us and walked toward the expensive vehicle. It looked recently washed and waxed.

"Hi, Mrs. Griffith. Are you bringing back that book about roses?"

"Yes, Rocky, but it's overdue. Can you tell me how much I owe the library?"

"Maybe, but my mom should probably do that. She's in charge now. Mr. W moved to Portland, Oregon. He's in the FBI, you know."

"Oh, I didn't know that. So, aren't you selling books any longer?"

"No, Ma'am. Most of the time we're in school. Maybe next summer. Did you know my dad is going to have a hobby store?"

Sandra interrupted the conversation by introducing me to the Griffiths; Oscar and Ellen. I had no idea that Oscar was a submarine captain, a rank above me. Captain Griffith asked where I had last served and I explained where I had been for the last eighteen months. The Griffiths said they wanted us to join them for dinner in the next week or so. The captain had three more weeks of leave before having to return to Groton, Connecticut, where his sub was being overhauled and upgraded. He expected this port call might be the last for his diesel ship; the nuclear vessels would soon be taking over the oceans' undersea patrols. Captain Griffith believed the future was undoubtedly progressing toward nuclear powered submarines.

The ladies had gone into the library to determine what Ellen's fine was for her overdue book. When they reappeared, Ellen was holding two more books. She held them up for us to see the titles: *Soil for Gardening* and *Japanese Rock Gardens*.

"My fine was only twenty cents, dear."

Oscar replied, "Imagine that—you didn't have to ask me for money."

Ellen pretended to hit her husband in the head with one of the books, which got us all laughing. Even though Ellen was a big woman, she and Oscar seemed to be a good fit. He was tall, maybe 6 feet 4 inches or so, perhaps six-years older than I, had crew-cut gray hair, and was lanky, no pot belly in evidence. He probably played center on his high school basketball team. His movements were smooth, almost calculated. His presence commanded respect.

We waved as they drove off. When the Cadillac neared the highway, Oscar beeped the horn twice, and we could see Ellen waving to us as they turned toward town.

Sandra and I walked toward the house, arm-in-arm. She asked, "What do you want for dinner?"

"Champagne, caviar, those little triangular pastries, and—."

Sandra laughed and pulled on my arm, "I do not run a French restaurant, dear. I think we'll have pesketty and meatballs."

I added, "And catsup. I know Rocky likes catsup, too."

The kids were on the floor looking up at the TV screen, watching The Cisco Kid. Rocky looked at me and said, "Dad, you should listen to what Pancho says. He's really funny."

I sat down on the sofa and Susan joined me, but her eyes were glued to the TV. She put her head on my leg, but kept watching the program. I could feel her chewing so I asked, "What are you eating, Suz?"

She didn't look up, but answered, "Gum."

I smiled and began to pay attention to the western program. About a minute later, I heard a siren. It couldn't have come from the TV, it was a police or fire siren, and it wasn't the varying whine from an ambulance.

Sandra yelled at me, just loud enough to overcome the TV sound. "That's a siren from a fire truck. I wonder where they're going."

I got up from the sofa and joined her in the kitchen. She was already looking out the window above the sink toward the highway. I went to the front door so I could get a more expansive view of whatever was taking place. Sandra and I stepped out on the porch. She was drying her hands on a kitchen towel. We looked across the road at our nearest neighbors, but could not see any signs of a fire a hundred yards away. The shiny red truck came into view and began slowing as it approached the turn to the lighthouse. When the truck turned down the gravel lane to our house, we glanced at each other. I was wondering what was going on. I looked around at the lighthouse tower and the adjoining buildings; there were no signs of a fire: no odor, no flames, and no smoke. Why had the fire truck come to the lighthouse?

Sandra said, "What in the devil are they doing here?"

The fire truck sounded a bit like a tank as it closed in on our house. The brakes squeaked a bit as the truck came to a stop, the engine idling. Two men climbed down from the cab and two other firemen came around from the rear. The big man from the cab shouted over the engine noise, "Where's the fire?"

"I checked our buildings, I don't see any smoke or fire. Why did you come out here?"

"Someone called in and reported a fire at the lighthouse. I hope it isn't a diversion from a real fire." He stepped toward me and extended his hand. "I'm Chief Bud Easton, my sidekick is Ron Ehrlick. He's our best driver."

I shook hands with both men and said, "I'm Leland Linfield and this is my wife, Sandra. I bet you know my kids. Most kids love to watch fire trucks."

They nodded to Sandra and Chief Easton commented, "We've met your wife. She and your boy, Rocky, and a friend of his, I think his buddy was Jerry, helped round up some Russian spies. Maybe you haven't heard that story yet."

I smiled, not surprised at the Chief's comments. "I've heard part of it. I've only been home a day. I've got a lot more to learn about my family."

Rocky and Susan were on the porch, eyes riveted on the shiny, red, throbbing truck loaded with ladders and hoses. Rocky waved and started toward us when the Chief looked toward the porch and waved. Susan ran out to Sandra and grabbed her hand, perhaps seeking safety from the big truck and the men dressed in firefighting gear.

We heard a voice emanating from the cab, apparently a radio call to Chief Easton. He excused himself and walked hurriedly to the cab, reached in and pulled out a walkie-talkie. He pressed a switch and spoke into the device. "Did you say the pier?"

The radio squawked back, "Yes, Chief, Sherner's Bait and Tackle Shop. We just got a call that it's on fire."

"All right. The lighthouse call was a false alarm. We're on our way."

Ehrlick had gotten into the cab when the radio came alive. He motioned to the other men to mount up. Chief Easton climbed into the cab and the engine roared out of its docile state, the truck pulled forward, turned sharply into the parking area, cut across the weed-strewn field and charged onto the highway heading for the pier.

Sandra cried out, "Lee! Did you hear what he said? He said our building is on fire. We'd better go down there. I'll call Mom and have her come over."

Sandra sounded a little irritated with me, but I couldn't blame her. I hadn't realized the significance of the name Sherner; I had only heard it once before, earlier in the day, when we signed the purchase papers. I felt a bit foolish, but I should have known the name. I used to pick up things like that during a briefing before a raid. I wish I had realized what was going on sooner; I might have ridden to the fire with the firemen. This was a time I needed to be able to drive legally. I had to get my license renewed—soon.

It seemed like it was taking forever, but Marty arrived in about five minutes. As she parked her car, Sandra and I climbed in our car, slammed the doors, and started to move down the lane toward the highway. She lead-footed it to the pier but we didn't want to interfere with the firefighters, so we parked a block away and walked to the action.

The fire engine was parked in front of our building, hoses lying limp, unrolled from the truck to the front of our building. One of the firemen was looking down at us from the roof.

"No smoke or flames up here, Chief. I think it's another false alarm."

Chief Easton saw us walking toward the building and he called out to Sandra, who had run ahead of me. "Mrs. Linfield, do you have a key?"

Sandra looked at me and I replied, "I've got the key." I reached into my left front pocket and pulled out the key to the front door and gave it to the chief. He and fireman Ehrlick went in the store and looked around, came outside, and announced, "There's no fire. Someone is messing with us. I'll have the sheriff check with the phone company and see if we can find out who placed the call. Here's your key." The chief returned the key and commented, "When you get the store ready, give me a call and I'll go through the fire regulations and precautions with you. We'll make sure the fire alarms are functioning properly."

"Thank-you. I'll buy some extinguishers to have on hand. Thanks for checking out the building."

"No problem, folks. We'll roll up the hoses, put the truck to bed, and go home for dinner. We all get hungry when the excitement calms down."

I had to smile at the chief's last comment. All the firemen looked like they had never missed a meal.

Sandra and I watched as the firemen put the equipment away and left the pier. I wanted to go in the building and see what the building contained, but thought it would be better to go back home to rescue Marty from Rocky and Susan so she could go home for dinner. Rocky and I would visit the building on Sunday as I had planned earlier.

As Sandra drove us home, I asked her a question. "Have you ever had a feeling like you were out of step with everyone?"

"I'm not sure what you mean, Lee."

"Well, I have been thinking about not reacting to the name Sherner when the Chief said the building was on fire. It's like I was a member of a book club and all the other members were talking about chapter 5, but I had only read through chapter 4. It's a feeling of impotence, or helplessness; having nothing to contribute."

"I'm sorry I was a little short tempered with you. I've been off my normal self since I quit working at the bureau. The first week I was home, I had to find things to do to keep busy while the kids were in school. I made lists and set up a new routine. I worried about forgetting to pick up the kids from school. But during those first seven days, I found out this job was open. We moved here and I had to do so many things, I didn't have time to think about much except setting up a new home. I'm still working on that. The library needs a lot of work, so we can work together and gradually, we'll get into a normal routine—don't you think?"

"I'm sure you're right. Next week I have to get my driver's license. I don't want to have to rely on you to ferry me around. I think I'll buy a pickup—something a couple of years old."

"You need to talk to Steve Morgan, Jerry's dad. He knows all about cars. He'll know if there is anything worthwhile in Crafton. Mom might know of something, also. She reads the paper, front to back, all the time."

"Is the paper a daily? Seems that Crafton is too small to have a daily."

We were nearing the turnoff to the lighthouse. Sandra glanced at me and answered, "The *Crafton News and Views* comes out on Sunday, Tuesday, and Thursday. The Sunday edition usually has one more page than the other days."

I laughed and said, "Weddings and such?"

"Uh-huh. Stanley Cross, the editor, will probably want to interview you about the store. We'll have to make a good impression when he comes by the new digs."

"Well, I want to paint the front and put up a sign. I imagine the fishing tackle will have to be separate from the models, maybe on one side, the hobby stuff on the other."

Sandra put on the brakes and parked about twenty feet from the porch. As we walked toward the house, she commented, "There's a cigarette and cigar machine in the store. Maybe we can exchange it for a pop or candy machine. Did you ever smoke when overseas?"

"Nope. I've never seen any reason to fill my lungs with smoke; smoking is a nasty habit."

Chapter 6

MY TIME IN CHINA

Everyone had contributed to a fairly long, conversation-filled dinner. Marty had been invited to stay, but she hadn't fed Surprise, so she went home, fed the dog and returned with him. After he sniffed my pants and let me scratch his back, he lay on the floor in the living room, not far from the dining room table. I occasionally glanced at the pooch to see if he was sleeping, but he just kept his eyes on us. I occasionally spotted him watching Susan and Rocky, but from time to time, looking me over. When it was time for dessert, he was on his side, asleep. I was happy to see that he never begged for table scraps. That, of course, could be explained because Marty had fed him earlier.

After dinner, we moved to the living room and Rocky asked me to tell us more about being in Manchuria. I reminded everyone about my bomb run on the bridge and losing power as I climbed in altitude and metal bits from antiaircraft struck my plane.

Susan was quick to remind me of my bloody face from a small laceration. "The engine was sputtering and smoke started streaming past the right side of the cockpit. I lost power at about 8,000 feet, nosed over and began to glide as far away from the North Korean border as possible, pretty much in a northwesterly direction. I wiped my face with my sleeve and decided the cut wasn't serious; the initial bleeding had slowed to a trickle. I had no clue as to the terrain below me, but I decided to raise the wheels and make a belly landing. I was afraid the wheels would catch something on the ground and cause me to cartwheel, or flip upside down. I didn't want to die while landing."

"How far did you glide, Dad?"

I knew Rocky was going to ask a lot of questions. I wasn't sure, but I said, "About ten or twelve miles, but that's just a guess." Everyone was listening intently, and I continued, "When my plane hit the ground, it skidded about forty yards, plowing some deep ruts into a field. When it stopped, I popped open the cockpit, climbed out on the wing, and dropped to the ground. I stood there a minute or so trying to get oriented. The sky was getting dark and I couldn't see any lights, so I could tell I wasn't near a city."

Susan asked, "Did you break your leg when you got down from your plane?"

"No, that happened much later when I was travelling through the mountains, leaving China behind and venturing into Russia."

Rocky said, "Gosh, I didn't know you were in Russia, too."

"Well, it took a long time to get there. You'll have to be patient to hear the whole story, okay? I'll skip some of the boring parts."

Rocky looked first at Sandra, and then Susan, and nodded.

"I was leaning against the plane when I heard a man's voice ask if I was American. I pulled out my handgun, crouched down to make a smaller target, and answered, yes. Then I asked who he was and he said something like this: *Me Zhang Lanfu. This my farm. I help you.*"

"My eyes had adjusted to the dim light and I could see a man a little taller than Rocky, dressed in a heavy coat, kind of like something a hunter would wear in the winter. He was standing beside a two wheeled cart that had a long box on it. Then he told me to take off my shoes, jacket, and hat, and give them to him."

"Wasn't it cold there, Dad? It was November." Rocky was paying close attention.

"It was getting cold. There were some patches of snow on the ground, but I think it had been melting during the day. The sun had almost set. Where was I going to go? I didn't have any choice but to follow his instructions."

Sandra asked, "But he wanted your coat. Didn't you worry about freezing during the night?"

"I didn't have to worry for very long. He had me help him take the box off the cart and open it up. There was a body of an elderly man inside. Dr. Zhang told me he was going to bury Mr. Yan tonight and my arrival interrupted his mission. Dr. Zhang was a doctor and also served as the local undertaker. We put my jacket and shoes on Mr. Yan and put him in the plane. Then Dr. Zhang told me to set fire to the plane, which I did with a flare. As we watched the flames grow, Dr. Zhang ran over to the plane and tossed my hat in the cockpit with Mr. Yan. After we put the box back on the cart, he had me get in it, and he closed the lid."

Susan pulled on my shirt sleeve. "How did you get out of the box, Daddy?"

"I didn't know where we were going, but I felt that I should trust Dr. Zhang. I tried to relax in the box but it was too small for me; kind of like trying to put a size ten foot in a size eight shoe. The ride was pretty rough; it felt like that cart was hitting every rut in the field, but it lasted only a few minutes and we stopped. Dr. Zhang opened the box and told me not to stand up. I was to keep crouched down so no one would see a tall visitor—maybe an American."

Rocky asked, "Could you still see your plane?"

"Yes. The fire was covering most of the fuselage and then there was a big blast; a gas tank must have exploded. Dr. Zhang told me to get in his house, because somebody would be coming by to see what was going on. Some of his neighbors weren't far away. Someone would tell the army about the explosion and they would find the wreckage of the plane. Dr. Zhang and I hoped the army would find Mr. Yan's bones and think the pilot was dead."

Sandra observed, "Dr. Zhang was a very smart man. How did he learn English?"

"He told me he studied English when he was in medical school. Most of the medical journals and many of the guest lecturers were English. His spoken English wasn't very good, but we were able to communicate. I didn't know one word of Chinese. Sometimes he forgot that I only knew English and he spoke to me in Chinese. When he did that, he laughed and tried again in English. As time went by, I was able to understand what was going on and he didn't need to say anything. We seemed to be reading each other's minds.

That first night I stayed in his house. In the morning we had a discussion that would provide an explanation of why I was staying with him. If we spoke English and someone overheard us, we would both be doomed, so Dr. Zhang decided I was to masquerade as a Russian, but I was unable to either hear or talk. He would instruct me how to speak with my hands. I was staying with him so he could help me learn how to communicate again. I had been injured in Siberia. Anyway, that was our story."

"But Daddy, you are American, not Russian."

Rocky came to my rescue. "Suz, Dad and Dr. Zhang were just pretending—it was fiction."

"Oh. I thought Daddy was telling us non-fiction."

I glanced at Sandra and received a smile. I got the impression that Susan's questions were not as significant as I thought; she was seeking a more superficial answer. "What I'm telling you is the truth, Susan, but Dr. Zhang and I were just pretending I was a Russian. If the authorities had known I was an American, Dr. Zhang and I would have been in trouble."

Susan nodded and said, "Oh, I get it." She smiled and looked at me, expecting me to continue. Sandra stood and started toward the kitchen.

"Would anybody like some popcorn?" The kids said, "Yes!" I got up and followed Sandra, but I went to the fridge as she was getting a large saucepan from the drawer near the sink. I was thinking of a cold beer all the way.

"Hand me the butter, dear."

I had already closed the door, but I transferred the beer to my right hand and reopened the fridge, grabbed the butter dish, and said, "Your command is my wish, my queen."

She stood there looking at me, shook her head and said, "You are so full of it."

I bowed, smiled, and handed her the butter dish. She cut a small slab of butter with a table knife and started toward me in a threatening manner, as if she was going to smear my face with the butter. I didn't move a muscle and stood my ground, but began to think about an escape. When she got very close, she dropped her hand with the knife and kissed me, then raised the knife and smeared butter on my nose. I should have known the kiss was a major distraction.

Sandra laughed, dropped another slab of butter in the sauce pan and turned on the burner under the pan. I measured out about a quarter cup of popcorn and poured it in with the butter.

"Aren't you going to wipe off your nose?"

"Nope. I want the kids to see how dangerous it is to be in the kitchen with you."

We stood there watching the pan on the stove. When the first kernel popped, we were both startled and laughed. Sandra grabbed a napkin from the counter and wiped my nose.

"Thank-you." I didn't think she would let me expose the butter on my nose for the kids to see. I was beginning to feel more relaxed now, knowing I was no longer alone in a strange land, wishing I was back with my family. I put my hands on her waist and gave her a kiss.

The top of the sauce pan was rising; the popping had almost ceased. Sandra grabbed the pan and set it on another unit. I set a large bowl next to the hot pan and she dumped the puffs into it.

"Hey, we make a pretty good team."

Just as I said, "Yeah, we could work at the theater," the kids joined us in the kitchen.

"What's taking so long, Mom?" Rocky was standing behind Suzy with his hands on her shoulders.

Suzy had her eyes on the bowl and said, "I get to add the salt."

"Just a minute, Susan, I have to melt some butter first. Then you can add the salt, but not too much."

Susan picked up the salt shaker. "Show me how much."

A couple of minutes later, the popcorn was ready. Sandra grabbed a wad of paper napkins and we went back into the living room to resume my story.

Susan had done a good job with the salt. As we ate popcorn and I sipped my beer, I told of the army coming to Dr. Zhang's house early that first morning. "A military officer came to the door and asked several questions, then barged into the house and looked around. I was lying down under a blanket in a small room next to the kitchen. Dr. Zhang told the military policeman our story. When they were leaving the room, the officer came back and hit me with a stick he was carrying, right above my left ear. It stung like blazes, but I didn't say a word. I just looked at him as I rubbed the sore spot. He turned and left the room."

Susan said, "That was mean!"

"Did you ever get a chance to beat him up, Dad?"

"No, Rocky, I never saw him again, but I wouldn't have done anything anyway. If I hit him, they would have discovered who I was. I couldn't risk drawing attention to Dr. Zhang and me."

"Mom, can I have a Coke?"

"Me, too. The popcorn makes me thirsty." Susan almost always wanted what Rocky asked for.

Rocky's question brought a quick response from Sandra. "You'd better not, you'll wet your bed. You'd better brush your teeth and take a sip of water."

"That's a good idea." I glanced at my watch. "It's time for bed. I'll tell you some more tomorrow night, okay?"

Chapter 7

THE STORAGE BUILDING

Everyone was up by 8:00 a.m., including Surprise. He had slept on Susan's bed. We had breakfast and were planning the cleanup of the storage building attached to the back of our house. When Sandra removed the padlock and swung the door open, I guessed the room was about ten feet by eighteen feet in size. There were two large decorative lanterns hanging from wires attached to an exposed ceiling joist. I couldn't believe they were part of the lighthouse. Perhaps Mr. Waicukauski or another lighthouse keeper had collected them. The floor was covered with old pipes, wires, nuts and bolts, and dirt in little drifts. In the right-hand back corner of the room were remnants of an out-of-date lighthouse lamp housing, covered with cobwebs.

I commented to Sandra, "We're going to have to cover the walls with insulation and drywall."

"Uh-huh. The ceiling, too." She looked up at the bare joists and spider webs. It looked like we were preparing a haunted house for Halloween.

"Yeah. Looks like we have a nine foot ceiling—more seams to tape and mud, but more room for shelves. Rocky, please get me a piece of tablet paper and a pencil. Susan, can you find me a ruler?"

I watched Susan confer with Sandra and then scamper from the storage building.

"I told her where the tape measure is. I hope she knows what I want her to get."

"That's all right, I can make estimates from the length of my shoe. It's almost a foot long."

Sandra laughed, not knowing if I was joking. I wasn't.

Susan returned with a tape measure and I estimated we would need about thirty sheets of dry-wall, but how were we going to get them to the lighthouse? Sandra was sure the building supply store would deliver, most all stores would deliver for orders over a hundred dollars. I calculated the amount of insulation, and took a guess at the pounds of nails, joint compound, and tape that would be required. When I completed my list, Sandra and Susan left for the house to call in the order.

While the ladies were gone, Rocky and I began moving the major pieces of junk that were scattered about on the floor. After Rocky helped me move two long, fairly-heavy pipes to the outside, he said, "I'll be back in a minute, Dad," and disappeared. I thought maybe he had to go to the bathroom. I followed him into the house to get a box to contain small items. Originally, I had thought we would discard the nuts, bolts, and other odds and ends, but I changed my mind. We would probably need a junk box to mine for useful items. I smiled when I thought that Sandra might accuse me of being a hoarder.

Sandra was in the kitchen pouring freshly brewed coffee into a Thermos and Susan was putting a handful of cookies into a plastic bread sack. Rocky was hanging up the phone.

"I called Jerry for some help, Dad. He'll be here in a few minutes."

"Good idea, Rocky. The more hands we have, the sooner we'll finish the job."

"You can tell us about the models we'll have in the store while we work."

"You know where I can find a box to contain the stuff on the floor out there?"

"Yeah, I know where there's one. I'll get it."

"Daddy, want a cookie?" Susan held out the bread sack and smiled.

"That's full of bread, not cookies."

"It's got cookies in it, not bread." She looked serious at first and then said, "Oh! You're teasing me! You're not s'posed to tease me, you know."

"Sorry, dear." I pulled a cookie out of the bag and said, "Thank-you. You know, you're my favorite daughter." I winked.

She caught on quickly and said, "You're welcome. You know, you're my favorite dad."

We all laughed.

Jerry arrived before I had finished the cookie. I watched Rocky and Jerry talking and walking toward the lighthouse. When I came out on the porch, I noticed the girl's bike leaning against the fence by the parking area. I wondered if Jerry's parents weren't very well off. When I was his age, my friends would have razzed me about riding a girl's bike and if my father had found out about it, I would have had a man's bike in short order. When I looked away from the bicycle, Rocky and Jerry were returning from the lighthouse. Rocky was carrying a medium sized cardboard box. No introductions were necessary, I had met Jerry at the school the day before.

"Hi there, Jerry. You're going to give us a hand?"

"Hi, Mr. Linfield. Yeah. Rocky said he could use some help. I'm pretty good at cleaning."

"You've got lots of experience?"

"Uh-huh. I vacuum and dust the house once a week. Saves Mom time after she comes home from working at the hospital."

"Good for you. You and Rocky can pick up all the junk on the floor in the storage building and store it in that box. Let's get to work."

It took nearly half-an-hour for the cleanup team to remove the floor debris, except for the old lamp housing. Upon closer inspection, I realized the pile of metal was not what I had originally assumed; it was the remnants of an old coal furnace. The parts were made of cast iron covered on one side with a thick layer of soot, interspersed with spider webs. Where would we put the heavy chunks of metal other than piling them outside, creating an eyesore? I informed Sandra of my discovery.

"What if we bury that junk?"

I thought for a moment and said, "I'd rather sell it to someone. We'd get a few bucks to buy wood for the shelving. Is there a foundry nearby?"

We stood there, alternately looking at the chunks of metal and each other. We both grinned. We didn't have a clue.

"I'll ask Mom."

That was probably a good idea, Marty knew just about everything there was to know about the area for fifty miles around.

We all heard three beeps of a horn. Susan ran to see who it was. Rocky and Jerry followed close behind. In about half-a-minute, Rocky stuck his head through the doorway and said, "It's the delivery truck from the building supply store. They want to know where to unload."

"Ask them if they can bring the materials back here." I didn't want to carry heavy supplies and put excess strain on my leg. If I reinjured myself, I'd not be able to work on the library—or at the store. I wondered if I was being over cautious. A husky man appeared at the door and said, "Hello."

I said, "Hi. Can you bring the materials in here?"

"I'll help, but I'm not with the delivery truck."

Sandra touched my arm and said, "That's Steve Morgan, Jerry's dad."

Morgan stepped into the room and we shook hands. "Sorry, I didn't know who you were. I thought you were one of the deliverymen. I'm Lee Linfield."

"Steve Morgan. Nice to meet you. Jerry told me you had returned from Korea. Jerry said Rocky was very excited; his day at school was torture for him. Hi, Sandra."

"Hi, Steve. We're going to fix up this storage room and transfer the books in here. Having the books on the lighthouse stairs was not a great idea. The elderly don't like climbing, and it's a little dangerous. Kids loved it though."

"How can I help? Put me to work, I've got four hours of freedom today."

"Any ideas about disposing of that pile of cast iron?"

"Sure. Let's load it into my pickup. I'll sell it for you. I know just the place for it, but they won't pay much."

"That's great. We were thinking of burying it." I smiled. "Probably not the best idea. As soon as we get the insulation and drywall in here, you can help me start hanging the drywall."

Steve nodded. "I'll help the delivery boys get the materials in here, they're not too stout. You and the boys can put the cast iron beside the pickup. I'll load it later."

As the materials began to pile up on the floor, I realized installing the insulation would go much faster if we had a staple gun, something I had not ordered. The rock wool batting was going on the walls and ceiling, although it would have been better to have had the insulation blown in above the overhead drywall. The insulation was going to be expensive, but I thought it was a better choice than building a fireplace or buying a wood stove. Sandra had said she would have liked a potbelly stove, but on second thought, it might not be a good idea to have a fire near all the books. The fireplace was nixed for the same reason, as well as the expense; we would use an electric heater and try to keep the door closed. We both laughed at the latter idea.

I signed for the materials and the two teenage delivery boys departed. We all stood looking at the stack of drywall and an even larger amount of rock wool.

Sandra broke the silence. "Where do we start?"

I didn't know how to answer that simple question, but Steve did. He pointed at the ceiling and said, "The ceiling is first, then the walls. I'll get some sawhorses and planks so we can reach the ceiling joists. We'll need two hammers."

Rocky went in the house to the tool drawer for a hammer and Jerry followed Steve to his pickup. They returned with everything we needed to start the project. Susan crawled on top of the drywall and started dancing as if she were on a stage. Sandra and I watched, smiled, and shook our heads.

Sandra laughed. "I think we've got a ballerina in the family."

With directions from Steve and his brawn, and my use of muscles I didn't even know I had, we had sheet rocked and insulated the ceiling in about two hours. Rocky and Jerry handed us nails and insulation and picked up things we dropped, mostly nails, but there was some danger and clatter when I dropped my hammer. Fortunately, no one was below me.

We were taking a break and admiring our work when Sandra sent a messenger to call us in the house for lunch. Movement at the storage room door caught my eye; it was Susan. She yelled, "Mom said to tell you lunch is ready!" She disappeared as quickly as she had appeared.

While we ate, Steve and I talked about hanging the rest of the drywall. He gave me some tips and said, "Start at the top and work down. Take your time. I have to leave for work this afternoon, so you'll be on your own unless you can get the boys to assist you. They can hold a panel in place until you can get a few nails to hold it. I imagine they'll get bored and want to wander off. Maybe you can somehow persuade them to help.

I'll try to get over after dinner during the week. We should have the job finished by next weekend."

"I sure appreciate the help you gave me. I really didn't know how to get started."

"No problem. Glad to help out. I'll call ahead during the week when I can get away. Good luck."

Steve went out to his truck, but I didn't hear the motor. I went out to see if he was having problems starting his engine, but he was putting cast iron pieces into the bed of the pickup. He was tossing the last chunk of metal in when I said, "Sorry, I could have helped you with that junk."

"Don't sweat it. It only took a minute."

I suddenly remembered that Sandra told me to ask Steve if he knew of any used pickups for sale. I mentioned it to him as he was getting in the cab.

"I'll see what I can find for you this coming week. I'll let you know as soon as I find something."

"Thanks, Steve."

I watched Steve's truck turn onto the highway and speed away toward town. Reflecting on how much assistance I had received for so little in return, I hoped we would become good friends; we had gotten off to a good start, but I hoped in the future I would have an opportunity to return the favor. I liked Steve. He was knowledgeable, quick witted, and strong as a gorilla. I smiled as I pictured him swinging from a ceiling joist by one arm.

"Dad, Jerry and I want to ride down to the pier. Do you need any more help?"

"I need you to help me for about fifteen minutes, then you can go. Okay?"

The boys followed me to the storage room and helped me put up three sheets of drywall, each held in place by a half-dozen nails, before I dismissed them. I finished nailing the drywall and called it quits for the day. I was worn out. My arms and legs were starting to tell me they had had enough for one day. I knew I was going to be sore tomorrow, but we planned to work at the craft store; the activity there would require much less muscle but much more thinking. I thought Sandra and I could handle anything that might arise, with occasional contributions from the kids. We had ideas and manpower. The kids would enjoy unpacking the boxes of merchandise we had temporarily stored in the house.

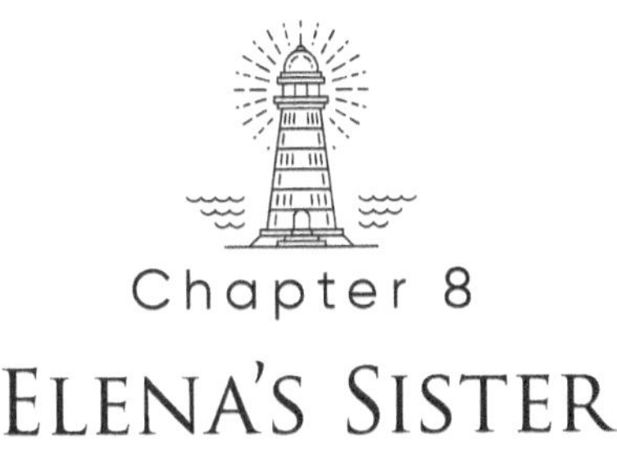

Chapter 8

ELENA'S SISTER

After Jerry and I helped Dad put up some drywall, we decided to ride to the pier and look into the windows of the soon to be craft store. I had told Jerry we were going to have models of airplanes, boats, and trains. We had imagined where they would be in the store. We both rode sitting down to the top of the hill; the base of the lighthouse was about thirty feet above the water, but we had to ride a slight slope up to Lighthouse Road and then pedal hard to climb a small hill to see down to the bay.

As usual, Jerry took off down the hill like a crazy man. I followed on Granma's bike, but had to brake quite a bit to keep from going too fast, the slope to the pier was fairly steep. Without brakes, I probably would have crashed before turning onto the road that ended at the dock not far from the building that Mom and Dad had rented to use as the craft store. Jerry skidded at the side of Lighthouse Road when he stood on the brakes and stopped before he quit sliding through the turn.

Jerry waited at Pier Lane for me to get to the bottom of the hill. I was always a little surprised he didn't tease me for not being able to keep up with him, but we were best friends.

We have had some minor disagreements, but never a fight.

We rode to the front of the building and parked our bikes near the front door. I put my hand on the window glass to block reflections, and looked into the store with my nose against the glass. It seemed to me nothing much had changed since the FBI had hauled Mr. Sherner off for trial. He had shot Lt. Nesbitt's girlfriend, Elena, Susan's and my favorite FBI agent.

When we were trying to see into the windows, a big shadow appeared from behind us.

We turned around and looked up at a big man in a blue and gray uniform. It was the Chief of Police that we had met after helping to capture the Russian spies.

"Hi, boys. What are you doing here? You're not thinking of breaking a window and stealing something are you?"

I knew then he didn't remember us, so I said, "No, Chief Simms. We haven't seen you since you were out at the lighthouse arresting those spies."

"Oh, sorry boys. I didn't recognize you in the daylight. Last time I saw you it was dark outside. You're Rocky and Jerry, right?"

Jerry said, "Yes, sir. Rocky's mom and dad are going to make Sherner's into a craft store."

"We were imagining where the models would be. Mom and Dad are going to start working here tomorrow. We're gunna help."

"Family business, huh?"

"Yes, sir."

"Will you have model trains? I have an HO train that I've been working on for years in my extra bedroom. Some day you boys will have to visit and see my layout."

"That would be great! Maybe my dad will bring us over, but he's pretty busy right now."

"I was thinking of sometime during the holidays." He stood there looking at us for a moment and then said, "Well, I'd better get busy. Bye, boys."

Jerry and I said, "Bye, sir."

Chief Simms walked away adjusting his hat. He was a big man, a little taller than Dad and a lot heavier. I'd bet on him if he ever fought a criminal.

"Hey, Rock. Take a look at that! I'll bet that boat cost some big bucks."

I followed Jerry's arm to see where his finger was pointing and there it was, the most beautiful boat I had ever seen, coming toward the pier. Two masts, polished metal accents gleaming in the afternoon sun, and *The Bahamian Wind* written in dark-blue on the white bow, meant someone with lots of money owned her. Standing ready to toss a bowline, a young girl looked along the pier, but nobody was there to catch the rope from the yacht. She yelled something toward the bridge and raised both hands in the air. Jerry said, "Let's catch the line and help tie her up. Maybe they'll let us on board to take a look."

I remembered the last time Jerry and I sneaked on board a boat and got in trouble, but this was a pleasure boat, not a three-hundred-foot long steel vessel from Russia. I wouldn't go on board a yacht like this unless invited. I was a couple of steps behind Jerry when the boat was a few feet from and drifting toward the docking area. We both caught the line and tied the line to a bollard. When we looked up, the girl had disappeared, but suddenly reappeared at the stern ready to toss us another line.

We ran to catch the other line and fastened it to another bollard about fifty feet from the bowline. I figured the yacht must be at least a sixty-footer. I'll bet it cost more than a new lighthouse. A man, about the size of Jerry's dad, wearing white pants and a white T-shirt with three red stripes across the chest, was placing a foldup set of steps to access the pier; the deck was a few feet below. We walked toward him to say hello.

"Hi, boys. Do you know a boy named Rocky? I think he would be about your age."

"My name's Rocky. I think I'm the only one in Crafton."

He said, "I'm Leroy Harris and this is my daughter, Millie." He climbed to the top of the pier and Jerry and I shook hands with him. Millie had followed her dad up the steps and stood a little behind him. She was about four inches shorter than Jerry and me, a blonde, and kind of cute. She was dressed just like her dad.

It suddenly came to me that this guy must be Elena's father, but I didn't know Elena had a sister, especially not one that was so much younger. I had almost forgotten that Elena's last name was Harris. The only time I remembered hearing it was when we visited her in the hospital after she got shot. I never called her anything but Elena.

Mr. Harris said, "I'd like to talk with your mother, young man." It sounded like I had done something wrong and he was going to make me pay. But what could I have done to the Harris's?

I stepped back and said, "She's up at the lighthouse with my dad and sister, Mr. Harris."

"Your dad? I thought your mother was a widow."

"No, my dad returned from Manchuria a few days ago. He surprised all of us."

"Well, then. I'd like to talk to both of your parents. I'll call a taxi. Is there a phone nearby?"

Jerry spoke up, "Crafton doesn't have a taxi, Mr. Harris."

"How far is it to walk?"

"It's too far, sir. We rode our bikes from the lighthouse. Maybe if you call my parents, they'll drive down here to talk with you. Is it important—something about Elena?"

"No, Elena's fine. She and Lieutenant Nesbitt are at a government conference in New York; something to do with the United Nations. This is about Millie."

He still sounded very serious. "Oh. You can call my mom and dad at 247. It'll cost you a dime."

He smiled at me, probably thinking that I figured a dime was a lot, but I was just warning him to have some change in his pocket. Jerry and I didn't have a cent between us.

"Is a public phone nearby?"

I pointed toward the start of the pier where the blue phone booth was. I had never seen anyone use it. There was a phone book in it, hanging on a chain. The paper had gotten wet and it had expanded and some of the pages were stuck together. Mr. Harris started walking down the pier. When he got to the front of our store, he stopped and turned around. "Millie, talk to the boys until I get back. It will only be a couple of minutes."

"Okay, father."

Millie sat down on the edge of the pier with her legs hanging over. "Sit beside me so we can talk." She patted the pier beside her.

Jerry sat on one side and I sat on the other. Neither of us could think of anything to say for a moment, but Jerry came through, "You have a really nice boat."

"It's not really ours. Dad and Mom are going to deliver it to the real owner in The Bahamas, but I can't go. I have to go to the fifth grade. That's why we're here. I'm going to live with the Linfields."

I couldn't believe what I just heard. "What?" I looked into her eyes.

Millie started laughing. "I'm not kidding. I'm going to stay with you 'til Christmas. I guess you didn't know. I wonder why your mother didn't tell you."

"She didn't say anything 'cause it's not true."

"Oh, it's true all right. My dad wants to talk to your mom about paying for my room and board for three months. He needs your mother or dad to drive down here to get my things and take them to your house. I bet your mom or dad will come down here to get me and my things."

"I don't think my mom will be here."

"Maybe she'll send your father.

"Nope. He doesn't have a license. It's expired."

"Okay then, your mother will come. You just wait and see."

Millie pushed off the pier and dropped to the deck. As she walked along the polished surface of the deck she turned her head and said, "I bet your mother shows up."

I shouted back at her, "I'll bet she doesn't." I looked at Jerry for some kind of support, but he wasn't saying a thing. "What do you think, Jerry?"

"I don't know. Millie sounds like she knows something. I think I'll wait and see. Here comes Mr. Harris. Let's ask him about what Millie said."

Mr. Harris stood a little behind us. We were still sitting where we were when Millie dropped to the deck. We looked up when he said, "Rocky, your mom and dad are coming to get Millie's things. Millie has a bicycle, she'll ride back to the lighthouse with you boys. She's a strong rider—you might not be able to keep up with her, but you'll have to show her the way."

Mr. Harris climbed down to the deck and said, "I'll start getting Millie's things brought up. Can you boys help with her things? She's got a lot of clothes and a bicycle."

That confirmed Millie's comments. I was having a hard time believing that Millie was going to stay with us, and I wondered why Mom hadn't told me about the arrangement. Maybe because she was so busy with Dad returning home. I was thinking it probably wouldn't be too bad, kind of like having a new dog in the family. At least I wouldn't have to be going around picking up her poop.

Jerry put his hand on my shoulder and said, "Looks like you have another sister, but it will only be for three months. We can still do our stuff together."

"Yeah, but why couldn't she stay with you?"

"You know her sister better than I do, and your mom and Elena were in the FBI at the same time. Maybe the Harrises have more confidence in your family than anybody else."

"Maybe you're right. Susan and Millie might get along, too. Suz won't be following me around all the time."

Jerry's eyes were following something on the deck. I looked around and saw what had attracted his attention. It was a young woman about the same age as Mom; maybe a little older than Elena, but I was just guessing. She was wearing a white blouse, blue shorts and no shoes. She had pink polish on her toenails.

Jerry poked me with his elbow and whispered, "Who is that? She's almost as pretty as your Elena."

I couldn't help noticing her blonde hair and pretty face, even though she had on a pair of black plastic sunglasses. Although I couldn't see her eyes, she turned her head toward us and said, "Hi, boys. Are you going to help get Millie's luggage up on the dock?"

"Sure. Can we come aboard?"

"Please do. Which one of you is Rocky?"

We dropped to the deck and I answered, "I am. Are you Elena's older sister?"

"Thank-you, Rocky. Millie is my daughter and I'm Elena's step mother." The sunglasses were smiling at me. "I'm Ronda Harris." She put out her hand but I didn't know whether to shake it or kiss it; the way she held it was like I had seen a queen meeting her subjects. Jerry helped out by stepping up to hold her outstretched fingers lightly in both his hands like a clam shell.

"Glad to meet you, Mrs. Harris. I'm Jerry Morgan."

"You are quite the gentleman, Mr. Morgan."

"Thank-you, ma'am. Rocky and I are best friends, but he's a little shy around pretty women."

I couldn't stand it any longer, Jerry had taken over the conversation. I had to set her straight. "I'm not shy, Mrs. Harris. I just haven't had as much experience with ladies as Jerry. I'm supposed to treat women with respect, especially when they live on a yacht." I smiled and she began laughing; just what I wanted.

She reached toward me and I shook her hand. I didn't use Jerry's method, just a regular handshake. Her hand was soft but she had a firm grip, almost like a man would have, but a man would never smell as good as she did. I think it was the scent of lilacs, but it could have been some other flower. One time, Mom said she sprayed a mist of scent into the air and then walked through it, but I think Mrs. Harris sprayed herself with perfume. Then, I thought about her strong handshake. I bet she played lots of tennis; rich women spend time playing tennis at country clubs while their husbands are working.

"You're very cute, young man. I think you and Millie are going to become good friends."

That bothered me a little. Why would a woman tell a ten-year-old boy he is cute? Isn't *cute* for babies? I could understand if she said I was handsome; Mom has told me that before, and I believed her, even if it wasn't completely true.

Chapter 9

DINNER AT SEA

Two men and a woman appeared from below deck carrying suitcases. The men wore fancy white shirts and black pants, the woman a light-yellow blouse and green skirt. They all had white slip-on shoes. I guess they didn't want to scratch or leave any marks on the deck. Maybe those shoes wouldn't slide on a slippery deck. Mr. Harris and Millie wore those shoes too, but Millie's were gray. I wondered how many crew members there were on the yacht. I didn't know the Harris's background, but maybe they couldn't sail a boat that big by themselves.

There were six suitcases for all of Millie's stuff. When our family travelled, Susan and I shared one suitcase. I wondered what could be in all that luggage. I hope she didn't have a bunch of dress-up clothes; they wouldn't be much good in Crafton. She probably had enough underwear so she wouldn't have to wash clothes but once a month.

Jerry whispered, "I think she has enough clothes for at least one weekend."

I laughed and said, "Maybe three days." I put my arm around his shoulders and talked into his ear, "Don't let them hear what we said."

Jerry and I started moving the suitcases up on the dock. Jerry got on top of the pier and pulled the luggage up as I lifted it high enough for him to grab ahold. When we had the six suitcases off the yacht, I saw our car coming down the pier toward the boat. Mom was driving but Dad wasn't with her. Mr. Harris was standing behind me, supervising.

"Don't forget Millie's bicycle, boys."

I turned around and saw a shiny, black woman's bike with cables running from the handlebars. My eyes traced the cables to the wheels. Her bike had handbrakes and small tires; just like a man's English racing bike. And it even had a speedometer. I couldn't take my eyes off that bike. I hoped Millie would let me try it out. I'd better be nice to her. I didn't think I would be strong enough to lift the bike up to Jerry, so I was going to ask Mr. Harris for help, but I tried and it wasn't very heavy. I lifted it up to Jerry and said, "Careful, Jerry, don't scratch it, it's beautiful."

Jerry hoisted it up and said, "Hey, it's a three-speed."

I hadn't even noticed the gear shift lever. I heard Mom. "Rocky, climb up and help Jerry load the luggage into the trunk and back seat." I looked away from the bike at Mom and said, "You didn't tell me about Millie. How come?"

"I'll tell you all about it later."

I heard voices behind me. The Harrises were climbing to the top of the pier, Mrs. Harris first and Mr. Harris last.

"Come on, Rocky. There's six of these things." Jerry was lugging two of the suitcases toward the car, almost dragging them. He was able to hold one of the cases above the dock timbers, but not both. Once I saw a drunk man walking downhill and Jerry's motion reminded me of him.

Mom had popped open the trunk when she stopped the car about fifteen feet from the steps to the deck of the yacht. I grabbed two more pieces of luggage, two smaller ones, thinking I would put them on the back seat. Jerry had gotten one case in the trunk and was pushing the second suitcase on top of the first.

"We can only get one more in the trunk, Rock—a small one."

I carried one of the smaller cases to Jerry and we jammed it in the rear of the car. It barely went in, but we were able to get the trunk closed. The other three smaller suitcases went on the back seat. There wasn't any room for the bicycle. Jerry and I walked over to where Mom and the Harrises were talking. They were talking about dinner. We stood there waiting for about a minute before I could break in.

"There's no room for the bike, Mom."

Mr. Harris said, "That's all right. Millie will ride her bike to the lighthouse when you boys ride back. She can go with you or find her own way. The lighthouse is easy to see from the top of the hill, isn't it?"

I remembered Mr. Harris saying she could ride her bike to the lighthouse.

Mom looked at me and then said, "Yes. The boys can show Millie the easiest way, but she can't get lost as long as she can see the lighthouse."

"That's right, Mr. Harris. We'll ride with her. There's only two left turns to our house."

"Okay, then. We'll expect you back at the boat at seven o'clock for dinner. Don't bother to dress up. We like casual."

Mom got in the car and gave the Harrises a little wave and then began turning around on the pier. She could have backed up all the way to the road, but I think she was a little worried about making a mistake and backing off the edge into the water. We watched as she got ready to drive away. She rolled down the window and said, "See you at home in a little while. Help Millie get up the hill, boys. Make sure she doesn't get hit by a car or truck on Lighthouse Road. The sun is going down in a bit and you don't have lights on your bikes. Ride on the shoulder."

"Okay, Mom."

Millie was already on her bike, waiting for us to get moving down the pier where our bikes were parked. As Jerry and I jogged along the pier, she rode past us and stopped next to our bikes. When we arrived at the craft store, she said, "Why don't you guys have bicycles for men?"

Jerry was ready for Millie's question. "These bikes were cheaper, there's less metal in them. You know, during the war, metal was hard to get." He glanced at me to see if I was going along with him.

I almost laughed, but decided to keep a straight face. Before long, Millie would know the truth; the bikes we had were the ones that were available. I had the same feeling about Millie as Jerry did. She was going to have to earn a place in our camaraderie, as Jerry liked to call it. He told me his mom said that is what we had. I thought it was just a friendship. I had never heard that word before. Someday we'll buy men's bikes—maybe when we get to high school. We'll be able to get real jobs then.

Jerry and I rode ahead of Millie to the turnoff to Lighthouse Road and waited for her to catch up. She wasn't that far behind us, and seemed to be taking her time, looking at everything as she rode. She reminded me of Mom when she's shopping, not wanting to miss any bargains. Mom would look at everything, touching all the clothes. I always wondered what she was thinking.

One car and a pickup went by as we got ready to go uphill toward the lighthouse. It wasn't dark enough for anyone to have their lights on yet. We should be home in about ten minutes. I hope Jerry will be able to eat with us on the yacht. I'll have Mom call for permission.

We were looking up the hill when Millie said, "I'll bet I can ride up there sitting down."

Jerry and I looked at each other and smiled. We had never done that on our bikes; we had never made it more than about half-way before having to get off and walk to the top.

"What'll you bet, Millie?" Her comment had been a dare to Jerry and me.

"I'll make you some cookies if I can't do it. If I can, you have to wash and wax my bike."

"What do you think, Rocky? Should we take the bet?"

"Yeah. I don't think she can do it. How long would it take to wash and wax her bike?"

"Not long. Let's see if she can do it."

Millie gave a little push and hopped on her bike seat. We watched her move steadily up the hill, her legs almost a blur, going round and round on the pedals, but the bike was climbing steadily up the hill.

"Come on, Jerry, let's see if we can make it without walking."

Jerry and I almost made it to the top on our bikes, but we had to walk up the last 100 feet or so. When we got to the top, Millie was not in sight. I hoped she had made it to the lighthouse without any problems. Jerry and I thought she would be waiting for us at the crest of the hill, ready to say, 'I told you I could do it.' We rode the rest of the way as fast as we could go to make sure Millie had made it okay. Her bike was parked next to the porch. We dropped our bikes in the grass and gravel near the porch and went inside.

Millie was sitting on the sofa beside Susan and Surprise. She was petting the dog. Millie didn't say anything, but we knew we were in trouble if we opened our mouths. The girls were watching TV. It looked like a puppet show was on so Jerry and I went in my room and sat on the bed.

Jerry said, "I should have known she could do it. I forgot about her having at least three gears. She used her lowest gear and went right up the hill."

"Oh, well. That job with her bike will only take about thirty minutes. We'll do it tomorrow if we have time. We'll use some of our car wax to shine it. With those small fenders, it won't take long. When I get a man's bike, it'll have gears."

"Yeah, and skinny tires. I'd like a blue one, not black." Jerry and I both liked blue.

"We need to call your mom and see if you can eat on the boat with us. I'll have my mom call her."

The oval table in the boat was big enough for eight, just right for all of us. Mr. Harris wanted to know all about Dad's ideas for the craft store and Dad asked about the trip Mr. and Mrs. Harris were going to take to The Bahamas. I don't know what Mrs. Harris and Mom talked about, I was listening to the men, but I think the ladies were talking about Millie going to school at Crafton; I heard them say Millie several times.

The lady we had seen earlier, dressed in green and yellow, was now wearing a pink blouse and black skirt and her nearly black hair was in a bun. She was our waitress and the two men we had seen before were serving the food.

Jerry and I looked over the items being served, but we didn't recognize much except some buns. There were glasses of water for everyone and the adults had wine glasses and coffee cups. The waitress, Margarita, gave me a plate covered with stuff I had never seen before. I looked at Jerry, he looked back and hunched up his shoulders. His plate was just like mine. Jerry pointed to a portion on his plate and asked Millie, "What is this?"

"That's squid. Try it." Millie gave me a funny smile—like she figured Jerry would spit it out, and then she'd laugh.

I found the same item on my plate and after studying it for a few seconds, I said, "I don't think I want to try it. I'd rather have a hamburger."

Mrs. Harris heard what I said. "I thought you boys would like to try calamari, but I guess I was wrong. What can I have Margarita prepare for you? You can have a hamburger if you really want one. We have plenty of ground beef."

Jerry and I both nodded our heads. Mrs. Harris rang a little bell that was sitting on the table next to her water glass. Margarita, the lady in pink and black, appeared and talked with Mrs. Harris. Margarita smiled and looked at me. "Would you like anything else, sir?"

She called me sir. What a surprise. I didn't know how to answer her. All I could think of was catsup, so I said, "Some catsup, please." Then she looked at Jerry and asked, "The same for you, young man?"

"Yes, please."

I could feel Millie looking at me, but I didn't glance in her direction. I wanted to eat something that I recognized, not some slimy stuff from an ugly sea creature. I suppose I would have to try it if I was shipwrecked and it was the only thing to eat or starve. I wanted to ask Millie what it tastes like, but I decided I'd better keep my mouth shut until my hamburger arrived.

When Millie leaned forward to drink some water, Jerry reached across Millie's back and poked me with his fork. "Try the salad, Rock. It's okay."

Chapter 10

THE ATTIC

We got home about ten-thirty. Millie had said her goodbyes to her parents and the crew of the yacht and we all climbed into the car. It was quiet in the car as Mom drove us to the lighthouse. Millie's bike was still at the front porch, so Jerry and I moved it around the house and out of sight from the road. Mom was worried that someone might take it, but I didn't think anyone would be coming around our house late at night. The light from the lighthouse made it easy to see without having any of the outside house lights turned on.

As soon as we got in the house, Mom asked Jerry if he wanted to stay over, but he said he'd better go home. We took Millie's luggage out of the car and piled it in the living room. Mom took Jerry home and was back in about fifteen minutes. She had probably talked with Jerry's parents. Granma said Jerry lived a hoot and a holler from the lighthouse. It seemed a long way when we rode our bikes. Jerry's house wasn't just down the street. While Mom was gone, we had some vanilla ice cream with chocolate syrup.

When we saw the car lights flash through the windows, Dad went out to meet Mom. They were talking about the attic as they came in the house. I knew there was an attic but I had never seen a way to get up there. There was a small square window at the end of the house below the peak of the roof, but it looked dirty on the inside, kind of brownish with white streaks as if it had leaked when it rained.

61

"How late do you stay up, Millie?"

"I usually go to bed about ten o'clock, Mrs. Linfield, but when we have company, I stay up 'til eleven."

"I'll show you your room. We'll move your luggage in there in the morning. Do you know which suitcase contains your night clothes?"

"Uh-huh, it's that small green one." She pointed at the suitcase on the top of the pile.

"Rocky, would you please take it to your bedroom?"

I sat there on the sofa kind of frozen. Millie and I were going to sleep together? I had slept in the same bed with Susan before, but she is just a little kid. Millie is my age. How is this going to work? I won't be able to sleep if she moves around or snores.

"Rocky, would you please take Millie's green suitcase into your bedroom and put it on the bed?"

"Uh, okay, Mom." I wondered what was in that little suitcase. I imagined some frilly pink pajamas like on store models in big city store windows. This is going to be something to tell Jerry about tomorrow.

Millie and Mom followed me into the bedroom and Millie looked at all the walls and up at the ceiling and then sat on the bed. I said, "You can put your things in that bottom drawer, it's empty." I pointed at the cabinet next to the door.

"Rocky, you will have to take your clothing out of the chest of drawers so Millie will have all four drawers for her things."

"Where will I put my stuff?"

"You're going to sleep in the attic as long as Millie is with us."

At first, I felt like I was being moved to a dungeon; I was being moved from my personal space for someone I hardly knew, and that someone was a girl. I was being taken from my home and being placed in an internment camp, just like the Japanese-Americans in the Second World War. I didn't even know how to get up in the attic. I wondered if it was full of dust, spiders or other bugs. Dad called me into the hallway.

"I'm going to lift you up so you can hook your fingers into that slot in the ceiling. Then I'll lower you down. Hang onto that groove and I'll grab the steps when they get low enough."

"Okay, but hold onto me."

Dad formed a step with his fingers from both hands interlaced and lifted me up where I could hook my fingers into the groove.

"Okay, you can lower me now."

As I was lowered, the steps to the attic followed me down. Dad grabbed the steps when my feet hit the floor and he forced the steps to the floor. A light was on up there. It must have come on automatically when the steps were pulled down. They weren't regular steps, they were too narrow. Regular steps would have blocked the hallway.

"Can I go up there?"

"Sure. I'll be right behind you."

Going up was a little scary when I got near the top; there wasn't anything to hold onto until I could reach the edge of the opening. When I got a little higher on the steps, I felt around with my left hand and grabbed hold of a narrow board attached to the attic floor. The last few steps were easy and I was standing in the attic. I was really surprised. It was beautiful.

I watched as Dad's head appeared above the floor. He looked around and said, "I think you're going to like this, Rocky. This is very good. The ceiling and walls are finished in cedar and covered with shellac. We might have to dust a little, but most everything looks nice and clean. Do you like it?"

"Yeah! This is really neat. I bet I'm the only kid in Crafton that has a place this fancy."

I sat on the soft bed and looked at Dad. He was too tall to stand all the way up, except in the middle of the room, so he got on one knee and looked around for a bit before he said, "I think we'll have to add some electrical boxes so you can plug in a fan, a radio, and a study lamp."

"You think I'll need a fan?"

"Maybe. The heat from the furnace will come up here, so you might get pretty warm, unless the ceiling isn't insulated. We'll have to wait and see when the snow comes. I'm sure you'll need a fan when summer arrives. The sun will cook the attic."

"I won't be up here in the summer, Dad. Millie will be gone by then."

"Oh, that's right. Mr. and Mrs. Harris should be back around Christmastime. I guess she'll only spend one semester in school at Crafton. I hope you'll help her adjust to her new surroundings. She doesn't know anyone here except you, Susan and Jerry, but I think she'll be in your class."

"She should be, she's my age."

"Well, let's go downstairs and get some of your things. We can toss them up here and you can get the remainder in the morning."

I could hear Millie in the bathroom brushing her teeth, the door was cracked open about two inches. Susan was in there with her, talking about not liking calamari. She was saying it tasted like wet pencil erasers. Susan started chewing on pencils when she entered the first grade a month ago. Mom said it was better than biting her fingernails. I think Suz was nervous about school.

Mom had told me to strip my bed and put clean sheets on it for Millie. The sheets on my bed had only been there for a couple of days and weren't dirty, but I think a guest should always get clean sheets. Kind of like staying in a motel. I was wondering how much Mr. and Mrs. Harris were paying us for taking care of Millie. Probably enough to pay for her food, the room didn't cost anything.

Mom came in the bedroom to check how I was doing with the sheets, and after inspection, she told me I had done a good job. The center fold in the sheet was right down the middle of the bed and the blanket was folded down under the feather pillows. The clean pillow slips smelled good; Mom had dried the laundry outside. My almost-clean sheets were in a pile on the floor. She told me to get whatever I needed from my room and change into my pajamas in the bathroom. She scooped up my sheets and said Dad was going to put some of my stuff in the attic. I was supposed to move the rest of my things tomorrow. It was too late to do any dusting up there tonight. Mom said she hoped I wouldn't have a fit of sneezing.

Dad took my pile of clothes, except for my pajamas, and said, "I'll put your things in the bureau for you. I'm going to give you an empty milk bottle in case you have to whiz during the night. I don't want you to fall down those steps in the dark. You might damage the floor." He smiled and I laughed.

"Thanks, Dad." Some of his jokes are very funny.

I looked down the hall and the bathroom door was wide open, the light off. I wondered where Susan and Millie were, but then I heard some giggling coming from Susan's bedroom. Mom was moving toward Susan's door when she said, "Time for bed, girls. You have to help at the store tomorrow, so get your rest."

I was going into the bathroom, but I watched Millie leave Susan's room and go into my old bedroom. She had on purple pajamas that covered most of her bare feet, except for her toes. The bottoms were a bit too large and they dragged on the floor. When she got in her room, she turned, glanced at me, said, "Night, Rocky," and shut the door.

As I changed into my pajamas, brushed my teeth, and washed my face, I wondered if Millie's pajamas were hand-me-downs from Elena, but I knew the Harrises had money. Maybe she just likes the color purple, and when they were shopping, that was the only size that would fit her that was the right color.

I wadded up my clothes, climbed into the attic and put them at the foot of my bed. I looked in the chest of drawers and found my clean underwear. Dad had done a neat job with my stuff, except for the socks; they were in a disorganized pile, just as they always were. He had put an empty milk bottle next to my bed. I don't think I could ever fill it up with one whiz.

I laid down on the floor at the top of the steps and said, "Good night down there." I don't know if anyone heard me, but I didn't want to yell. Susan was probably already asleep.

Dad said, "Good night, Rocky. I'm going to put the stairs up so nobody walks into them during the night. Don't try to ride them down in the morning, I'll pull them down. I put a piece of twine where I can grab it."

As the stairs came up, I felt like I was in a castle and the draw-bridge was being lifted to protect the people inside. I hoped I wouldn't have a bad dream and start yelling during the night. Just before the stairs were all the way up, the light shut off. It was almost black, but I stood frozen in place for a few moments. I remembered seeing a string hanging down from the light on the ceiling. Then I could see momentarily, the lighthouse light from that dirty window gave me a chance to locate that string. I pulled on the string to turn on the light so I could see my bed. It was about three steps away, so I pulled the string, the light went out, and I felt my way to the bed. The next thing I knew, it was morning.

I hadn't used the milk bottle, but I did have to go when I woke up. I put on clean shorts and a T-shirt, and the rest of my clothes from Saturday. The stairs were already down; Dad must be up—maybe making coffee, but I couldn't smell it yet. I wondered what time it was. I need to get a clock for the attic; a wind-up with an alarm. I went downstairs and into the bathroom to brush my teeth; I had a terrible taste in my mouth. It was probably something from the hamburger, it couldn't have been from the squid. Those were really good burgers that Jerry and I had on the yacht. The cook had put a slice of tomato, two dill pickles, meat, and lettuce between those buns. I had added the proper amount of catsup.

After flushing the toilet, I went in the kitchen. Dad was just putting the coffee pot on the stove.

"Good morning. How'd you sleep up there?"

"Good morning, Dad. Really good. I didn't even dream."

Chapter 11

NEWSPAPER REPORTER

Sunday was cool and blustery. Although it was light after seven in the morning, it felt like the sky was going to be cloudy and gray all day. After breakfast, we loaded the car with the boxes of models, glue, paints, and other stuff Dad and Mom had bought in Edgewater. Dad kept looking at the clouds and saying that he hoped it wasn't going to rain until after we had all the boxes moved into the store. Millie was not afraid to work or get dirty, she helped Susan move the boxes stored in Susan's bedroom onto the porch.

The box with the model trains was the heaviest, and Susan called out to me to help Millie. Susan wasn't able to lift her side of the box. Suzy held the screen door open for us and Millie and I carried the heavy load out to the car. Dad and Mom packed the car full. There wasn't enough room for us in the car, except for Suzy. She was going to ride on Dad's lap. Millie and I were supposed to ride our bikes. I telephoned Jerry and he said he would come over and get his bike in the afternoon, but he might not be able to come to the pier. I told him we would see him at school tomorrow if he didn't show up at the store.

"You guys be careful on the road. Sunday drivers are sometimes thinking of their sins and not concentrating on driving. If you aren't at the store in about ten minutes, we're coming after you, so no fooling around. Okay?"

"Okay, Dad."

"Okay, Mr. Linfield."

Dad got in the passenger seat, lifted Suzy onto his lap and got comfortable. Mom rolled down her window and said, "See you on the pier in a few minutes." Millie and I watched them drive to the highway and start toward the waterfront.

"Where'd you put my bike, Rocky?"

"Stay right here, I'll get it." I wanted to hold onto the hand grips on that bike, and as soon as I could, I wanted to ride it and try out the gears. Racing Millie's bike against Jerry's or mine, would be like racing a new sports car against a Model T. I wheeled her black three-speed from behind the house out to the front porch and held it until she was ready to ride.

She smiled and said, "Thank-you."

Her smile really made me feel good. I picked up my bike from the ground, and we started riding toward the highway. Although Millie could have gone much faster than I could, she stayed beside me all the way to Pier Lane. She used her brakes most of the way down the hill just like I did. I think she worried about falling and getting her skin torn off by the gravel or the blacktop. I had the same thoughts. There was no reason to take chances and have to go to the hospital.

When we arrived at Pier Lane, I watched her shift gears, stand on the pedals, and rocket away from me. There was no way I could catch her, I just pedaled along looking around the bay for boats I hadn't seen before. The only big difference that I noticed was that the yacht was no longer tied up at the pier. Mr. and Mrs. Harris and crew were on their way to The Bahamas. I wondered if I would ever see that beautiful boat again.

Mom and Dad were unloading the car when I got to the store. Millie's bicycle was parked at a bike rack in front of the boat rental store next door. Randahl's Rentals was bigger than our store, painted blue with black trim. Randahl's neon sign was turned off. The last time I had seen it on, it was flickering. It probably burned out.

I parked my bike next to Millie's three-speed and went over to the car. I didn't see Millie.

"Where's Millie, Mom?"

Mom was picking up a box from the back seat, but she put it down, turned toward me and said, "She's inside, sweeping. Maybe you can hold the dust pan for her."

I went inside the store and looked around, but didn't see Millie. I walked toward the back of the store and called out, "Millie?"

"I'm in here, Rocky."

There was a big closet with a curtain instead of a door. She pushed the curtain aside with the broom handle so we could see each other. She was sweeping some bits of paper, lint, and what looked like brown rice, from a small pile between two cabinets full of books and fishing supplies. There were several spools of fishing line.

I recognized the brown rice, but it wasn't rice. It was mouse turds. Our science teacher had shown us pictures of mouse droppings last year. He told us not to touch them or breathe the dust from them; they could cause disease.

"Don't sweep up that stuff that looks like rice. It's mouse poop."

"Mouse poop?"

"Yeah. You don't want to touch it or breathe the dust from it; it'll make you sick."

"So how do we get rid of it?"

"We'll spray it with bleach and then vacuum it up. Have you seen a vacuum in here?"

"Maybe."

"Maybe? What do you mean?"

"There's a small closet back there." She pointed toward the rear of the store. "I've never seen some of that stuff before. I just took a peek and slammed the door shut. I wasn't looking for a vacuum."

"I'll look."

The closet was narrow, but pretty deep. I pushed some fishing rods and small buoys out of the way. There was a small, black-and-gray upright vacuum behind an extra shelf that was standing on end. I just hoped the machine worked. To get it out, I had to remove almost everything from the closet. There were more mouse turds on the floor next to the shelf.

Millie had followed me with the broom. I told her about the droppings and she said, "What would mice eat in here, there isn't any food."

"Yes there is. There's candy in those glass bottles next to the cash register. I'll bet some was dropped on the floor and the mice ate it. Did you see any place to plug in the vacuum?"

"No, but there must be one where the cash register is, unless it uses a crank." She laughed and then frowned, hunching her shoulders. "Everything in here looks old."

"I think the cord is long enough to reach back here." I left the vacuum standing near the back closet and unwound the cord. It must have been twenty-five or thirty feet long. Millie picked up the plug and pulled on the cord as she made her way to the register.

"Okay. I plugged it in. Try it."

I flipped the switch and the vacuum motor and floor light came on. I was a little surprised that it worked. Millie came running back to me with a spray bottle of bleach. She made a mean face and said, "Where are those dirty mouse turds?" She held the spray bottle like a six-gun.

I started laughing and held out my hand for the bottle of bleach.

"I'll spray, you vacuum."

It only took us a couple of minutes to get all the mouse droppings vacuumed up. I rewound the cord on the vacuum handle and put the machine back in the closet.We made a pretty good clean-up team.

Mom and Dad had transferred all the boxes from the car to the store and were standing by the cash register talking and pointing at cabinets and counter-tops where they thought the merchandise should go. Mom was pointing at the cigarette machine and said, "Can you take that thing out of here? It's in the way."

Dad motioned for me to help him. We picked up the machine and moved it outside underneath the right front window. I heard Mom say that she hoped someone would steal it. Dad smiled and said, "She doesn't mean that. We're going to trade it in for a candy machine."

"Good. I like Babe Ruths and Butterfingers." My mouth began to water as I recalled biting into peanuts and chocolate.

"Say, I like Babe Ruth candy bars, too. That's the best buy for a nickel."

The man's voice came from behind me. I didn't recognize it, so I turned around to see who it was. He was younger than Dad and wore brown pants, a white long-sleeved shirt, and a wide black tie. He looked a bit uncomfortable. He was probably cold and should have had on a sweater. He stuck out his hand and said, "I'm Jack Timmons. I'm a new reporter for *The Crafton News and Views* newspaper."

I shook hands with him and said, "I'm Rocky Linfield, this is my dad." I pointed to Dad, who was rolling up his sleeves. The men shook hands and Dad asked the reporter what we could do for him.

"Actually, Mr. Linfield, I've come to see your son."

I looked at him wondering what he wanted with me. I had never talked with a newspaper reporter before, but I remembered Granma once said you have to be careful about what you say to them, they don't always report what you say accurately.

Dad said, "About what?"

"I've been looking for a story and I dropped by the police station on Friday. I heard two officers talking about two boys and a woman that helped catch some Russian spies. I pried one of the names out of them and it was Rocky. I was out of town yesterday, but this morning I asked around and was told to visit the lighthouse, but no one was there. One of your neighbors sent me to Mrs. Makler and she said Rocky was probably down at the pier. I would like to interview the young man and have him tell me the story about the spies. I think it would be a good addition to the paper—local color."

Dad put his hand on my shoulder and said, "Rocky, do you want to talk to Mr. Timmons about your summer experience? You don't have to if you don't want to. The story will be in the paper and everybody will know about you, Jerry, and your mom."

"Do it, Rocky. You'll be famous!" Millie had been standing in the doorway and had overheard Dad and me talking with the reporter, but I didn't think she knew anything about the capture of the spies, unless Elena had mentioned it.

I wasn't sure what to say, but I felt like I needed to tell the story for Jerry, too. I didn't know what Mom would think. I'd better ask her. I wasn't sure Mom wanted everyone in Crafton to know she had worked for the FBI, but I was pretty sure they knew Granma had been an agent.

I turned my head toward the door and shouted, "Mom!"

"You don't need to shout, Rocky. I'm right here." She was standing just inside the door looking over Millie's head. "What can I do for you?"

"This man is a reporter for the newspaper. Can I tell him about the spies?"

I could tell Mom was thinking about it, because she didn't answer right away.

"Well, all right, but only if he'll promise that I can read the story before it appears in the paper."

I looked at the reporter. He smiled and said, "I promise."

The reporter and I sat down beside the cigarette machine. I could smell the tobacco. He pulled out a notebook from his back pocket and a pencil from his shirt pocket.

I said, "Where do you want me to start?"

"How about when you first came to the lighthouse?"

Millie came over and stood beside me. "Can I listen?"

"Sure." I tapped on the timber beside me and she sat down.

Because of all his questions, it took almost an hour to tell Mr. Timmons the story. Millie didn't say a word, but she seemed to take in our every word. I was going to say, "*That's all*," when Jerry showed up. He parked his bike and was walking toward us.

I said, "That's Jerry Morgan, Mr. Timmons. He can answer any of your questions. The fireworks were his." I introduced Jerry to the reporter.

"Did you tell him about the Russian spies?"

I nodded my head and said, "Yep. The whole story. I don't think I left anything out."

Jerry sat down beside Millie. She turned her head and spoke softly to him, "You and Rocky are going to be famous." Jerry smiled.

SCHOOL FOR MILLIE

While I was telling the reporter about Jerry's and my kidnapping, and later on helping to catch the spies, Mom and Dad had reorganized the display cabinets in the store. I don't remember hearing them moving stuff around; I guess I was too involved with the story. The reporter thanked me and said he would contact Mom before the write-up appeared in the paper on Thursday. I gave him our home phone number. He recognized it as being the number for the lighthouse.

It took all six of us about an hour to put all the models and other hobby supplies in the cabinets so the arrangements looked nice and it was easy to find things. Suz slowed us down a bit because she couldn't read and had to ask lots of questions, but Mom helped her. We put the old stuff that was in the dusty cabinets in the empty boxes. We cleaned the cabinets, inside and out. It was 5:30 when we finished, locked the door, and started home. As Dad, Mom, and Suz got in the car, Mom said there was still a lot to do before we could open the store for business. Millie, Jerry, and I rode our bikes to Jerry's house so Millie could meet Mr. and Mrs. Morgan, then Millie and I pedaled to the lighthouse. On the way, I showed her where Granma lived, but we didn't stop.

For Sunday dinner, we had waffles, like we did many times before Dad went to Korea. While we were eating, Millie asked me, "Were all those things you told that guy true?"

"Sure. Do you think I would lie to somebody from the newspaper?"

"I'd bet it's happened before." Millie had that determined look.

"Not from me. I might have left out some of the details, but that's all."

"Well then, I think you, Jerry and your mom are heroes. You're the first heroes I've ever met. I'm going to keep a copy of the paper when the story comes out. I want you to sign it. It'll be one of the treasures from my stay in Crafton, something I'll always remember."

"A scrapbook item?" I thought she was making too big a deal out of it.

She smiled, "Uh-huh. I'll put it with my first yacht travel pictures."

When Millie and Mom had cleared the table and we were about to have some ice cream, Millie was walking around the house from room to room. I wondered what she was doing.

"What are you looking for, Millie?"

"Surprise. Where is he? Did he run outside when we came in?"

Mom answered, "My mother came over and got him when we were down at the pier. We'll go over to her house tomorrow so you can meet her and see Surprise. During the week, Surprise stays with her. My mother's name is Martha Makler. She's not a regular grandmother."

Millie came over and asked me, "What did your mom mean when she said her mom's not a regular grandmother?"

"Granma is a former FBI agent. She'll investigate you." I didn't grin.

Millie stood there frowning for a moment and then said, "I'm not worried. I haven't done anything wrong."

"Well, you'd better be careful around her. She's a crack shot with a forty-five."

Millie smiled, pushed me lightly in the chest, and said, "Oh, you're joking. I'll get you for that."

"I'm not joking, just wait and see." I didn't want to tell Millie how active and smart Granma was. I figured she would find that out for herself.

While Mom and Dad did the dishes, Millie, Suz, and I watched some of Ed Sullivan. I was wondering how difficult it would be to learn to juggle, when Mom came into the living room and stood there watching TV for a minute. Just as a commercial for Alka-Seltzer came on, Mom said, "Millie, we need to get all your things out of the suitcases and into the dresser and closet. While we're doing that, you can tell me what you want to wear to school tomorrow. We might have to iron something."

"Okay, Mrs. Linfield."

When we heard what Mom said, Suz and I looked at each other and nodded. We both were thinking the same thing. Suz went to the TV and pushed the on/off switch and the screen went blank. Suz went to her bedroom, but I sat there on the floor for a moment thinking about having Millie in my class. I hoped she wouldn't show how smart she is. If she does, the other kids won't like her. I'll have to clue her in on the way to school.

Dad had lengthened the cord on the stairs to the attic so I could jump and grab it. I pulled the steps down and when I was on the third step, Mom called to me.

"Rocky, you need to take these things up to your room." Mom had piled a bunch of my shirts and pants on a chair outside the door to Millie's bedroom. I grabbed an armful of my clothes, looked in my old room and saw Millie opening up a suitcase and piling her things on the bed. There were two empty cases standing on end by the closet door. I wondered where we were going to store all those empties, but it suddenly came to me, they were going to be put in the attic for me to guard. Christmas was still three months away. It seemed like that was a long time to have to live in the attic. At least it wasn't full of spiders; it was a nice room.

I took three armfuls of clothes up those skinny stairs before I sat down on my bed for a moment. I put the shirts in one stack and the pants in another. My underwear was already in the top drawer of the dresser. I glanced at the opening in the attic leading downstairs and wondered how long after the war was over that Japanese Americans got out of the internment camps; maybe Granma will know. I heard Millie call my name.

"Rocky, there's one more bunch of your things on the chair. Do you want me to bring them up?"

I thought for a moment and then said, "If you want to. You can see what my attic room looks like. Be careful on the stairs." I could hear her taking one step at a time, slowly coming up. When her head appeared through the hole in the floor, I reached down and grabbed her right arm so she couldn't fall. She looked at me and smiled.

"My, this is very nice. Thanks for helping me up the steps. I think I had too big a load."

I decided to say something funny, so I asked, "How much do you weigh?"

She scowled and threw my clothes in a heap on the floor. "Thanks a lot. Couldn't you just thank me for bringing up your things?"

"Thank-you, Millie. I didn't mean that you were fat or anything. I meant it as a joke."

"Well, I don't think that was funny. Do you treat all the girls that way?"

"No, just the ones I like." That seemed to help because she smiled and started down the stairs. After she had taken three steps, she stopped and said, "I have to iron a blouse. I'll see you in the morning. Good night."

"Okay. Good night."

When I woke up in the morning, I could smell coffee and hear rain drops hitting the roof. I got into my school clothes and went down to the bathroom. Suzy was brushing her teeth, but I could see the mirror over her head, so I combed my hair and went into the kitchen. I had to pee, but I decided to wait until the girls were finished with the bathroom.

"Morning."

"Good morning, Rocky." Mom and Dad said the same thing—it almost sounded like one voice, but it was from a very small choir.

Suz and Millie joined us at the table and we had Cream of Wheat and strawberries. Millie didn't look like she was dressed for school; she still had on her pajama top over a plaid skirt, and no shoes, just white socks. We had to hurry to get to the bus, so Suz and I ate quickly. I wondered why Millie was taking so much time. *Wasn't she going to school with us?* Suz and I put on jackets and headed out the door, but after I had taken a few steps, I stopped and shouted back at the house. "Come on, Millie, you'll make us all late."

Mom came out on the porch and said, "I'm taking Millie to school today. She has to register before she can be assigned to a class."

"Okay. Tell her I'll see her in Miss Hill's class. That's room 127."

Suz and I got on bus 4. The driver, Mr. Trondell, said hi and called us by name. He knew the first name of every kid that rode with him. He wore glasses, was partially bald, and always wore a maroon sweater during the winter months. Sometimes he whistled as he drove. The lighthouse stop was the last pick-up before we got to school. The bus was never full even if no one was absent that day. Jerry was usually on bus 7, but sometimes he would have to ride bus 3 when he was almost late. He would have to run about three blocks to catch bus 3. Bus 7 stopped two houses from his place on the corner of eighth and Tietan.

I watched the classroom door all morning, expecting to see Millie arrive with the principal, Mr. Howell. But the morning went fast and only kids that had to use the restroom came and went. No adults or Millie showed up. I thought maybe she got sick and stayed home with Mom and Dad.

I was surprised at lunchtime. The cafeteria was open from noon until 12:30 for 5th and 6th graders. I went through the line, got spaghetti, orange Jell-O with fruit in it, and chocolate milk. I sat down at a table with Billy O'Reilly and started eating, all the time looking around to see if Millie might be there. I saw Jerry sitting beside a girl, but I couldn't see her face, they were turned away toward the windows.

Billy said, "Wha'd yah do this weekend?"

"I worked at the library and down at the pier. Mom and Dad bought Sherner's store. They're going to sell hobby stuff—you know, model planes, boats, and trains. What'd you do?"

"Oh, I worked outside with my dad. We cleaned up the yard and chopped some firewood."

He paused as he looked over at Jerry, then said, "Who's that girl with Jerry?" He pointed toward the windows where Jerry had been sitting.

Jerry was walking toward the return tray area, but I couldn't see who was behind him until he turned to go around the table closest to the cleanup rails. It was Millie! I wasn't quite finished with my chocolate milk, but I had to talk with Millie. Where had she been all morning? Why was she eating lunch with Jerry?

I planned my way to the return tray rails so Millie and I would bump into each other. After she placed her tray on the stack to be washed, she looked right at me.

"Oh! Hi, Rocky."

"Hi, Millie. Where have you been all morning. I've been watching for you, but you never came to class."

"I'm in sixth grade, same class as Jerry. He's been showing me around."

"I don't get it. How did you get in the sixth grade?"

"I'm not sure. I was given a test when I registered, and they said I was ready for grade six. That's all I know about it. Maybe your mom can explain it better."

"Uh, okay. Well, stick with Jerry, he'll watch out for you. Some of the sixth graders can be mean."

"All right. Thanks. We'll ride home together. I've got to go, Jerry's waiting for me." She pointed at the hallway door. Jerry waved when I looked at him, so I waved back. I watched Millie walk toward Jerry for a second and then I grabbed my chocolate milk container before it was taken from my tray, sucked it dry with the straw, and tossed the empty into the big waste basket at the end of the rails.

All afternoon, I kept wondering how Millie got put in grade six with Jerry; she was a whole year younger than him. I didn't learn much that afternoon, but Miss Hill started us making some Thanksgiving art projects with scissors, colored paper, and paste. I made a turkey without a head beside a chopping block with blood on it. Miss Hill said she thought it would be better to make a live bird, so I added a head and threw the chopping block in the waste basket. She said that my live turkey was much better. I thought my first picture was more realistic.

When three o'clock rolled around, the bell sounded and I met Suz and Millie standing alongside bus 4. Suz was climbing on the bus when I heard a loud car horn from behind the bus. I looked back and saw a brown pickup. At first, it reminded me of the Russian spies and I felt like I should get on the bus, but the horn sounded again with three short beeps. I stepped back from the bus to get a better look at the truck and saw Dad sitting in the driver's seat. He waved at me and motioned for me to come over to the pickup.

"Get the girls and we'll drive home together."

I was kind of excited that Dad had come to pick us up. He got his license and bought a pickup during the time Suz, Millie, and I were in school. I ran to the bus door and yelled at Suz and Millie, "It's Dad, he's gunna drive us home. Come on." I looked at Mr. Trondell and explained that we were going to ride home with my dad.

He said, "All right. You're sure it's your dad, Rocky?"

"Yes, sir. It's him."

"Okay. Help the girls off the bus. That last step's a big one."

Chapter 13

A HINT OF TROUBLE

Millie climbed in beside Dad, then I got in. Suz got on the running board and I pulled her up onto my lap and shut the door. I hoped we would go right to the lighthouse because my legs would go to sleep with Suz sitting on me for very long. When we were about half-way home, I noticed Millie's jacket was of brown corduroy with two pockets, each one big enough to carry at least two sandwiches. The sleeves went almost to her wrists. I reached over and touched her sleeve to see if it was really corduroy. It was—and soft, just like my white pants. Her skirt was the same plaid one she had on at breakfast. It had fall colors: red, yellow, light-green, and light-brown. Her blouse must have been the one she ironed last night, but the only part anyone could see was the white collar.

Suz was first in the house when we got home, then Millie and me. The TV was on, but Suz was in the kitchen getting a cookie from Mom. Dad had said he would be inside in a minute, he wanted to check something on the truck. Millie went right in her room and changed her clothes, then came into the living room and started watching TV with Suz.

I went in the kitchen to see Mom. She was busy washing something at the sink.

"Mom, did you know Millie got in the sixth grade?"

"Yes, Rocky. The principal gave her a test and he decided she should skip grade five."

I wondered how they did that. "I waited for Millie in class all morning long. I found out at lunch she was in Jerry's class. She was eating with Jerry."

"That was nice. She knew someone she could talk to. Being new to a school is sometimes difficult, especially if the student doesn't make friends easily."

"Yeah, I guess so, but I was hoping she would be in my class. We could do homework together."

"Well, you could invite Jerry over, they could do their homework together, and then all three of you could do things together."

"But, Mom, that's not the same."

"Don't worry, Rocky. You'll figure something out."

After school on Tuesday, Jerry and I washed and waxed Millie's bike. She watched us like a teacher watching a second grader write her first word in longhand. It took longer than I had thought, almost an hour. Our cold fingers looked like prunes after having them in the cold soapy water. The waxing went faster, the bike was already dry. We had Millie inspect our work and she said it was all right. She found a spot where we had missed wiping off the wax.

She told us we should wash and wax our bikes, but Jerry said it wouldn't do much good, they were almost ready for the junk yard. I had to agree with him. I figured that Granma's bike was older than all our ages added together. The original seat had worn out and Granpa put a newer one on about ten years ago. The seat was free. Granma said the newer one had been taken from a bike a car had run over. Nobody got hurt though; the bike was in a driveway and a car had backed over it.

Thursday evening was kind of exciting. The paper had come out in the late afternoon. I had been home from school for about an hour when the phone rang. Dad and I could hear it from the library. The outside of the house was the inside wall of the library building, so we could hear Suzy, when she yelled, and usually the phone, too, unless we were hammering or sawing.

Dinner was at 6:00 p.m. Mom asked Dad and me if we had heard the phone ringing.

"We sure did, hon. Were the calls about the library? People wanting books?"

"Nope. They wanted to know if the article in the paper was real. I told them it was. I answered four calls."

"They asked about the stuff I told the reporter?"

"That's right, Rocky. I reviewed it for the reporter on Tuesday. He said it would be in today's paper."

"Geez, Mom. You didn't tell me. Where's the paper?"

"It's on the little table below the phone."

I picked up the paper and there it was, on the lower half of the front page. I spread the paper out on the living room rug and began to read. Millie got down on the floor beside me on her knees and elbows. She finished the story before I did.

"That's almost identical to what you told the reporter, Rocky. He only left out some small details—they didn't matter."

I was thinking Friday was going to be a nothing day, but now I realized kids were going to make a big deal out of it. I'd better warn Jerry. I didn't know if Morgans took the paper. I called him and he said what I was thinking, we would both have a day of being pestered.

But Friday wasn't so bad. Miss Hill asked me if she could read the article to the class and I said she could. Afterwards, I had to answer questions, but there were only three. The rest of the day was just a regular day. When I saw Jerry at lunch, he told me his teacher, Mr. Dix, did the same thing as Miss Hill. I think they must have talked about it early Friday morning in the teacher's lounge. I think Miss Hill smoked.

Each night after dinner that week, Mr. Morgan had come over and helped Dad with the drywall and the electrical wiring in the new library building. I had homework so I didn't help Dad during the week, but Friday night we all painted the whole inside white. Suzy got tired after a short time and didn't want to do it anymore. She said her arms hurt. Mom put her to bed early.

Dad worked mornings at the store and then all afternoons and evenings in the library. I helped him after getting home from school. He called me his gofer. The first time he called me that, I thought he meant an animal doing dirty deeds, but he told me what it meant. We stayed up late Friday to finish painting, including some of the shelves Dad had made. Millie baby-sat Suzy when Mom came out to supervise Dad and his gofer. We didn't need any direction, but I think Mom felt better after checking how we were doing.

Jerry and his dad couldn't come over Saturday morning; Mr. Morgan had to work. I helped Dad finish nailing the shelves to the walls so they wouldn't fall over with a load of books and hurt someone. Mom had gotten some pieces of gray and blue rugs from a carpet dealer where they sold cheap remnants. We tacked the rugs to the floor; gray ones around the entrance and blue ones below the books. The floor looked nice. Mom said we should take off our shoes, but a second later, she said, "I'm kidding!"

It was about ten a.m. when we started moving books from the lighthouse to the new library. Mom put waxed paper on all the shelves to keep the books from sticking to the fresh paint. She supervised placing the books on the shelves in alphabetical order. There were some titles that were confusing because they started with the word *the*, so we went with the second word.

We were eating lunch when a car drove up and honked three times. Dad looked out the window and said, "I don't recognize who it is, but they're a nice looking couple."

I immediately thought of Lt. Nesbitt and Elena, so I said, "Is she pretty, Dad?"

"Uh-huh, very."

It had to be Elena. I got up from the sofa and laid my sandwich on my paper napkin and said, "Millie, your sister's here."

"Really? How do you know? You haven't even looked outside."

"I can tell by the horn beeps, and Dad said the woman was very pretty. It has to be Elena. Come on, let's see if I'm right." I grabbed Millie's wrist and pulled her off the sofa. She followed me out on the porch.

I was right, it was just who I thought, but I wondered why they were here. Granma's neighbor, Lt. Nesbitt's mother, usually told Granma when Aaron and Elena were coming to visit, but Granma hadn't called Mom to let us all know they were coming to Crafton. Granma hadn't brought Surprise over either. I began to think something might be wrong.

Before Elena could step onto the porch, the ladies had a group hug. I waited until the ladies' hug was over to have my hug with Elena and shake hands with Lt. Nesbitt. Dad introduced himself and shook hands with

Lt. Nesbitt and Elena. Jerry and Mr. Morgan had met Aaron and Elena before, so they just said 'hi.'

I asked the lieutenant, "How did you get time off to visit us?"

"We took two days off so Elena could talk with Millie in person."

"Oh." I figured it must be something important, but Mom had warned me before about being too nosey, so I didn't ask what it was all about.

Mom said, "Let's go inside and sit down. You can tell us what brought you to Crafton. I hope it's not about spies."

Elena and Aaron smiled, but the smile left their faces as we all sat down in the living room. Elena sat beside Millie on the sofa, "Millie, can we go to your room?"

"Sure. I want to show you my room, anyway. It used to be Rocky's, but he has moved to the attic. It's nice up there. I think he likes it."

Elena whispered something to Mom as she passed by. I couldn't hear what was said.

Mom brought in a plate of sandwiches and put it on the coffee table. Dad carried in a big bowl of potato chips and a stack of paper birthday napkins left over from Suzy's party.

I picked up a sandwich and watched Elena go into the bedroom with Millie and close the door. Elena seemed to be more like Millie's mother than her sister.

Mom said, "Rocky, would you please turn on the TV?"

"Okay." I got up and turned on the TV. It was on CBS channel 6. Army was playing football against Dartmouth. Army was ahead twenty-three to seven. Dartmouth wasn't doing so hot. I went to the sofa, took a bite from my sandwich, and sat down.

Mom said, "Turn up the sound a little, please."

I looked at her, wondering why she wanted the TV so loud, but I did what she asked. After I finished the last of my sandwich and got a glass of milk in the kitchen, I came back to the sofa. Half of Millie's sandwich was still on her napkin, just as she had left it. No one had moved it and Millie hadn't come from the bedroom. I wondered what Elena and Millie were doing. It wouldn't take long for Millie to show Elena her room, they should be back to watch the game and eat. I wanted to turn down the sound on the TV, it was too loud, but I didn't want Mom to have to tell me to leave it the way it was. I guess I was a little confused.

Dad said, "As soon as we're through eating, let's work on some more books. We should be able to finish in another hour or so."

Mom looked around the room and said, "Does anyone want more to eat? We have some apples and a lot more potato chips. I've got Cokes, coffee, milk, tea, and water to drink. Drinks are pretty much serve-yourself, just come in the kitchen and I'll show you where things are."

The bedroom door was still closed. It had been at least fifteen minutes since Millie and Elena went in there. I wondered what they were doing; the bedroom was just a simple bedroom, there wasn't much to see. Maybe Millie was showing Elena some of her new clothes. I couldn't think of anything else that would take so long. Did Mom want the TV loud so we couldn't hear them arguing?

The bedroom door opened and Millie followed Elena outside. Mom went outside with them and after a minute or so, Millie was hugging Mom. Elena put her arms around both of them.

The game ended: Army 37, Dartmouth 7. Dad turned off the TV, took some dishes into the kitchen, and said, "Time to get back to work, men—and Susan."

We all went outside. I was the last out of the house, following the others around the corner toward the library, but Mom stopped me and handed me the lighthouse key.

"Rocky, would you take Millie up to the gallery? I think she would like to see out into the ocean. The water is beautiful today."

Chapter 14

THE GALLERY

"Sure, Mom." I couldn't understand why Mom wanted me to take Millie to the top of the lighthouse, except to show her how much you could see from there, but maybe Millie would tell me what the sisters had talked about.

Millie stood beside Mom and Elena, with her arm around her sister's waist, not moving toward me or the lighthouse, so I took her hand in mine and moved a step. She seemed to resist, so I gave her a little tug. "Come on, Millie, it'll be fun. Are you afraid of heights?"

"No!"

She sounded mad at me for thinking she would be afraid of climbing to the top of the lighthouse. I looked at her eyes and saw they were red. She must have been crying. What had happened in her bedroom? That's when I realized Mom had asked me to take Millie to the lighthouse gallery to get her thinking of something else. I wonder what Mom knew?

"It will only take a few minutes. Come on. I think the ocean will be beautiful this afternoon. You'll see some birds and far off ships."

She began to walk with me toward the lighthouse, slowly at first, but then at normal speed. When we got to the door, I gave her the key to unlock it so she would have more things to remember about going to the gallery. The door always squeaked when it swung open.

"It's kind of dark in here, Rocky." She looked back at me, squinting from the dim interior to the open sunlit doorway.

"There's a light switch on the wall to your left. Flip it up."

With the lights on, Millie could see the steps that circled the inside wall up to the trap door that led to the gallery.

She pointed up and said, "We're going up there?"

"Uh-huh. Think of climbing to the torch on the Statue of Liberty, but not as high as that." Millie started for the steps and I grabbed a blanket from a box next to the old library desk. Mom had decided to keep the desk where it was so visitors would have a place to sign the guest book. We had used the blanket to skid boxes of books across the floor before carrying them to the new library room. The material was a little dirty, and a few holes had appeared from the friction with the floor.

I was surprised by Millie's climbing speed. I had a hard time keeping up with her. She stopped when she reached the five-step metal ladder that went straight up to the gallery. She looked down at the floor and then at her fingers, she was getting white knuckles from holding the railing so tightly.

I said, "You can't fall, just hold the railing normally. I'll go up first and shoo any birds away so they don't scare you. They can surprise you if you're not expecting them to flutter off."

I started up the ladder, but I accidentally dropped the blanket. I told Millie to toss it to me when I was completely through the opening. Before I could turn around and ask her to throw the blanket, it came sailing through the trapdoor opening. I caught it and said, "Thanks."

Her head popped up above the gallery floor and then she scrambled through the opening and sat down on the blanket. I had folded it making a place big enough for two. Her eyes looked more normal now and I watched her look out across the water, but her face was frozen like in an old photograph. I had expected her to say something like: "*It is very pretty from here,*" or "*I can see so far from here,*" but she didn't say anything, she just sat there and stared. I wondered what she was thinking, so I asked, "What's on your mind, Millie?"

She opened her mouth but couldn't seem to talk, but then she looked at me and started crying. Tears were running down her cheeks. I pulled my shirt tail from my pants and wiped her tears.

"Can you tell me what's wrong?"

"My parents have disappeared. The police in The Bahamas found the boat. It had run ashore. There was blood inside the boat. Elena said the authorities think Mom and Dad were killed."

"What? How could that happen?"

"I don't know. They didn't have any enemies, they are nice people."

"I thought they were nice. What about the company they work for?"

"Elena's going to check out the company. It's called World Sea Transfers."

I thought about what Millie had told me. I knew what she felt like. I had been through the same thing when we were notified that Dad was shot down over North Korea. We didn't know if he was alive or dead, but I hoped for the best, and it turned out okay. He came home more than a year later.

"Maybe the blood was from one of the crew, not your parents."

"Millie said the police were checking on that, but they wouldn't know for about a week. They have to get everyone's medical records."

I told her about Dad and how we carried on without him for more than a year. I think she began to feel a little better.

"What did you do when you heard your father had crashed?"

"I worried a lot and said a prayer."

"I don't know how to pray. I've never gone to church."

"You don't have to go to church to pray. Just talk to God."

"Out loud?"

"I think that's the best way. I suppose you can say it in your head, but I like to talk to God—like He's a friend. Just think about what to say and talk to Him."

Millie closed her eyes and sat for a minute, then looked out toward the horizon and said, "God, please protect my parents. Keep them safe—Amen."

"Good job, Millie."

She still had hope that her mom and dad were all right. She moved closer to me and said, "Could you put your arms around me?"

I had never held a girl before, except for Suz, and she was my sister. I hesitated—kind of frozen in place, but just for a moment. I put my right arm around her shoulders and pulled her closer. She put her head on my shoulder and said, "You're nice and warm."

"I just ate a sandwich and drank some warm water to wash down the salt from the potato chips." I thought about what I had just said and felt kind of stupid, but Millie didn't say anything, she just looked across the water. "See those two sailboats?" I pointed with my left hand.

"Uh-huh."

"They have a race every Saturday; the Lanes and the Humphreys. Whoever loses has to buy lunch for the other couple. They've been doing that for years. Granma told me."

"How old are they?"

"I think about fifty. Mr. Lane is a banker and Mr. Humphrey sells Chevys."

"What about the wives?"

"They used to teach school, but they quit to have children. I think their kids are all in college now. The Lanes have two girls and the Humphreys have two boys. One of the girls is named Lois—like in Superman. The other one is Rhonda."

Millie was trying to smile. She was looking out across the ocean water. "Can you tell me something about the ocean, something I might not know?"

"Hmm." I had to think for a little bit. Millie was pretty smart, so it had to be something more difficult than the name of a fish. "Okay. How did the people over 2,000 years ago know the earth was a sphere?"

She thought for a minute and said, "I think they thought the earth was flat. Weren't they afraid of sailing off the edge?"

"Some of them were. They must have had bad eyesight and needed glasses."

"Don't you need a telescope to figure it out?"

"Nope, just good eyesight. When a ship sailed away, it didn't just get smaller and smaller and then disappear, the first thing to go out of sight was the hull, the last thing to disappear was the top of the mast—usually a flag was at the top. So, the earth had to be shaped like a ball."

"So good eyesight and brains were all that was necessary."

"Uh-huh. Do you want to go down now?"

"No. I want to stay here for a while. Do you want to go down?"

"No. I kind of like it here with you."

"Me, too. But should we help with the books?"

"Nah, Mom has enough helpers."

We sat there for about thirty minutes watching the two sailboats racing around the outer buoys and observing seagulls gliding down to the rocks below, sitting for a few moments, spying on objects in the water, and then flying off. Most of the time, when on the rocks, they stayed near the water. I assumed they were looking for something to eat. The last time I was down on the rocks climbing around to see if I could find anything interesting, I noticed most of the rocks fairly high above the water were covered with bird poop. I figured most of it came from seagulls, but why didn't they poop over the water? Maybe they had to relax to go. One more thing to ask Granma about.

"I wish I had a paper airplane. I want to see how far it would glide from here. Next time we come up, let's see whose plane will glide the farthest."

"Do you always want to compete, Millie?"

"My dad said it's good to have friendly competition. I'm just remembering what he told me. I don't always win, I just try hard."

I heard a car below us, squishing gravel in the parking area as it slowed down. The brakes squealed as it came to a stop. I couldn't tell whose car it was from so far above. The car looked little from the gallery. The driver got out. It was Granma. She opened the back door and Surprise jumped out, barking as he ran to the front porch.

I called down to her, "Granma, everyone's in the new library—behind the house."

I wasn't sure she knew where we were putting all the books, but right after yelling to her, I realized Mom must have told her about the changes in the library. Granma looked up and waved. Millie and I waved back. We watched her walk around the house and disappear through the library door.

"Let's go down, Millie. I want to ask my granma something."

Millie folded the blanket into a nice square. I went down the ladder first so I could help her if she needed it. She dropped the blanket on my head just as I touched the metal floor at the bottom of the five-step vertical ladder. I had to refold the blanket, and when finished, Millie was standing beside me, grinning, and said, "Gotcha!" She took off down the stairs before I had a chance to say anything. She seemed to be feeling much better, the trip to the top of the lighthouse seemed to have lifted her spirits. Mom was pretty smart sending us up to the gallery.

I dropped the blanket on the chair at the sign-in desk, went outside, locked the lighthouse door, and followed Millie into the library building.

Mom was introducing Millie to Granma when I entered the building. Surprise was trotting around the bookcases, sniffing the books. Mom said, "Rocky, would you watch Surprise so he doesn't pee on anything?"

"Here, Surprise." He came to me and I picked him up and took him outside. I carried him to the front porch and tied his collar to a piece of clothesline rope attached to the column at the corner of the porch. He didn't like it and began biting at the rope. I went back to the library just in time to hear some good news.

Granma was standing in front of Millie holding her hands. Granma said, "Millie, your parents aren't dead, they were kidnapped. The FBI just phoned me; they couldn't get in touch with Elena to tell her."

Millie hugged Elena. Their cheeks were wet. Millie came over to me and hugged me and kissed me on the cheek. It was a little embarrassing. I'm sure I turned red; I felt hot. No girl had ever kissed me in front of a bunch of people, except Mom and maybe Granma.

"Thank-you, Rocky."

"For what?"

"You taught me how to pray."

"You're welcome."

Suzy smiled.

Chapter 15

ELENA'S PLAN

Granma picked up a pencil and wrote a phone number on a library book check-out card. She gave the card to Elena and said, "You need to call this number. They're waiting to hear from you."

"Is it an FBI number?"

"CIA."

I had never heard of CIA. "What's CIA, Granma?"

"That's the Central Intelligence Agency, Rocky. They can operate outside the United States."

"Like in the Bahamas?"

"That's right."

Elena had left the library as soon as Granma said CIA, but she was gone for just a moment. She stuck her head back into the room and looked at Mom. "May I use your phone, Mrs. Linfield?"

"Of course. You can phone anywhere you like—and call me Sandra."

Suzy played with Surprise on the new rugs. Mom, Dad, and Lt. Nesbitt sat on the bench next to the door and Granma sat in the padded librarian's chair. Millie and I walked around the room looking at the titles of books, occasionally pulling one out to look more closely. Some of the covers gave a reader clues about what was in the book. The adults were discussing something, but Millie and I weren't listening. Elena returned after about fifteen minutes.

"Sandra, I need to talk with you. Let's go in the house." Elena looked very serious. The CIA must have told her something important, maybe dangerous.

They were gone for five minutes. Dad had mounted a clock above the library door and I noticed the time when Mom left with Elena, so I knew how long they were gone.

Mom came in the library biting her upper lip. Elena was right behind her. Elena looked at Millie first, then Lt. Nesbitt. We were all watching them. Mom spoke first, "Elena has asked me to go with her to The Bahamas. We're going on another boat, almost identical to the one Mr. and Mrs. Harris were on. Tomorrow, we're going for some training with the CIA in Washington, D.C. We'll be back on Friday and leave on the boat, The Bahamian Isles, Saturday noon."

Dad was a little upset, I could see it in his face and hear it in his voice. "Sandra, what are you thinking?"

"We believe the kidnappers will try to take our boat. They'll think it will be easy to take advantage of two defenseless women. They'll be wrong. Mother will stay here with you and the kids and help with the library and you will be able to work at the store. We're thinking it will only take about two weeks and we'll be back. The boat's crew will have an experienced captain. The other two crewmen will be from the boat company. One of them is a good cook, and they're expert seamen. We'll have plenty of firepower—and brains."

Dad was quiet for a moment and then said, "Well, I know you two will have a monopoly in the brain department, but I don't know about your abilities with firearms."

Granma spoke up, "Don't worry about these two ladies, Lee, they can outshoot most men—including you."

"Yeah, Dad. Mom is a great shot with a rifle, and I've seen Elena shoot a pistol. They don't miss."

"I guess I can't doubt two of my family. That makes me feel better about the enterprise."

Millie had been moving slowly toward Elena. She grabbed Elena's right hand and said, "I want to go too, they're *my* parents."

"You can't go, Millie, it will be too dangerous, and besides, you have to go to school." Elena was holding Millie's hands and looking into her eyes.

"Elena, I can miss two weeks of school. I can make it up in two days. That's not a problem."

I decided to try to help Millie. "She's right. Jerry told me Mr. Dix's class is easy, and Millie is smarter than Jerry. He told me so."

Elena didn't make a big deal out of telling Millie she couldn't go to The Bahamas, she just didn't bring it up again. Mom, Elena, and Arron Nesbitt left for Washington, D.C. after dinner. They were going to drive straight through, a little over 500 miles. The ladies made some sandwiches and Aaron bought some soda while Mom packed her suitcase.

They left Crafton at 7:30 that evening. Millie's eyes were filled with tears, and when Suzy saw Millie's watery eyes, she started crying too. Dad, Granma, Suzy, and I gave Mom a hug and kiss and Dad said, "Have a good trip. We'll see you Friday." We all yelled "Bye!" as they drove away. I watched the car's red taillights disappear.

Millie grabbed my arm and began pulling me toward the porch.

I was resisting. "What are you doing?"

"I have to talk to you. Right now!"

"What about?"

"Let's go up to your room. No one can hear us up there."

Millie went into the house, jumped up, got a good grip on the twine and began pulling the stairs down from the ceiling. She didn't weigh that much but the steps were lowering as she briefly hung from the cord. I latched onto her waist, so she wouldn't fall, and pulled down until her feet touched the floor. The stairs were coming down on their own. She went up as fast as she could and sat above the top step. I followed her and sat on the attic floor with my legs hanging through the opening.

"Okay, what is it?"

"Do you want to go to The Bahamas with me?"

"Are you serious? Sure! But how are we going to get on the boat without anybody seeing us?"

"Well, I haven't thought of a way, but we've got five days to figure it out. I know where we can keep out of sight on board. I discovered good hiding places on the boat Mom and Dad were on and the new boat is supposed to be almost identical."

"Good, that takes care of one problem, but we have to sneak onboard."

"I know. We'll figure it out. We're both pretty smart."

We could hear people coming into the house. Dad said, "What are you guys doing?"

"We're just talking."

"I don't like you dangling your legs through that hole, Rocky. I'm afraid you'll slip and fall."

"Okay, Dad, we'll sit on my bed and talk."

As Millie and I moved over to my bed, an idea hit me. I sat next to my pillow and Millie plopped down at the foot of the bed sitting sideways.

"I just thought of a diversion. Jimmy Franklin's older brother has a small boat and he's out of school now. I think his name is Billy; he's kind of a goof-off. He likes to pull pranks on people, especially tourists that don't know about his practical jokes."

"What could we have him do for us? Would we have to pay him?"

"I'm sure he'll do something for us for five bucks. I've got a couple of dollars, how about you?"

"Mom and Dad gave me ten dollars before they left for The Bahamas. I still have seven dollars."

"Okay. Take my two dollars and give me your five. That should be enough to pay off Billy."

"What are we going to have him do?" She pulled a five dollar bill from her pocket and gave it to me. I forked over my two bucks.

"I'll tell him to bump into the side of the yacht and make a big deal out of it. I just need to tell him when to do it. We'll hide on the pier and when he makes a commotion, we'll sneak aboard."

"Oh! That sounds wonderful!"

"You'd better go back downstairs now. Dad will start to wonder what we're doing if you're up here too long. We'll talk again after dinner."

"Okay, we'll chat later."

"Be careful going down, the first couple of steps are a little scary."

I put the five dollar bill in my pocket and sat on the bed thinking about the time for Millie and me to sneak onto the boat. I hadn't thought for very long before I heard, "Rocky, come down for dinner." It was Granma. I wondered what we were going to eat. When Mom cooked, I could almost always tell what was for dinner, the smells from the kitchen travelled into the attic. My mouth started to water when I smelled something from the kitchen.

Granma had made omelets. They were full of vegetables. I put catsup on my serving, but the girls used butter, salt, and pepper. Millie used lots of pepper, but it didn't seem to bother her. I would have sneezed putting it on my eggs. After dinner, Millie and I put on coats and sat on the porch to discuss our plan. I made sure the door was closed before we said anything.

"Tomorrow at school, I'll ask Jimmy if his brother would like to make five bucks for doing something at noon on Saturday. I probably won't know until Tuesday—when I see Jimmy again."

Millie thought for a minute and then said, "You'd better get Billy's phone number in case the time changes. You might have to call him."

"Good idea. I'm hoping we can leave before lunch and hide on the pier until Billy does his thing. When he starts a commotion, we'll sneak aboard. Oh! I just thought of something—we should probably pay Jimmy two bucks for his trouble."

"What do we do about Jerry? Should we tell him what we're going to do?"

I had considered that and answered quickly. "I don't think so. If he knows, he might get into trouble for not telling on us."

"But he's your best friend."

"I know, but he'll understand."

"What about weapons?"

"I've got a pocket knife and a slingshot." I figured she would laugh.

"Are you a good shot?"

"You bet. I can hit a soda bottle with a marble at twenty yards, seven out of ten shots. What about you?"

"I can shoot a pistol. I shot a thirty-eight before at a target range. I did pretty well, but I don't have a gun."

"I'll find out if Granma has a gun. We can borrow it, but I might have to break into her house."

Millie scrunched up her face. "That doesn't sound good."

"I'll see what I can do. Let's go back inside, my feet are getting cold."

Chapter 16

CONSPIRACY

Jimmy Franklin wasn't at school Monday and Millie ate lunch with Jerry as usual. I glanced at them as I chewed on some carrot sticks dunked in mayonnaise. Millie was laughing. When they got up to dump their trays, Millie looked at me, smiled and gave me a finger wave. I didn't talk with her until we rode home on the bus. We sat in the back where we couldn't be overheard. Suzy sat in the front with one of her classmates that gets off just before we do.

"Jimmy didn't come to school today. I'll have to talk to him tomorrow."

"I hope he isn't home sick all this week. What will we do then?"

"I think Jimmy's brother still lives at home. If Jimmy doesn't show up tomorrow, I'll call the Franklins and ask for Billy."

"Hmm. That will save us two dollars. I've been thinking we should have some money to spend in The Bahamas. What if we need a taxi? And we'll need some food, of course. Do you have any more money?"

"I think Suz has a couple of bucks I can borrow, but I think we'll need more than that. I can't ask Suz to loan me her money. She'd blab and we'd get messed up."

"I can sell my bike. I'll bet I can get at least fifty for it."

"No! You can't do that. Let me see if Granma will loan me some money." I didn't want Millie to sell her bike, I haven't had a chance to ride it yet. It would be like me getting a new BB gun for Christmas and then selling it before I had shot or scratched it.

"You'll have to tell her a lie, Rocky. Do you want to do that?"

"I don't think she'll mind as long as I pay her back. I'll ask her when we get home. Dad will be at the store. Make sure you're with Suzy so she doesn't hear anything."

"Okay. There's the lighthouse. Let's move up front."

After taking off my shoes and changing my pants, I sat on the bed thinking of what to say to Granma about the money. When I looked down from the attic, Suzy and Millie were coloring and watching TV. Granma was reading something. I think it was *The Reader's Digest*. It was about four o'clock when I heard Granma get up and move to the kitchen to begin cooking dinner. I wondered what we were going to have tonight.

I was in my stockings and kind of sneaked down to the hallway and then to the kitchen. I wanted to talk to Granma in secret. If Suzy knew about the loan, she'd blab. That's for sure.

"Granma, could you loan me fifty dollars?"

She looked at me like I was from outer space. "Good heavens! What would you do with fifty dollars?"

"I was looking at a boy's bike down at Mitchell's hardware the other day. Mr. Mitchell said if I could put down fifty dollars, he would hold it for me. It's metallic blue with chrome fenders. It's beautiful, Granma."

"What do your mom and dad think about it?"

"Oh! I don't want them to know. I want to do it on my own—show them I can be responsible. I'll pay you back, Granma. Jerry and I are going to earn money taking care of yards next summer and washing cars. Maybe even get more books for the library, if Mom will pay us like Mr. Waicukauski did."

"Let me think about it, Rocky. I'll tell you after dinner."

"Okay. Thanks, Granma."

"Suzy's watching a TV show. Would you please set the table?"

"Sure, Granma." I stood there a minute counting how many places we would need. The table could seat six, but we only needed five places tonight with Mom, Elena, and the lieutenant gone. I wondered how far they had travelled yesterday, whether they had arrived in Washington late at night or early in the morning. I bet they were tired after the trip.

When Granma said that was all I needed to do, I went into the living room and sat on the sofa beside Millie. We looked at each other for several seconds, but I had nothing to say and she couldn't ask any questions with Suzy listening. I just shrugged my shoulders.

Dad arrived home about ten minutes later. He said he was going to take a shower. I noticed his limp as he walked toward the bathroom. I could tell he was tired. When Dad was worn out, his limp got worse. He must have moved cabinets and done a lot of walking today. After dinner, he seemed to have gotten his energy back. Maybe he had just been hungry. I know that makes me tired.

Dad and Granma did the dishes and the rest of us watched TV. I had to do some reading for Tuesday, so I went up to my room after about an hour of watching the tube. There had been a commercial about a color TV. Not very many people had them. Ours was black and white. Someday, I'll bet everyone will have a color set.

I had just started reading when I heard the phone ring. I was hoping it was Mom telling us she had gotten to Washington without any problems. I laid on the floor and stuck my head through the stairway opening so I could hear better than when sitting on the bed. Dad was talking. He said beautiful, so I knew it was Mom. He only talked for a minute and then hung up. I'll ask him about the call when I finish reading.

It was 9:35 when I was done with my assignment. I took my book downstairs and put it on the table next to the door so I wouldn't forget it in the morning. The girls had gone to bed, so I sat on the sofa beside Granma. Dad had fallen asleep in the overstuffed chair. He looked very peaceful. I didn't want to wake him up to ask about Mom.

Granma whispered, "Rocky, I've decided to loan you the fifty dollars. I'll go to the bank and get it in the morning."

"Oh, thank-you, Granma. I promise I'll pay you back." I gave her a hug. "Who was on the phone?"

"That was your mother. She said everything is going fine. Not to worry."

I went to the bathroom to brush my teeth. Millie's door was closed so I couldn't tell her I got the loan from Granma. I'd tell Millie in the morning on the bus or whisper to her at breakfast. I hoped Jimmy Franklin would be at school tomorrow. I didn't want to call his brother, I didn't even know him. He might tell me to buzz off.

It was Tuesday, October 14. It was chilly. When we climbed on the bus in the morning, Suz sat with one of her friends. Millie and I sat behind them so we could talk. Millie lowered her voice, almost to a whisper.

"What happened, Rocky? About the money, I mean."

"I got us fifty bucks. Granma's going to the bank this morning to get the cash."

Millie smiled, "I knew you could do it. I hope you see Jimmy today."

"Me, too."

I was a little worried about our plans, it was already Tuesday morning. We only had three more days to get everything ready. We couldn't carry a suitcase on board with us. We would have to have some kind of backpack to carry our things from home to the pier Saturday before noon. If Jimmy didn't show up by Wednesday, we would have to figure out another diversion, but I didn't know anyone else that we could pay to distract the people on the boat.

I didn't have to worry about Jimmy very long. He showed up at school. I talked to him during morning recess. I didn't ask why he wasn't in school Monday. He said he would talk to his brother, but the trick might cost me more than five bucks. I didn't want to use up any of the fifty I was getting from Granma. Millie and I would need to hold onto that money as long as possible. We had no idea how much things would cost in The Bahamas.

"I don't have any more than five dollars for your brother, but I think I can get you two."

"Uh—I'll see what I can do. I think Billy will do it. He usually does stuff like that just for a laugh. He told me he likes to make rich people squirm. Five bucks would be a big reward. I'll let you know tomorrow. Okay?"

"Okay. Thanks, Jimmy. See you in class."

The recess bell rang and everyone had to return to class. I hadn't seen Millie. I wondered what she was going to do about things we would need while we were hiding on the boat. I hoped we'd have our own porthole. I'd hate to be hidden away for a week or so without any sunlight and not be able to see the ocean. As I thought more about the trip, I realized we would need a bathroom. Then it came to me that we could dump things out of the boat through a porthole. I had to ask Millie if one of the hiding spots had an opening to the sea. We had a lot to talk about.

On the bus ride home, Millie and I talked about where we would hide on the boat. The first place she thought of was on the main deck toward the stern of the boat where some firefighting equipment was stored. I didn't think there would be a fire while we were on board, so the place would be safe. She said she could sneak out at night to go to the bathroom, but in case of an emergency, we could dump things overboard from a rectangular hatch that swung open. It was a ventilation louver. We would need a screwdriver to open it. My scout knife had a screwdriver blade. She thought the two of us would take up too much space and not have any freedom to move, so it was not the best place to hide.

Another space was higher up on the top deck below the main mast. Sail mending materials and tools were stored there along with an extra mainsail. Also, there were two louvers. Millie said there was one problem with the top deck space.

"When the boat moves around in choppy seas, we might get seasick. When I checked out that space, I felt seasickness coming on, so I got out quickly and went below. That's when I found the third space."

"Is it big enough for two?"

"Uh-huh, but we'll have to move some things around. The stuff in there seemed to be disorganized."

"Stuff?"

"Two deflated lifeboats, some life preservers, and a carton of signal flares. That room smells like the inside of a new car. The door has *EMERGENCY* stenciled on it. It's at the top of the stairway that leads to the galley, the crew's quarters, and the bathrooms."

"That sounds like the best place for us, Millie. We could sneak into the bathrooms at night when everyone's asleep."

"Not everyone is asleep at night, Rocky. Someone's always on duty watching for problems—like ships and islands, but the watch officer is usually on the bridge, two flights above."

"Isn't that too far away to hear anything?"

"The watch officer might hear a toilet at night; it's very quiet on the boat then."

"Okay, then. We don't flush." I looked at Millie and laughed. She smiled and pinched her nose. If someone on the boat discovered the toilet hadn't been flushed, I imagined they would just flush it and forget about it, but if it happened again, that could be a problem.

"How many toilets are there on the boat?" I hoped there would be several.

"Umm. One on the bridge, two below the main deck and a urinal near the engine room. Why?"

I explained what I had been thinking and Millie agreed that we'd have to be careful about flushing. "We'll have to take at least one roll of toilet paper with us—for emergency use. What can we put things in? We'll need a bag of some sort, won't we?"

I remembered that Jerry had some war surplus army backpacks. They were just the right size to carry an extra pair of underwear, some candy bars, and toilet paper. I nodded. "Yeah, we sure can't take one of your big suitcases. Ask Jerry if you can borrow two of his army backpacks. Tell him you and Granma want to go for an all-day hike on Saturday."

Right after I said that, I began to think about where we could store the packs until we needed to get on the boat. We didn't have a place to hide them at home. "We have to find a place to put the packs until we get on the boat. Any ideas?"

"No. I'm sorry, Rocky." Millie's eyes were almost running over.

"What are you sorry about?"

"You have all the answers. I'm not contributing anything. I asked you if you wanted to go with me, but I don't have any ideas."

"Yes, you do. We just haven't gotten to your ideas yet. Remember, you know all about the boat. I don't know anything about it—except it floats." I grinned.

We had been home for less than a half-hour when Granma handed me two twenties and a ten. I gave thirty to Millie and I put twenty in my sock drawer. I figured we should ride around and see where we could store our packs and pick them up Saturday morning on the way to the boat.

Chapter 17

GETTING READY

Millie and I put on sweaters and jackets and talked to Granma in the kitchen before we rode to search for a temporary storage place for the travel-packs.

"Mrs. Makler, do we have any peanut butter or chocolate chip cookies?"

"After school snack, huh?"

"Well, yes, but Rocky and I are going to ride around after school and see if we can get more books for the library. We're going to borrow some backpacks from Jerry. With all that riding, we'll need something to munch on."

I hadn't made a suggestion, but Millie had thought of a way for us to be seen with the packs and riding at any time of day, especially when we had to go to the pier on Saturday. What good thinking! She had worried that she didn't have any ideas. Now we can keep the backpacks in plain sight. We just need to put our bikes out of sight when we sneak on the yacht.

"I'd like some of both, Granma. I can taste them already. Your cookies are always so good."

"Thank-you, Rocky. Do you two want to help make them?"

"We're going over to Jerry's to get the backpacks. Maybe Suzy can help you. She loves licking cookie dough off her fingers."

"Okay. How long will you be gone? It's getting dark pretty early these days and you don't have lights. You should be back by five o'clock."

"All right. We'll check the time over at Jerry's. See you before five."

"Bye, Mrs. Makler."

"Bye, now—and be careful."

During the ride to Jerry's, I asked, "How far *is* it to The Bahamas, anyway?"

"I checked the world globe in the school library on Monday. The islands are about 1,200 nautical miles from here."

I had never heard of a nautical mile. "Geez, Millie, what is it in regular miles?"

"That's not necessary. Dad said the yacht travels between twenty and twenty-two nautical miles per hour."

I did a quick calculation—about sixty hours. "So it's going to take us two and a half days to get there."

"Umm." Millie looked around for a second and said, "That's right—if we don't stop along the way."

"Why would we stop? Doesn't the yacht have everything the crew needs?"

Millie stared at me for a couple of seconds and said, "What if someone needs a doctor?"

"Yeah, I didn't think of that."

Millie laughed. "You made me think hard about that one, Rocky."

Jerry was sitting on the front porch tossing pebbles onto the street when we arrived. Millie parked her bike with her kickstand and I let mine drop on the lawn. After saying hi to Jerry, Millie asked, "Do you have some backpacks Mrs. Makler and I could borrow?"

"What for?"

"Rocky's grandmother and I want to go for a hike to watch birds and other fall wildlife on Saturday afternoon. We want to carry binoculars, a camera, and some snacks, but we want our hands free while walking around in the trees and across Wild Weed Creek."

"Oh, okay. I'll get them for you. Does Rocky need one too?"

I answered, "Nope. I'll be helping Dad at the store on Saturday."

"Wait right here, I'll get them." Jerry disappeared into the house for less than a minute and returned with two war surplus olive-drab Army backpacks all wadded up. He held them out to Millie. She gave me one.

"Is that the only color you have?"

I almost laughed but I wanted Jerry to think that Millie was serious, so I kind of bit my tongue.

"Gee, Millie, the Army doesn't put on fashion shows. I can see the enemy watching for a soldier wearing a pink backpack and shooting him as he crawled through the brush—certain death."

"Oh! I guess different colors wouldn't be so good for the Army. Well, thanks, Jerry. We have to go back home. Rocky's grandmother wants us home by five o'clock."

Jerry turned and looked through the screen door. "Our clock says 4:38, you'd better start back home. Hope you get good use out of the packs. Have a nice hike."

Millie and I each put on a pack and got our bikes ready to ride. As we began to peddle, I yelled back, "Thanks, Jerry! We'll see you at school tomorrow!"

"Bye, Jerry!" Millie waved.

As we got off our bikes at the lighthouse, I said, "That was really funny when you asked Jerry if that was the only color he had. I about cracked up."

Millie smiled and said, "I wanted him to think that I was fashion conscious. I didn't want him to think we were going to do anything but what I had said."

We could smell freshly baked cookies as soon as we stepped onto the front porch. I was cold from riding. The sun was dropping low in the sky and the cool air blowing past my noggin made my nose and ears cold. I think Millie was a little better off with her long hair protecting her ears and neck. When we got inside and moved to the kitchen, Suzy said, "Where'd you get those shoulder bags?"

"They're not shoulder bags, Suz, they're Army backpacks. We're gunna ride around after school and find more books."

"Oh."

Granma said, "Take off your coats and have a cookie. You'd better put those surplus things in your rooms."

Granma and Suzy were making at least two dozen of both peanut butter and chocolate chip cookies. I watched Granma press a fork down on a ball of cookie dough and then again at a right angle. The center of the peanut butter cookies looked like the reverse of a waffle, little square bumps poking up. I picked up a warm cooked one and took a bite. My taste buds exploded. Millie had grabbed a chocolate chip cookie and was nibbling toward a cluster of three dark-brown chips. We looked at each other, smiled, and nodded. Granma's cookies were the best. I poured three glasses of milk for us to wash down all the cookie bits.

"Okay, that's all until after dinner. Scat!"

"Thanks, Granma. That was really good."

Suzy smiled and said, "Yummy."

Millie followed with, "I second that."

At school on Wednesday, Jimmy said his brother would bump into the yacht Saturday noon, maybe a couple of minutes after. I shelled out seven dollars to Jimmy and made him promise to have his brother complete the deal. If we didn't have a diversion, we were sunk; Millie and I would never get to The Bahamas. After the bus ride to school that morning, I didn't see Millie again until we were on the bus going home at three o'clock.

Millie pulled on my jacket sleeve. "Is Jimmy's brother going to do it?"

"Uh-huh. Jimmy promised me, at Saturday noon, or a few minutes after. We'll have to be ready."

"Oh! This is getting exciting. Now we have to find a place to store the bikes."

"As soon as we get home, change into something warmer. We'll ride down near the pier. I have an idea where to look for a storage place. I'm going to wear a cap today. Yesterday, I about froze my bean."

"I'll get us some cookies to put in the packs. Don't eat them. Okay?" Millie was really serious.

"Okay. Maybe we should have some cheese, too. Something that won't spoil in three days. How about some apples?"

"Rocky, *fruit* will make you poop."

I laughed. "We'd better not take any beans."

"Now you're not being serious."

At school today, while Miss Hill was reading a story to us, I was thinking about hiding our bikes. As Millie and I were nearly to Pier Lane,

I signaled Millie to stop about half-a-block short of the street. There was a footpath that seemed to go behind the row of stores on the pier. I had never paid attention to it before, but now I was looking more closely at things. The path looked like it might go right behind our store. The dirt and gravel were overgrown with weeds but we could wheel our bikes over the rough walkway. As we started through the weeds, I could see there were some bad spots where soil had slid down the slope and made humps of dirt across the pathway.

"Be careful Millie. If you slip, push your bike away so you don't fall on it and get hurt."

"Okay. I'm following your footprints and tire tracks."

We made it safely to the trashy areas behind the stores. There were fire escapes, some leaves and bits of paper, probably blown in by wind, and a few waste cans behind the stores. I recognized the back of the craft store. This was going to be perfect. We could leave our bikes and walk behind the stores until we reached the mooring spot of the yacht. No one would be able to see us, unless someone was putting garbage in the trash cans.

"What a good spot, Rocky! I hope this isn't our last bit of luck."

On the way back home we walked our bikes most of the way up the hill so we could talk.

"Let's not put anything into the bags until Friday night. Hide your things around your room so Suzy won't snoop and find the backpacks full of our baggage. I don't think she'll try to come upstairs; she's afraid she might fall. Oh! Make sure you wrap the cookies in an old bread sack. Suzy's got a nose for cookies like a shark has for blood."

"I've been thinking, Rocky. When should we leave for the pier on Saturday?"

I thought for a minute before I answered. We were almost at the top of the hill when the lighthouse light came on. Millie was startled and almost dropped her bike.

"Oh, gosh! That scared me."

"I know what you mean. The first time it happened to me, I was in the lighthouse. I heard a noise and thought the top of the tower had broken. The noise was the circuits closing."

"So, when should we ride to the pier?"

"We'd better go right after Mom and Elena leave for the boat. They said they would set out for The Bahamas at noon. I hope they're on time or Billy's diversion might not work. We'd better pray that luck is on our side."

After dinner, Millie, Granma, Suzy and I played Monopoly for about an hour. Millie and Suzy had lots of property and money when we quit. Granma and I were bankrupt. Dad watched boxing and fell asleep in the big chair. We were all going to help Granma with the dishes, but Dad told us to get our clothes and homework ready for tomorrow. Suzy put on her PJs and Millie and I started getting things ready to put in our backpacks. I put my stuff beneath my clean underwear in my chest of drawers. I don't know where Millie put her things—maybe in one of her empty suitcases.

Thursday was a good day at school. Jerry, Millie, and I ate lunch together and told some jokes. We joined in a kickball game, fifth graders against sixth graders. The sixth graders won, but I didn't care. Millie and I were prepared for the trip to The Bahamas except for sneaking on board the yacht. That was our last mountain to climb.

After school, Millie and I took off on our bikes looking for library books. We visited some houses that Suzy and I had never been to, but we only got one book from a nice old lady that walked with a cane. She had us in and we talked with her for about twenty minutes. No one answered the door at most of the houses. The people might have been at work, or they saw us coming. Granma gave us a quarter for the book. It was about the South Sea Islands. Millie said it was too bad it wasn't about The Bahamas.

At lunch on Friday, Jerry wasn't in school. He hadn't told Millie he would be absent. I ate with Millie and we talked about Elena and Mom coming back from Washington, D.C. We thought they would be at the lighthouse when we got home. We had to act normally so they wouldn't expect anything.

When we got home, I noticed the parking lot was empty, except for Granma's car. I don't think it had moved all day. Elena and Mom must not be back. I wondered if they were on the way. Suzy had said she was going to watch for a car carrying Mom and Elena, but when we got off the bus, Suzy raced ahead of Millie and me. We saw the screen door slam when she disappeared into the house. The door was open when we got to the porch.

"Susan, you didn't close the door."

"That's okay, Granma. Millie and I have it."

Millie stopped by the kitchen to talk to Granma. I went to my room, took off my jacket, and put on my slippers. We weren't going to look for books because we didn't want to miss any time with Elena and Mom when they got home. I was really curious about what training they had when in Washington at the CIA. I hoped they could tell us about it if it wasn't secret. I went back downstairs and into the kitchen. Granma was making brownies. She said the cookies probably wouldn't last through the weekend.

Millie and I looked at each other and smiled; we knew where most of the cookies had gone. They were waiting to be taken to The Bahamas. When the first pan of brownies came from the oven, we could hardly wait for the nutty brown cake to cool. Suzy had chopped the walnuts and wanted to cut the brownies in the pan and lick the knife, but Granma was afraid Suzy would chop off a finger. She asked Millie to carve the cake into smaller pieces. Suz got the first bite and danced around like she was in heaven hopping from cloud to cloud. Millie and I each ate one piece, but didn't try to take any for the trip to the islands until later.

The phone rang. I was closest, so took it off the wall mount. It was Dad. He said he had a long-distance call from Mom. Elena and Mom would be home in a couple of hours; we shouldn't wait for them before having dinner. He would be home at six-thirty. I told Granma so she could schedule things.

Granma said, "Since you guys have had a snack, you won't mind eating a little later than usual. Why don't you all go out and play? You can burn off the brownies and get some fresh air in your lungs at the same time."

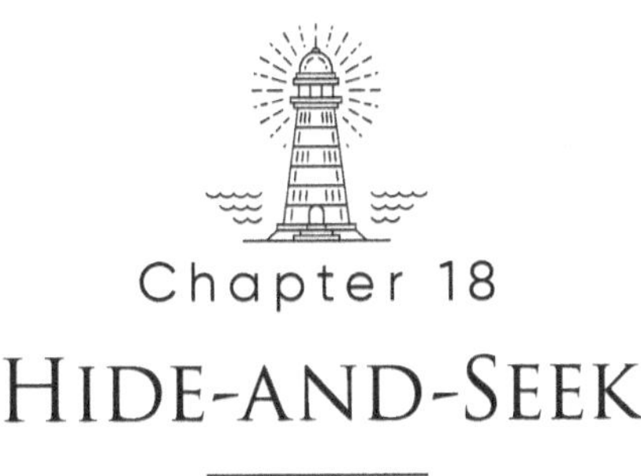

Chapter 18

Hide-and-Seek

Millie and Suzy put on their coats as I was going up to my room to get my shoes. When I went outside, they were sitting on the porch.

Suzy said, "Let's play hide-and-seek. Rocky, you're it." The girls laughed, got off the porch, and started to hide. I said, "Okay. I'm looking for you after the light has gone around three times." I pointed up to the top of the tower. "Go!" I closed my eyes for about fifteen seconds, guessing how long the light rotated, and then cried out, "Ready or not, here I come!" I had heard some footsteps go around the corner of the house toward the library, but I couldn't tell who I had heard. The other feet seemed to go toward the parking lot. The lot was closest, so I began searching there. Someone had to be behind Granma's car, but when I peered around the hood, no one was there. Then I heard a yell.

I had heard that high-pitched scream once before when Ensign Thorndike had been shot. It was coming from Susan. "Ah-h-h-h! Rocky! Granma! Someone's in the library!" She saw me, but ran to the porch. "Granma! Get your gun!"

Granma, wearing her apron over her housedress, stepped out on the porch carrying her pistol. "You kids, get in the house! Lock the door!" She looked around. "Where's Millie?"

"I'm here." Millie's voice came from Granma's car. Millie was under it. She stuck her hand out, I grabbed it, and pulled. Millie said, "Not so hard, Rocky. You'll skin me on the pebbles."

"Sorry." I relaxed my tug a little. "Granma wants us to get in the house."

"I heard her. I'm not deaf."

I laughed. I still had her hand, so I pulled her up from the ground and we ran for the porch. Granma had a flash light in her left hand and her .45 in her right. She was sneaking around the corner of the house toward the library building. I was the last inside. I slammed the door and turned the deadbolt lever.

"What did you see, Suz?"

"Just a—a shadow, but I smelled something. You know, like when Daddy makes a fire in the fireplace."

Millie said, "Like burned matches?"

"Uh-huh. I don't like that smell. It hurts my eyes, too."

Millie sat down on the sofa beside Suzy and held hands. They both looked up at me. I thought we would all be safer if we went to my bedroom and pulled up the stairs. I started to tell the girls to go to my bedroom, but there was a rap on the front door window. I stepped over to the hallway and looked at the door. Granma was standing on the porch looking into the house.

"Rocky, please unlock the door. Whoever was there is gone."

I unlocked the door, turned the knob, and Granma came into the hallway holding her gun at her side. She relocked the door and turned to enter the kitchen. Suzy and Millie had their eyes locked on the forty-five. Granma started to say something, but went in the kitchen. I heard some metallic clicks and then she came into the living room.

"Someone tried to start a fire in the library, but Susan must have interrupted whoever it was. I found a couple of burned matches and some singed check-out cards in the wastebasket. We're lucky there wasn't a bunch of wadded up paper to start burning."

"How did a person get in the library, Mrs. Makler? Isn't the door always locked after three o'clock?"

"I'm not sure, Millie. Perhaps I forgot to lock the door, or maybe a picklock got in. But why would anybody want to start a fire? Burning books is such a malicious act."

Suzy told us what happened. "I was trying to hide. I turned the knob on the library door and it opened. I went in, closed the door, and stood against the wall. I could smell the burned matches and thought I'd better get out of there. I was afraid somebody might say that I had burned the matches. I reached for the door knob, but someone hit my hand and opened the door. I ran out and yelled."

"You sure did yell, Suz. I'll bet Dad heard that down at the store. He probably thought it was a police siren."

"Rocky, what did I tell you about teasing Susan?"

"I'm sorry, Suz, but your yell was really loud."

"Well, I was really scared. I'm just a kid, you know."

Granma explained, "When you ran out, whoever was in there must have departed. I went in, turned on the lights, and looked around. Nobody was there."

I was thinking about diversions so I said, "Maybe someone wanted us to come out of the house to fight a fire and they would sneak in the house and take something."

Granma looked at me. "What would they want from the house? We don't have any valuables."

"I have a gold necklace in my bedroom, but who would know about it? I've never worn it in Maine. I wore it once in New York when we picked up the boat that my mom and dad took to The Bahamas."

I commented, "It would have to be worth lots of money for someone to follow you to Crafton. Is it that valuable?"

"Not really, it's just a simple gold chain. Mom and Dad gave it to me for my birthday last June. I don't think it cost very much—probably less than twenty dollars."

When Dad got home we clustered around him and told him what had happened. All three of us were talking at the same time, but he managed to figure out what had happened. He took a flashlight and went out to the library to look around. After a couple of minutes he came back in the house and told us the same thing Granma had said when she went out there with her gun. He was carrying the library wastebasket and dumped the scorched checkout cards in the fireplace.

After dinner we were watching TV when the phone rang. Granma was closest, so she answered.

"Hello. Hi, Sandra—okay—I'll have Lee come and get you."

When Dad heard his name he got up and was moving toward Granma and the phone.

"Bye." Granma hung up the phone and told Dad, "Sandra and Elena are down at the pier. They want you to come and get them."

Dad frowned. "Why are they down at the pier? Couldn't they just drive here?"

"They're on a yacht. It just docked."

Dad pulled on his jacket and asked Granma if he could borrow her car. I guess he thought his pickup wasn't comfortable enough for the ladies. I didn't think they would mind riding in the pickup. I guess the seat isn't as soft as a car seat.

"Here are the keys, Lee. There's plenty of gas." Granma dropped her keys into Dad's right hand. He sorted through them and found the car key.

He looked at us on the sofa, smiled, and said, "I'll be right back with our overnight guests." I could hear the jingle of the keys as he went out the front door.

Granma stood in front of us blocking the TV. "I want all of you to pick up any of your things laying around the house and put them in your room before the ladies arrive." She backed up to the TV and turned it off. "Now, please."

We all walked around, but only found a couple of things to put away. Suzy opened the hall closet, threw her boots in, and closed the door. Millie and I took our coats to our bedrooms. I sat on the edge of my bed and thought about making sure I didn't slip and say anything about Millie's and my plans. I had to act normally. I didn't think it was going to be hard to do, Suzy was going to be excited about seeing Mom and Elena and would be nosey, asking them all kinds of questions. I just had to be quiet and listen to them talk about the CIA. I had planned on doing that ever since they left for Washington. I knew a little about the FBI, but I didn't know anything about the CIA.

I sat there for about fifteen minutes thinking that any minute I'd hear Granma's car arrive and voices outside. All I could hear was Suzy and Millie talking in the living room and Granma asking them if they wanted a cookie or a brownie. I kept listening for the car. I watched my alarm clock for a couple of minutes before I decided to pack all the things I needed for the trip to The Bahamas. It seemed like it took longer than the five minutes the clock showed and my pack was ready to go. I wondered if Millie had packed yet.

Why weren't they back yet? Dad had been gone for almost thirty minutes. What were they doing? I went downstairs after I slid my backpack under my bed behind my stack of Lone Ranger comics. Nobody could see that far under my bed without getting on their hands and knees.

I was thinking about the stuff in my pack when I suddenly remembered that I had forgotten my slingshot. What was I going to use for pebbles? Then it came to me—my bag of marbles, but I couldn't take them all, not a quart jar full. I poured them out on my bed, separated the black and white ones, wrapped them in a handkerchief, and added the slingshot and marbles to my pack. They didn't take up much room.

I heard the car wheels scrunching the parking area gravel and went down to the living room and waited for the front door to open. Dad held the door for Elena and Mom and they came in talking.

"We're home." Mom's voice could be heard over the TV. Suzy had turned it back on. She ran to Mom and threw her arms around Mom's waist.

Suz said, "How was your trip, Mommy? It's so good to have you back home."

"Our trip was great. After four days of intense training, we travelled by rail to New York City and came the rest of the way on the yacht. What a beautiful boat!"

Granma had made coffee and placed a tray of cookies and brownies on the dining room table. She had even made Kool-Aid for Millie, Suzy, and me. We sat around and talked with Mom and Elena for almost an hour before Millie and I were surprised by what Elena said.

"I think we should all go to bed. Tomorrow's going to be busy in the morning. Sandra and I have to get down to the pier by ten o'clock—that's when we're leaving for The Bahamas."

Millie and I almost froze in place when we heard ten o'clock. Millie looked at me and motioned with her head toward her bedroom. Then she said, "You can use some of my suitcases if you want. Rocky and I'll get them for you. Come on, Rocky."

I was sitting on the living room floor, got to my feet, and moved toward my old bedroom. As soon as Millie and I were in the room, I whispered, "I've got to call Jimmy and tell him to have his brother do the job at ten instead of twelve o'clock."

Millie leaned toward me and whispered back, "Is it too late to phone tonight? It's almost ten-thirty."

I thought about it for a second and said, "I'll try now. If I don't get him, I'll try again in the morning."

"Okay. Let's ask your mom and Elena what size luggage they need."

"Good idea. I'll take a big one out to the living room. Then I'll call Jimmy."

"All right, I'll carry out a smaller one."

When everyone was looking over the suitcases, I grabbed the phone, stepped into the kitchen and called Jimmy. His mom answered and I asked for him. I waited a few seconds.

"Hello."

"Hi, Jimmy. This is Rocky. Tell your brother to bump the yacht two hours earlier. Okay?"

"Okay. I'll tell him ten o'clock."

"Thanks, Jimmy. Bye." I put the phone back on the wall and joined the others.

Chapter 19

SAYING GOODBYE

Granma drove home to take care of Surprise and stay the night at her house. She told us she would be back in the morning to deliver Surprise and cook breakfast. Elena was to sleep on the sofa. When I went to bed, I hoped God had heard my prayer, and I hoped Millie had also asked God for a little help. Billy Franklin had to bump his boat into the yacht at ten o'clock in the morning. If he didn't, Millie and I wouldn't be going to The Bahamas.

I woke up smelling pancakes and coffee, but it was still dark in the attic, so I turned on the reading light above my pillow. I rubbed my eyes and looked at my alarm clock; it was ten after seven, time to get up and get into my travelling clothes. As soon as I was ready to go, I went downstairs. Elena was sitting up watching TV. The sound was turned down so low so I could barely hear it. I wondered if she could read lips.

"Good morning, Rocky." Granma's voice came from the kitchen.

I looked at Elena and replied, "Morning." Although Elena was sitting up, I don't think she was awake, or she was thinking about something very complicated. She had been quiet last night, too. I started to wonder if she had been brain-washed by the CIA, but I didn't really believe the CIA would brain wash one of their own agents.

"Rocky, come get some pancakes." Granma had put a stack of them, five or six high, on a plate in the middle of the table. The chunk of butter and bottle of maple syrup were waiting. She had put the syrup next to my plate. I thought she had confused the syrup with catsup. Granma knows I really like catsup, but not on pancakes.

Other than the noise from me sliding my chair, the only other sounds came from the coffee maker and Millie. She was wearing grayish-brown pants and a sweater with a light jacket tied around her waist. "Hi, Rocky. Did you have a good sleep?"

I had taken a bite of pancakes and couldn't talk, so I just nodded. As soon as I swallowed, I asked, "How was your night? Any dreams?"

"Uh-huh. I dreamed I was on a rowboat and the waves were coming over the sides. I was afraid I would drown. Then I smelled coffee and pancakes and knew I was dreaming." She pointed into the living room and said, "What's wrong with Elena? I said hi to her and she didn't say anything."

I frowned at Millie, afraid she was going to give something away talking about a boat, but Granma didn't say anything and Granma was the only one really awake.

"Good morning, everyone." Elena had walked into the dining room in her bare feet and was just standing there looking at us as if we had ignored her when we got up. We all said good morning. "I'm going to get dressed. Is the bathroom empty?"

Mom ran down the hallway and into the bathroom. Elena crossed her arms on her chest, leaned against the wall in the hallway and sighed. "I guess I'll wait."

Granma handed her a mug of coffee. "Here you are, dear."

"Thank-you, Mrs. Makler."

"Elena, my middle name is Vera. Why don't you call me Vera?"

"Oh, thank-you, Vera. I thought Mrs. Makler was a bit formal."

Suzy, still in her pajamas, came into the dining room and sat next to me. "Can I call you Vera, Granma?"

Granma hesitated for a moment and then said, "No. Call me Granma. When you get older, you may call me Vera."

"How old?"

"Ten years from now."

"Then you'll be an old lady, Granma."

I could hear Elena laughing in the hallway. I could see her from my chair. She had her hand over her mouth.

By eight-thirty, everyone had gotten dressed and had finished with breakfast. Mom didn't want to eat pancakes. She said she might throw up on the boat. I wish I had thought of that, I might have the same problem, but maybe the boat will be steady and I won't get seasick.

Dad had planned on being at the store by eight o'clock, but today he was going to take Mom and Elena to the pier at nine and then open the store for business. That would give them an hour to get their things onboard and stowed in their rooms. Mom said they were going to have rooms next to each other. Elena said their spaces are about the size of Suzy's bedroom, but the ceilings aren't as high, only six and one-half feet. Suzy's bedroom has a nine-foot ceiling.

Dad took us kids outside to play catch so Mom and Elena could get packed without being bothered. Granma had brought Elena's clothes from Mrs. Nesbitt's, her next door neighbor. I think Elena and Lt. Aaron Nesbitt, Mrs. Nesbitt's son, are going to be married before long. He won't be going to The Bahamas, he has to go on some type of naval maneuver near Nova Scotia. He'll be on a destroyer.

"Lee, could you come and help carry our luggage?" It was Mom calling from the porch.

Dad tossed me the softball and went in the house. I tossed the ball to Suzy and she surprised me, she caught it, but throwing it back was a disaster. If we had a barn, she couldn't have hit it from ten feet. Millie was trying to keep from laughing. She had to turn away from Suz so she could laugh. I think she bit her tongue to keep Suzy from hearing anything.

Millie said, "Let's put the ball away and watch them load the truck. We'll see how much stuff they're taking with them."

As we walked toward the porch, I noticed a dark-blue car parked on the road next to the turnoff to our house and the lighthouse. I had never seen that car before. I could see a man behind the wheel looking at something, maybe a map, but it could be a newspaper. He's probably from out-of-state and checking a map because he doesn't know the roads along the coastline.

Suzy, Millie, and I sat quietly a few minutes before Mom came out carrying a medium-sized suitcase, followed by Dad with a big one. Millie poked me and said the big one was hers. Elena came out carrying two suitcases, both of medium size. I wondered why Mom had so much more stuff than Elena. Dad tossed all the luggage in the back of the pickup and after checking his watch, said, "We'd better get going, it's a couple of minutes after nine. Ladies, you need to say your goodbyes."

Suzy ran up to Mom and wrapped her arms around Mom's waist. Mom gave Suz a hug and kissed her on the forehead. I gave Mom a hug and said, "We'll see you in a couple of weeks. Right?"

"Yes. If it takes longer, we'll send you word of our delay, but I can't imagine any problems. Just mind your dad and your grandmother. Take care of Surprise!" She smoothed my hair with her fingers and kissed my nose.

I laughed. "Okay, Mom. Have a good trip."

I don't know what Millie and Elena said, but when I looked at Millie, I could see a tears running down her cheeks. It surprised me a little because we were going to The Bahamas with them. Maybe Millie was just acting and doing a really good job.

Granma came out carrying Surprise and gave both Elena and Mom a hug and then went back in the house. I wondered if Granma thought Mom was going to be in danger and didn't want to make a big deal out of saying goodbye. But maybe that was just my imagination.

"Ladies, let's get down to the pier and get you on that boat." Dad was getting into the pickup.

Mom and Elena climbed into the pickup and Dad started the motor. We could see Mom and Elena wave to us from the rear window. When they got to the highway, they turned right and disappeared over the hill. That blue car started moving before the pickup was out of sight. I had to wonder if Dad's pickup was being followed by the sedan.

"We'd better get going, too, Rocky. I hope we can get some more books today."

"Are you guys going to ride your bikes?" Another question from Suzy.

"Uh-huh. We'll give you some of the money we get for the books. Mom should pay us the same as Mr. W. did."

"So I get one-third?"

"Yep. Why don't you take Surprise for a walk? Make sure you have a leash on him. You'd better stay away from the water; it's pretty cold now."

Millie and I went into the house and put on our loaded backpacks. As we went out the door, Granma said, "Where are you going?"

I stopped and turned around, partly to hide my full pack, and partly to answer her.

"We're going to look for books over on the other side of the bay. We've got some lunch, but we won't be gone too long."

"All right, but be careful and stay away from the heavy traffic roads. I'll expect you back by two or three o'clock at the latest."

"Okay, Granma. See you later—probably after three."

I was relieved that Granma didn't search our backpacks. Millie and I rode to the highway and headed toward the pier. We had only ridden about half-way to the hilltop when Jerry rode up behind us and said, "Where are you guys going?"

Millie answered, "We're riding to see Mrs. Hughes to pick up some books and then we're going to have a fall picnic at Armadale Park." She pointed at her watch and said, "Look, Rocky, it's already 9:30. We're going to be late if we don't hurry. Bye, Jerry. I'll see you Monday in class."

We rode away from Jerry. I shouted back, "See you Monday!" He gave me back a weak wave. On the way down the hill, I thought of all the lies I had told in the last week, but it was for a good reason. Millie had to help get her parents back from the kidnappers and I had to help Millie. Besides, Mom and Elena might need me to help them get some bad people, like when I stabbed that man with the barbeque fork and shot cherry bombs from the lighthouse gallery at those spies trying to sneak ashore. Boy, it all seemed like a long time had passed since that happened, but it had only been about two months ago.

When we got to the pathway to the back of the pier stores, we hopped off our bikes and started walking them. "What time is it?"

"Nine thirty-eight."

"Hurry, Millie. We have to be in position." I could see Dad's pickup in the parking lot. He must be in the store. He won't see us.

Wheeling our bikes at a half-run, half-walk rate got us behind the stores in about a minute. We dumped the bicycles behind the craft store, underneath the fire escape, and ran the rest of the way to the end of the pier where Mr. Riley sold boat motors and parts. "What time is it?"

Millie took a deep breath, "It's nine forty-one."

"Okay, we can wait here for a few minutes." We were behind Riley's store, but I could see the yacht and across the bay. I spotted Billy's boat moving slowly toward the pier and the yacht. I looked at Millie and grinned. "I think this is going to work."

She squeezed my arm. Both of us were out of breath, but I don't think it was from running. It was from being scared. My heart was really pumping. I tried to relax, but I was having a hard time doing it. We had to get aboard without being detected.

"Where do we go next, Rocky?"

"See those barrels? Right behind them. You'll smell the gasoline. A little bit spills each time they pump some out for a boat. Try not to breathe the fumes; turn your nose away or pinch it with your fingers."

I counted eleven barrels, separated into two bunches. Some were probably full and the others empty. The empty ones had spaces between them where we could hide. We had waited a few minutes, but it seemed much longer. "What's the time?"

Millie sighed, "It's nine fifty-six. Should we move behind the barrels?"

"Yeah. Stay low and follow me."

We darted across an open space about twenty feet wide and ducked behind three barrels arranged almost in line. We sat down and waited. One, two, three minutes went by and then I heard Billy's outboard engine. He was fiddling with the engine, making it sound like there was something wrong. If I didn't know better, the sound would have fooled me. Suddenly there was no sound at all. It was deadly quiet. Then we heard a big thunk. It sounded like the hull of the yacht was vibrating. We could almost feel it. I think Billy hit the yacht harder than he had originally planned. I hope he didn't damage the hull. His boat was too old to worry about damage.

Millie looked at me and put her hand over her mouth; I could tell she wanted to laugh. I smiled and whispered, "Get ready!"

We heard a yell but we didn't recognize the voice. I couldn't tell if it was from Billy or someone on the yacht. Then I heard Mom. I stuck my head up above the gas containers and looked down the pier. Nobody was looking our way. "Go, Millie!" I couldn't tell what was being said because we were sneaking on the yacht, being as quiet as possible, and not paying attention to the words.

It only took us about five seconds to get from the pier to the emergency equipment room. I tried the door, but it wouldn't open. I couldn't see a lock but it just wouldn't open.

"Hurry, Rocky!"

"I'm trying. The door must be locked."

"It can't be, it's an emergency-center door."

"Okay. You try it!"

Millie tried, with the same result. Someone was going to see us if we didn't get in there. Then she turned the lever to the left and the door popped open. We were both in in about three seconds. I pulled the door shut and we both sank to the deck on our butts. Millie put her right palm over her heart. I put my head between my knees and said, "Thank-you, God."

We could hear voices from outside. "Aren't you Billy Franklin?"

"Yes, ma'am. Aren't you the lighthouse lady? What are you doing on this big yacht? Did you come into some money? I hope I didn't damage your vessel, it's a beauty."

"No, I didn't come into any money. I'm going on a trip for the CIA. There doesn't appear to be any damage. Could you please move your dinghy away from our boat?"

"CIA? Oh, I'm sure sorry about bumping into you. It's not a dinghy, Mrs. Linfield, it's my fishing boat, bought and paid for. The engine got a cold today."

"Sorry, Billy. Please move your fishing boat so we can move away from the pier. If we hit you, you'll probably sink. We wouldn't want that."

"Okay. I'll shove off and drift out of your way. Have a good trip."

"Thank-you, Billy. Get some cough medicine for your motor."

Millie and I had heard almost everything and were trying to keep from laughing. We both covered our mouths with our shirts and hands to keep from making any noise. Mom was really great when she called Billy's boat a dinghy. She knew about Billy's goofball pranks and I wondered if she thought anything was suspicious about the collision.

A minute or so later, we could feel the engine vibrations and we were moving, slowly at first, but then picking up speed. We must have been out of the harbor area when the engine noise was a steady hum and kind of soothing. We were on our way to The Bahamas. Goodbye, Crafton.

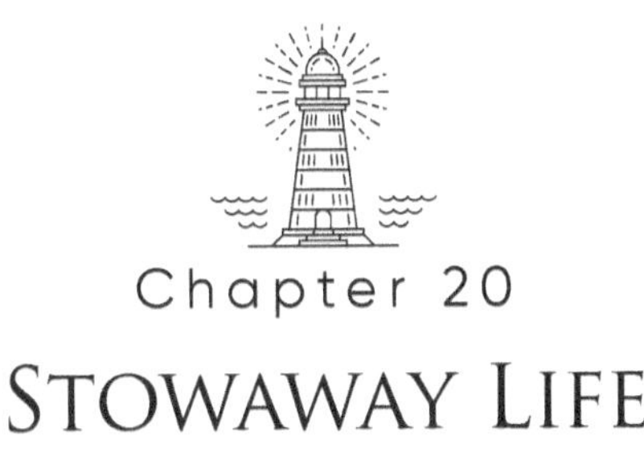

Chapter 20

Stowaway Life

The interior of the emergency equipment room was not as disorganized as Millie had recalled from the other yacht. The two inflatable life boats were stowed as nearly cubic packages wrapped with a thin plastic rope and a lever to be twisted to expand the small boats. According to the instructions printed on the outside label, it seemed each boat could hold five people, maximum six, depending on size. What surprised both of us was a porthole and a louver; we had expected only a louver.

"Rocky, we have to put something over the porthole so nobody can see in."

I looked at the porthole and figured one of our backpacks would cover the round window. I emptied my pack, putting some things in my pockets and giving my extra underwear to Millie to store in her backpack. I put my slingshot and marbles behind the collapsed lifeboats. Then I hooked my backpack over the porthole window. Not much light could get into our little hideaway. With the porthole covered, there was only a little light coming from a space under the emergency door.

Our room was about four feet high, but big enough for us both to lie down. As my eyes got used to the dim light, I saw some folded, gray fire blankets stacked in the corner. We would be able to lie down on them—better than on the hardwood deck. We could use our jackets for pillows. Sleeping was not going to be an uncomfortable problem.

The only other equipment in the storage area was a half-dozen red fire extinguishers, each about the size of a half-gallon of milk. Millie and I decided to stack them right inside the door. If anyone wanted one, it would be easy to get to. In the need to fight a fire, no one would look much farther into the room when they saw the extinguishers, at least that is what we hoped. But Millie was pretty sure there wouldn't be any fires to worry about. I had to agree with her, at least that was my thought, too.

For the first three or four hours, we listened to the creaks and groans of the boat and tried to identify the voices we heard from sounds coming through the louver and from the hallway. There were two men, a woman named Fiona, Mom, and Elena; altogether, seven of us were on the yacht. One of the men, Charles, was the captain. He sounded like he was the oldest person on board. The other man, Vern, was usually below in the engine room. I'm guessing at him being about Mom's age. Fiona seemed to be older than Elena, but younger than Mom, maybe in her early thirties. I think she was the cook, but she also did laundry and cleaning. She was kind of a maid. I think it's hard to tell how old a person is from their voice.

When we heard voices, we identified who was talking and what we thought they looked like, except for Elena and Mom, of course. We had to whisper to remain undetected. Millie fell asleep first, leaning against me with her hands folded in her lap and her head on my shoulder. I listened to her breathing for maybe ten minutes. I woke up at least an hour later. I could smell coffee.

Millie moved suddenly, as if startled, opened her eyes, and sat up straight. "What time is it?"

"I don't know. I can't see your watch."

She held her wrist nearly touching her nose and said, "I can't read it anyway. I'll have to move over to the porthole to be able to see." I could hear Millie crawling toward the porthole.

"Be careful. Don't move the backpack. Someone might see it move. We need a watch made for blind people—one with Braille numbers."

"Why didn't we think of that?"

I knew she was grinning and I almost laughed. I wondered how many things we didn't think of. While Millie was trying to read her watch, I moved over to the blankets and unfolded one. I spread it out on the deck and then added another one to make the floor softer. I laid on my back and moved my legs like I was riding my bike. My legs were getting stiff just sitting there in one position. There was a brief burst of light and then darkness.

"It's five forty-seven, Rocky. Shall we dine at six o'clock?"

"Yes, Madame. I shall prepare our meal. What would you like for a beverage?"

"A spot of tea would be satisfactory, Master Linfield."

I smiled and knew that we were both having fun. We had been on the yacht for eight hours and hadn't had any problems. We were in good shape and none of the crew knew we were on the boat.

"Did you sneak a peek through the porthole?"

Millie was quiet, but after a few seconds, she said, "Uh-huh. Are you mad at me?"

"Not really, but you risked giving us away. Wha'd you see?"

"The ocean."

That was what I'd expected. Millie crawled back beside me and opened her backpack. I couldn't see what she was doing, but I could hear her rustling through some papers. Then I felt something touch my lips. She was trying to stick a cookie in my mouth. That's when I discovered her night vision was better than mine. I probably would have poked out her eye with a cookie.

I reached up, took the cookie in my right hand and took a bite. It was one of Granma's best: chocolate chip. There was more rustling of paper and I smelled a brownie. Then I heard Millie chewing.

"Did you know you gave me a chocolate chip cookie?"

"Uh-huh. And I got a brownie."

"How'd you tell in the dark?"

"I wrapped them differently with wax paper."

"Pretty smart, Millie."

"Thanks."

"You're welcome." I grinned, thinking of Suzy. "What else do you have in there?"

"Would you like some cheese—maybe a carrot?"

We suddenly froze in position and didn't move at all for about ten seconds. Someone had walked by the emergency supplies door going to one of the bathrooms. We heard the click of the door lock and after a couple of minutes, the toilet flushed. Water was running for a few seconds, the sound of the door lock repeated, and then footsteps going past our little room.

Millie poked me and said, "I'm glad we couldn't hear everything."

"I know what you mean. I'd like a piece of cheese, please."

"Put out your hand, Rocky."

I felt a hand bump my arm on the side and then a piece of something cool was placed in the palm of my outstretched hand. I smelled it first. It was a chunk of cheese.

"Thank-you."

"You're welcome. I have a carrot. I'll chew quietly."

I could barely hear the crunching between her teeth. At least she didn't snap off a piece of carrot, making a noise, and she chewed with her mouth closed. Even though we were whispering, we didn't know if anything we did or said could be heard outside of our space. We both knew we had to be sure not to drop anything, especially if it was hard.

We heard more footsteps in the hallway and didn't move until we knew the person had returned, passing by in the opposite direction, whistling. Mom and Elena didn't whistle, so we expected it was one of the men. We had heard the same clicks of the bathroom door as before. The flushing had been very quiet.

We didn't hear anything else, except for some creaks and groans of the boat, for nearly fifteen minutes. The hum of the engine was present, but like a bee hive far away.

"Rocky, I have to pee."

"I wish you hadn't said that. Now, I have to go. How long can you hold it?"

"Not much longer or I'll have an accident."

"Crack open the door and take a sniff. See if you smell food."

The light coming in from the hall seemed very bright, almost like looking into a flashbulb. My eyes adjusted quickly though, and I could see everything in our room.

"I smell their dinner. Something smells really good."

"Okay. They're having something to eat. Run down to the bathroom. See if you can find an empty bottle for me. Remember, don't flush!"

Millie was out of the room in a flash. She couldn't have been gone longer than twenty or thirty seconds. I watched her come back on her tiptoes, carrying an empty Coke bottle; just what I needed. She handed the bottle to me and crawled back into our room. I shut the emergency equipment hatch and leaned against it. We were in complete darkness again until our eyes adjusted to the dim light rays that came under the bottom of the door.

Millie exhaled and said, "Oh! I feel so much better."

"Let me trade places with you so I can pee in the bottle. I hope I don't fill it up."

Even though I was turned away from Millie and knew she couldn't see me, I couldn't get the flow started. I had never peed in the presence of a girl before.

"Millie, make a hissing noise—like running water."

I tried to think of waterfalls, and water running from the taps in the sink and bathtub. In my mind I watched the water in the toilet swirling after flushing. That did it. I started filling up the bottle. I hoped it would hold all my water. I could hear the sound changing as the pee level started up the neck of the bottle and then stopped. I zipped up and held the bottle so it wouldn't tip over. I wonder if I'll ever be able to pee without help when someone is in the bathroom with me. I need to talk with Dad about it.

"Do we have something to seal the bottle? If it tips over, we're doomed."

Millie didn't answer immediately. I heard something but couldn't tell what she was doing. "Here, Rocky. Stuff this in the neck of the bottle and stand it up in the corner behind the lifeboats. It can't fall over there."

She had rewrapped the cookies and given me a good-sized piece of wax paper. I squeezed it into the shape of a cork and jammed it into the top of the Coke bottle. Millie had come through again.

"Do we have any water to drink, Rocky? I should have gotten a drink when I went to the bathroom, but I was afraid I would be discovered, so I got out of there fast.

"I have some water. When I was trying to find a gun at Granma's, I got a canteen from her garage. I couldn't get in the house, it was locked up tight. I'll get it for you. We'll both get a drink and you can refill it in the bathroom in the morning."

The canteen was with my slingshot and pocketknife. We both took a couple of swallows. Millie said the water tasted like metal. I wondered how she could come up with that. We were both getting tired so I unfolded the last two fire blankets to use to keep us warm as we travelled on the ocean. I thought of a question for Millie.

"Do you know how warm it is in The Bahamas in October?"

"Un-huh. I looked it up in the school library. The daytime temperature in usually in the eighties."

"That's good. We won't need sweaters and jackets during the day."

"I'm wondering how long we'll be there."

"As long as it takes to get your mom and dad back. No longer. We have to get home and go back to school."

"What do you think will happen when your dad and grandmother find out we're gone?"

"Geez, I don't know. I'll bet they've already found our bikes and figured out we're on the yacht. Granma and Dad are both pretty smart."

"Yeah. I'll bet they're trying to get in touch with the boat already—just to tell Elena and your mother we've disappeared."

"Well, I hope they don't contact anyone until we're in The Bahamas."

"Me, too. If they find us, they'll probably sail to Florida and send us back home."

"I'm tired. Don't think about it anymore, Millie. Let's go to sleep."

Chapter 21

LISTENING

Sunday started off the way we ended Saturday, cooped up in that little room, afraid to make any noises above the sounds of two people breathing. When we figured out the crew was eating breakfast, Millie made another visit to the bathroom. She poured the contents of the Coke bottle in the toilet and flushed after she had gone to the bathroom. She realized what she had done and hurried back to our room without filling the canteen.

"I'm sorry, Rocky. I flushed on account of habit. What are we going to do?"

"We have to wait to see if anyone heard it. Maybe they're not all eating together. The people not there could have flushed the toilet."

We sat in fear of discovery for nearly thirty minutes, but nothing happened. While we waited, I noticed the boat was bouncing around more than yesterday. We must be riding waves instead of smooth ocean water.

"What's that noise?" We could hear what sounded to me like rain drops hitting the roof over my attic bedroom.

"I think it's starting to rain. I hope it doesn't get too rough. We might get seasick." I wanted to pray, but I figured that would be useless. If we had rough weather, God couldn't do much to keep me from throwing up; it would just happen. But then Millie said something that made good sense.

"I don't think we'll get sick. We hardly ate anything yesterday."

"I sure hope you're right." As I sat there, I began to think: What are we going to do when we arrive in The Bahamas? Are we going to come out of our hiding place and say "Surprise?" Maybe something will happen and we'll know what to do.

Millie and I talked it over and she agreed with me. We would have to wait and see. If we popped out of our little room without a good reason, we would make Elena and Mom madder than—hell. That was the only word I could come up with. I could think it, but I'd better not say it out loud.

We both had two cookies and a sip of water for breakfast. We talked about nearly everything for about an hour. We were both getting tired of whispering. Millie held her watch in the dim light coming under the door so she could tell the time.

"It's ten o'clock, Rocky. We've been on the yacht twenty-four hours."

"Another day and a half and we'll be there. I think this is the worst trip I've ever been on." I realized that Millie might take that the wrong way, so I said, "Not because I'm with you, Millie, but because we're trapped in this little space with nothing to do."

"I understand. I feel the same way. We should have a flashlight and something to read."

"I wish we could hear what my mom and Elena are saying. I mean, what is going on? I wonder what the plans are to find your parents."

"I've been thinking about that, too. If my mom and dad were kidnapped, don't you think the kidnappers would want some money, a ransom, or something?"

"Uh-huh. I don't get it. If we hear some voices, let's crack open the door and listen. Maybe we can tell what's happening."

The up-and-down motion of the boat had stopped and then I couldn't hear the engine. At first I thought something was wrong, but then we heard noises from above us. In a couple of minutes, the yacht had tilted and we were sliding toward the porthole. That's when I realized the boat was sailing under wind power. The engine wasn't necessary.

I didn't have to tell Millie what had happened. She knew more about sailing than I did.

"The boat is listing, Rocky! The fire extinguishers! They're going to fall over and slide. We've got to move them or we'll be discovered."

She was right! We had to act fast but as I tried to get to the cylinders, I kept slipping on the blankets. I shoved them out of the way so I could crawl uphill toward the door without slipping. Just as I got to them, the one on top slid off the pile—but I caught it, keeping it from banging against the deck.

"I'm coming, Rocky." Millie was crawling up behind me, I could tell by her voice she was getting closer. "Hand me the extinguishers, one at a time, and I'll put them against the port wall. When they're moved, we'll use the blankets to keep them from sliding around."

It took about ten minutes to get the cylinders moved and covered so they couldn't make any noise. We rearranged our floor blankets and stretched out with our feet to port, helping to hold the extinguishers in place. After that emergency, I hoped the wind didn't shift so the boat would list to starboard. As we were rearranging things, Millie explained port and starboard to me.

"Where does the crew eat dinner, Millie? How do we get there? Is there only one way?"

"Holy cow! One question at a time. Okay, dinner is served one deck below us in the bow. If the sails are out, the captain will eat on the bridge. You can get to the dining area two ways; I'll tell you the best way first."

Millie gave me instructions so I could get close enough to hear what was being said during dinner with the least chance of being seen. We were going to have to risk being found, but one of us had to listen to what was being said by Mom and Elena. I would try first. If I wasn't successful, Millie would try again at lunchtime tomorrow. Our last chance would be during dinner tomorrow night. We only had three chances left before we reached the islands. We didn't want to risk it at breakfast, people got up at different times.

We took naps until lunchtime and both of us woke up a few minutes before noon. There was some commotion on deck and we heard some yelling, but we sat quietly, listening for every morsel of sound that could help us figure out what was going on. I sat there hoping no one would suddenly open the emergency supply door and see us, but the noises from above stopped. I could hear another, familiar sound return after about ten minutes. It was the engine. I also noticed the list was gone, we were moving on the water with the deck almost level.

Millie and I did some leg and arm exercises and sat up on the top of the lifeboats instead of the floor. Millie said she worried we wouldn't be able to walk when we left our room if we stayed lying down for too long. We planned an exercise program to keep our muscles in the best possible shape while we hid out. We decided to do the program three times a day. After we did the exercises the first time, we relaxed and had lunch. We each had a cookie, a brownie, and a hard-boiled egg, followed by a swallow of water. We'd have to get more water soon.

In the late afternoon, we heard thunder and it began to rain, but the yacht just kept plowing steadily ahead. The boat seemed to be moving pretty much at the same speed all the time. The only time the yacht changed speed was when it was using wind power. Then it was like a relay race where all the runners ran at different speeds.

Millie took a quick peek through the porthole and said, "The deck is wet and water is running off the glass. It's getting dark, too, but the waves aren't very big."

I was glad she had looked outside, now I had something else to think about. I was getting tired of picturing things in my brain about school and other places in Crafton. There was one thing I never got tired of though, the lighthouse. I hope there are lighthouses in The Bahamas. But after a few minutes, I began to worry about sneaking to the place Millie had told me it would be fairly safe to listen to the diner's conversation. I knew I shouldn't eat before I tried to listen to Mom and Elena, my nerves might cause me to get an upset stomach and throw up.

According to Millie, it was five minutes after six. I was sitting next to the door. I heard footsteps and held my breath until they passed. Someone was going to the bathroom. I heard the door open and the lock click. Millie had told me to call the bathroom the head. That's the term sailor's use for the toilet. I waited for the footsteps to pass by again and then I opened our door. I could smell food. I waited for about ten more minutes and then went into the hallway. Following Millie's directions, I sneaked to where I could hear people talking. I listened for about five minutes, got scared I was taking too much time, so I returned to the equipment room.

"What'd you hear?"

"Nothing important. They were just talking about the yacht and ocean travel. I guess they don't know we aren't home. Maybe when you listen, we'll know more."

"Well, I know they have a radio. Before long someone will tell the captain we're missing."

"Yeah. That's what I'm worried about. They'll search the boat and find us. Then we won't be able to help find your parents. They'll put us on a plane and send us home."

"If they get a message and start looking for us, we've got to swim ashore."

"I hope we're close to land. I swam about a mile in the dark once and it's pretty scary."

"It might not be too bad if we have a life preserver and are together."

"I'm worried about sharks. They feed at night. I checked it out at the school library."

"Dad told me to punch them in the nose if they get too close."

"Good idea, but if you don't see one coming—."

"Let's not talk about it anymore. Okay?"

Millie opened her backpack and pulled out stuff for dinner. We had cheese, two cookies, and a pickle for dinner. Afterward, she said, "Would you like some wine?"

At first, I thought she was going nuts, but then I realized she was back to her old self.

"What do we have on the menu?"

"I have a bottle of aqua—fifty-two. Would you like a sip?"

"Ah, fifty-two. That was a good year for the grape."

I don't know why we were having fun in our double-size casket. I was so tired of hiding—eating carrots, cookies, cheese, and drinking metal tasting water, I was almost ready to give up and eat dinner with the crew. But when Millie talked about saving her parents, I became enthusiastic again. I had to help her find her mom and dad. I didn't know for sure if she would be helping me do the same thing if my parents were kidnapped, but I felt like she would. At least, she had asked me for help, not anyone else. Maybe I was the only one that could help her.

We did our exercises and used our fingers and the end of a carrot to brush our teeth. Then we made up some tall-tales and talked about them for over an hour. I tried to go to sleep but couldn't for a long time. After what I thought had been at least an hour, I said, "Are you asleep?" There was no answer. I started doing multiplications and got up to the twelves before I fell asleep.

When we woke up, Millie was sitting there humming. I don't think it was a song, she was just humming. Maybe it was to the engine. That was the only thing we could hear. Not really hear, but feel some vibrations through the boat.

I rolled over, so I was turned toward her, and stretched. "Morning."

"I was wondering when you'd wake up. I've been asking you questions, but you've been ignoring me for the last half-hour."

"Sorry. I had a late night at the office."

Millie covered her mouth and laughed. "We sound like an old married couple."

We whispered our daily plans, at least until Millie had her turn trying to hear what was being said at lunchtime. After taking care of toilet chores, we had a muffin and cheese. I was surprised when given a muffin, I didn't know we had any. Millie said she was down to the last layer of food at the bottom of her pack. I had a few cookies left with my slingshot and ammunition.

At eight o'clock, we figured we had about fourteen hours to go and we'd be in The Bahamas. That was if we had averaged twenty knots per hour. I wished we knew what our present position was.

The morning went very slowly, but we heard a lot of footsteps moving up and down the hallway. We thought everyone was trying to use the bathroom about the same time. I thought that maybe we were closer to The Bahamas than we realized and people were getting cleaned up to go ashore. But the activity stopped after about thirty minutes and everything went back to normal.

Millie and I napped for a while and then talked over what she would do when everyone was having lunch. We decided to eat after she got back from eavesdropping. I think I was more nervous than Millie. She was pretty cool. When it was time, she sneaked out and tiptoed down the hall.

I cracked the door just enough so I could hear if anything went wrong. I don't know what I was going to do if something did go wrong. I knew for certain that I wasn't going to jump overboard. I began to worry after about ten minutes. The time might have been less, or more, I didn't have Millie's watch. I suppose I could have used my heart beat for a clock, but it hadn't occurred to me then.

I heard rapid footsteps and was sure it was Millie, although I waited until she tapped on the door before I opened it. She came in, shut the door and exhaled, as if she had been holding her breath for ten minutes.

"Wha'd you hear?"

"The captain told Elena and your mother that your dad sent a message that you and I had disappeared. They have no clue where we went. Jerry told your dad we had gone to the park and were going to try to get more books for the library. Your dad thinks we were kidnapped. He called the police. Suzy is staying home from school with your grandmother."

She took another deep breath and exhaled. "I wish we could tell them where we are."

"Me, too. But we can't let them know we're going to The Bahamas."

"So you don't think they'll search the boat?"

"Nope. I'm sure they think we're somewhere in Maine, not a thousand miles south, and with them on the same boat. Mom and Elena would be very surprised to find us here."

"If we have to go overboard and swim to an island, what do we take with us?"

"Your backpack, but with only our clothes, the marbles, and my slingshot—and the money, for sure. Leave everything else here."

"For them to find?"

I thought for a minute and said, "Before dinner, we put everything back the way it was when we got on board. Whatever isn't in your pack, we put in mine with one fire extinguisher. When we get in the water, we'll let my bag sink."

"Oh, that sounds good! They'll never miss one fire extinguisher."

Chapter 22

GOING ASHORE

"Millie, are you a good swimmer?"

"I can do all right, what about you?"

"I get tired real fast if I don't have a float to hang onto. Where can we get into the water—where they won't see us?"

"At the stern. There's a life preserver on the back wall we can use. Nobody'll notice it's gone. It's something no one pays any attention to."

"We'll splash if we jump in."

"We don't have to jump. There are some handholds and foot notches so we can back off into the water. We won't make any noise at all."

"Okay. We've got our plan ready. I just have to listen at dinnertime."

We exercised and napped until five-thirty and got our things ready for leaving the boat. The sky was gray again and a few drops of rain were falling on the deck. Dinner was served at a couple of minutes after six. We checked our packs, stacked the blankets, and put the extinguishers back where we found them, except for one. I noticed the engine noise had stopped. Millie said the other noise we had heard was from the anchor.

We gave the crew five minutes to get settled and then I sneaked to our listening place. I stayed for about ten minutes before I returned to our room.

"Lots of news, Millie. Dad and Granma caught a guy trying to burn down the library. Surprise was going crazy—barking at the front door, so

Dad went out and looked around. The library wall was starting to burn near the door. Surprise sniffed around and started running toward the shoreline so Dad followed after throwing some dirt and sand on the fire. Granma had her gun and shot the fire bug. He had tried to shoot my dad."

"Is that it?"

"No. I'm just out of breath." I took several breaths before continuing. "The firebug was from New York. Someone with a Russian accent hired him to kidnap you. He didn't know the name of the man that hired him, he just had a number to call after he had you. He thought you were in the house. The fire was to get the adults away so he could grab you."

"Why would he want me?"

"Granma threatened to blow off his knees if he didn't talk, so he told her the Russian wanted to get Elena's family and make her watch as he killed them—and then he would kill her. The Russian is the cousin of the man Elena killed at Granma's house. He wants revenge."

"Wow! I guess I'm lucky I wasn't in Crafton."

"Oh, one more thing. We're anchored about 500 meters off the northeastern coast of Abaco Island."

"Oh! That's in The Bahamas. We're really there!"

"We've got to go, Millie, before they get up and start moving around the boat."

"I'm ready. Here's your pack, it's kind of heavy."

We crept to the port deck and moved as quickly as we could toward the stern, without running. The sound of two people running, even small ones, would be heard. Millie pointed at the life preserver and I snatched it off the wall. She was already halfway down the side by the time I got to the top of the handholds and notches. It was getting dark, so I hoped we could get away from the yacht without being seen. It had to be that way.

When my legs dropped below the surface, I was surprised; the water was warm, not like the ocean water near Crafton last summer. I let go of my pack and it made a slurping sound and sank into the deep water. No one will ever find it. Millie was treading water beneath the overhang of the yacht, out of sight of anyone on board. I stuck my left arm through the hole of the preserver and paddled over to her. That's when we heard, "Sandra, your husband found the kids' bikes behind the craft store. He thinks they've been hiding on the yacht. Let's start searching." It was the captain's voice.

We stayed out of sight and worked our way toward the bow and waited until we couldn't hear any noises coming from the boat. As we floated, hanging onto the preserver, I noticed a dim light reflecting off the hull of the yacht, off and on, off and on. I looked around and saw where the light was coming from—a lighthouse. I pointed to it and Millie nodded that she could see it.

I whispered, "That's our target. Let's wait a little longer, for the sky to get darker."

"But the sharks. What are we going to do?"

"We just have to chance it. We've been lucky so far. Are you getting cold?"

"No, the water's warm. It's like sitting in a bath for a half hour and the hot water has cooled to just warm, time to get out of the tub and dry off."

We floated there for about ten minutes before pushing off toward the rotating light. I was reminded of swimming away from the Russian ship, hanging on to that piece of wood to keep me from sinking. But this was fun, I had someone to swim with. It wasn't so lonely, and the stars were different. Polaris was low in the sky. Everything was new, and different. We paddled for about 100 yards before we began kicking. We were far enough away from the yacht so the crew couldn't hear us. We couldn't hear any voices.

I think the water was carrying us toward the shore. We seemed to be covering the distance from the yacht to the island at a good rate. The light kept getting higher and higher as we moved closer to it, but it seemed to be moving to the right.

"Rocky! Something touched my foot!"

"Did it bite?"

"No."

"Then don't worry about it. I think you just touched bottom. The water isn't very deep here. Try to walk."

"Yes, I think it must be sand, it moves when I step on it. We can walk ashore now."

"Let's float a little farther—until the water is shallower. I don't want to step in a hole and go under, or get cut on coral. Ocean water doesn't taste so good, either."

In ten minutes we were standing on shore in the sand. We weren't very tired, but we flopped on the ground to relax and look around. At first, the only things I could make out were the lights on the yacht and the lighthouse beacon, farther north, sweeping around and around. The ocean currents had swept us several hundred yards south of the lighthouse. It was slightly chilly, our wet clothes certainly weren't helping us stay warm. I needed some dry underwear.

"Do you think our clothes in the backpack are dry?"

"I wrapped them as tightly as I could and used all the wax paper from the cookies to cover them. They might be dry. I'll check."

My eyes had adjusted to the light from the beacon that made it to the ground around us. It wasn't bright enough to read a comic book, but I could see Millie and the beacon's rays reflecting off her eyes. Her eyes twinkled like the stars near the horizon. She wiped her hands in the sand until they were dry and then unwrapped our clothes.

"They're dry! I want to change."

"Go ahead, I won't look."

"Let's sit back to back. When I've changed, you can change."

"All I have in there is dry underwear; no dry pants or shirt."

"That's all right. I don't care if you're in your underwear." She smiled and said, "It might smell like cookies."

"Yeah, but I care." I wouldn't care, if Millie was related, like my sister, but she's not. What would she tell the girls in Crafton when we get back home?

"Rocky, look over there." She pointed to the south, just off the sandy beach.

"It looks like a small house. Let's check it out."

I took off my tennis shoes and socks and started across the warm sand. Millie was wringing out her wet clothes as she walked beside me. She had her shoes, tied together with the laces, around her neck and the backpack slung over her left shoulder. I still had my wet pants on, but I had taken off my shirt and put on a dry one. My wet jacket was tied around my waist.

The house wasn't a house, it was a picnic building with three tables. The roof looked like it was made of plywood, maybe something left over from the war. We laid our wet clothes out to dry on top of one of the wooden tables. I had taken off my wet pants and shorts and put on dry shorts, but I left my jacket on to cover my lower half, at least my private parts area.

We were both rubbing our arms and legs, trying to keep warm. Even though the daytime temperature was around eighty, the temperature seemed to have dropped at least ten degrees after the sun went down. We discovered the sand below the picnic tables was still warm from the daylight sun, so we sat down back to back to keep as warm as possible. I felt Millie's stomach growl and a few minutes later, my stomach growled. We both laughed.

"I'm really hungry, Millie. Is there anything to eat?"

"A couple of carrots and a small piece of cheese. We'll have to find some food in the morning. Want half of what we have?"

"Sure. We might as well live it up. Still have your money?"

"Uh-huh. How about you?"

"It's in my wet pants, drying out. Should be dry by morning."

We had our evening meal and lay on the warm sand, listening to the surf. The last thing I remember thinking about was rats.

We woke up early in the morning. The sky was a light gray and the sun was just thinking about coming up. Millie announced the time as six thirty-eight. Her waterproof watch was about our only valuable possession, and that wasn't worth very much. I didn't include my slingshot and marbles. Up to now we hadn't needed a weapon.

My pants, shirt, and jacket were dry, but smelled a bit like an ocean beach. After I dressed, I tied my jacket around my waist as before. Millie had done the same with her jacket. We both checked our money and it was all there. After stuffing all our things into the backpack, I stuck my arms through the webbing, and hopped a couple of times to get the canvas bag settled on my back. Millie didn't need to carry our things and my slingshot was right on top of the clothes so I could get it easily. I was surprised when Millie pulled a small comb from her pocket, ran it through her hair, and then handed it to me. I didn't have much to comb, but I used it anyway, just in case there was some seaweed hiding.

Millie stood on top of one of the picnic tables and scanned up and down the beach. Besides where we had spent the night, the only man-made thing she could see was the lighthouse. We decided to go inland and try to find something to eat. We hiked across sand and rocks for about ten minutes before coming to a single-lane road. We followed the road going south. There was no traffic at all. We just kept walking as the sun warmed us.

We stopped every ten minutes or so to scan the area, looking for a town, or something. We couldn't see any houses. I began to think we were on a deserted island shipwrecked like Robinson Crusoe.

"What are we going to do, Rocky? We're almost out of water."

"How much do we have left?"

"Enough for one swallow each."

"See any birds?" I was hoping they would be near some water, a small lake of fresh water. Just thinking of a lake made me thirsty.

Millie's head swiveled and she said, "Nothing but sand and sky. Maybe we should have gone north."

"Maybe you're right. Maybe someone lives at the lighthouse, like us in Crafton. Want to go back the other way?"

"Let me think about it."

We sat down like Indians, in the middle of the road, and looked at each other. Millie raised her left eyebrow and shrugged her shoulders. We were in a pickle. Our water was almost gone. We couldn't go very far. We had been sitting for about five minutes when we heard an engine. The noise was getting louder, so we stood up and moved off the road watching the road as the noise approached from the south.

It was a jeep.

Chapter 23

PINKY

I didn't think the jeep would stop, but the driver must have wondered what two kids were doing at the side of the road. The driver was a large Negro. He smiled and waved as he zoomed past us and then skidded to a stop on the sandy road. Millie ran toward the multicolored jeep. He backed up until he got to Millie and then stopped, turned off the engine and got out. He was tall, had on shorts and a colorful shirt, open at the neck, but was barefoot.

"Vut you doin' way out here by you self?"

I reached Millie and grabbed her arm before she started blabbing. I took over; I didn't want her to tell him her real name. What if he was one of the kidnappers?

"We're just walkin', lookin' for somethin' to eat."

"Vere you from, if I may ax?"

"Boston."

"I knowed it!" He slapped his leg and smiled. "You may'landers. Brother an sister?"

I nodded and Millie followed what I did. "She's a year older than I am. I'm Jerry and she's Irene." I figured if I used Jerry, she would be used to the name and not call me Rocky.

"Velcome to duh Bahamas. Nice to meet you. I's Pinky" He stuck his finger in his chest and then held out his big right hand, but I froze for a second. I had never met or even touched a Negro before. I thought his skin would be rough like the paws of some kind of animal. Millie shook his hand so I did too. His hand felt similar to Mr. Morgan's hands, like he worked with tools a lot. "Bet you vonder how a black man git duh name Pinky."

"Yes, sir."

"Well, you git in dis jeep an I tell you. I take you to Miss Carla's house an you can eat an tell your story." He slapped his big hand against the seat and we climbed in beside him. Millie looked at me kind of funny-like as if to ask me why I was making up false names. I couldn't explain it to her with Pinky listening.

He started the jeep, shifted gears and spun the tires, forcing us against the back of the bench seat. Millie was surprised and grabbed my leg to keep from falling off the seat. I grabbed the side of the jeep and held on tight. Pinky laughed and started singing, words of a song I had never heard.

"Born on duh beach of shiftin' sand,
'Tween duh ocean and duh sky,
Buried on duh cay, middle of duh land,
Only dem birds visit vere I lie."

We listened carefully to Pinky's words, watching the weeds and sand fly by. The lighthouse could be seen on the right but it looked like a toy in the distance. I tried to read the speedometer, but there wasn't one, just a gaping hole in the dashboard. I looked at Millie. Her hair was flying in the wind. She said, "Wow!" All I could do was grin. I don't think either of us had ever gone so fast. I guess there wasn't any speed limit, and if there was, Pinky wouldn't have paid any attention. He seemed to be a part of the island, this was his life.

In five minutes we could see some buildings coming onto view. Pinky slowed the colorful jeep to a crawl. I guessed that was so we could see where we were. He cut the engine and coasted to a stop in front of a two-story house surrounded by a white picket fence. Pinky swung his legs out and motioned for us to follow him.

"C'mon you voy'gers. Vee git you somethin' to eat."

We climbed the four steps to the covered porch. Pinky knocked on the screen door twice and guided us into the house. It didn't look like a regular house. Each room I saw had a table in the center with from four to six chairs against the walls. I guess whoever sat at the tables chose their own chair and moved it to the table. Pinky grabbed two chairs, and motioned for us to sit down. He picked up another high-back chair and sat across from us.

Pinky called, "Miss Carla!" and a lady with gray hair, wearing a red and white striped apron, came to our table. She wore glasses and looked about the same age as Granma, maybe a little younger. She wasn't fat, but she had a round face and sparkling eyes. She was a little lighter in color than Pinky.

"Who you have here, Pinky? Vere did you find dese nice people?"

"Out on duh road. Dis is Irene an Jerry—don't rightly know duh last. They's hungry so I bring dis chirren to you. I gat money."

"We can pay. We have some money—American money. Is it good here?"

Miss Carla put her hand on my shoulder and said, "No need to pay, dearie. Duh first meal to small tourist is on duh house."

"Do you have pancakes?" I looked at Millie and she nodded—pancakes were all right with her.

Miss Carla's face grew from just friendly to like a little smiling Christmas angel's, "You can have near anythin' you like. I can make almost any dish from anywhere in dis whole big world. I'll have you some pancakes shortly."

Millie glanced at Pinky. "Can we wash our hands, sir?"

"Oh, I's not a sir, I just a lowly beachcomber. He winked. Come wid me, I show you duh toilet."

We followed Pinky down a hallway to the back of the house. He pushed open a door and we went in and locked the door. Millie turned on the water and turned to me. "Why don't we use our real names?"

"What if Pinky or Miss Carla are part of the gang that took your parents? If they knew you were Millie Harris, you'd be in real trouble. Me, too."

"I didn't think ahead to that, Rocky. What should we do?"

"Let's ask questions to see if they saw your parents. Maybe they know where someone could be hiding them."

Millie smiled, "I'm sure glad you came along. Working together we will find them. We'll pretend to be looking for Mr. and Mrs. Morgan, but we'll describe my parents."

We used the toilet, washed our hands, and went back to the table where Pinky was waiting. There was a stack of pancakes in the middle of the table, two small metal teapots, and a plate of butter. I watched Pinky reach with a fork and stab a couple of pancakes off the top of the stack, put a little butter on them, and pour syrup from one of the little teapots. Millie and I followed his example and we were soon stuffing our faces. It was our first real meal in over two days. Miss Carla joined us and sat down at the table.

"So how is it?"

"Really good," Millie answered. "May we have some milk?"

Pinky said, "How 'bout a spot a rum?"

"Pinky! You know better!" Miss Carla gave Pinky a dirty look. He just smiled.

"I don't think so. Milk or water would be fine."

I watched Pinky lean back in his chair, clap his hands, and say, "Jest teasin'." Then he laughed, a deep rumble from his giant chest. I noticed he wore a silver chain with a cross and dog tags around his neck.

Miss Carla scolded, "Pinky, you be nice!" She watched us eat for a minute and then looked at Millie and said, "Just vere is your parents, dearie?"

"They said we could walk to the lighthouse where they would meet us, but they weren't there. We looked for a road and were waiting for someone to come along. We were rescued by Mr. Pinky."

"So you don' know vere they is?"

Pinky was listening very closely. He pulled a small notebook from his short's back pocket. Miss Carla tossed him her pencil and he got ready to write.

"Tell how they look. Maybe I see 'em."

Millie described her mom and dad and gave Pinky their ages. Before Millie had finished, Miss Carla said, "I think they here tree, maybe four, days back. They with tree men I never see before. But they couldn't be your parents, you see them this mornin', didn't you?"

Millie looked at me. I could see it in her eyes. She wanted to tell Pinky and Miss Carla the truth and so did I. I nodded my head, said, "Go ahead and tell them."

Millie started telling the real story. It took us more than a half-hour and eight more pancakes to explain how and why we came to The Bahamas.

We were interrupted only once during our explanation. Two ladies came in Miss Carla's and asked for directions. When they left, Miss Carla said, "So you chirren is not related at all? I would have thought you brother an sister. Sure you had me fooled."

Pinky said, "I, too. You good actors."

"I'm sorry we lied, but we didn't know who you were."

"No worry. We need figure a way to hep you. Duh law people on the islands are busy down south. Pinky is the only man dat looks out for us here in duh north."

I was really surprised. Pinky sure didn't look like any policeman I had ever seen. "You're a policeman?"

"No, not policeman. I a lookout for United States Navy when war is going. I watch for German subs from old lighthouse. Now I watch out for people on Abaco."

"This town is Abaco?"

"No, no. Town be Shallows Town. Island be Abaco."

I nodded. "Where would those men keep Millie's parents? You said there's an old lighthouse. Would they be there?"

Pinky's eyes moved around like a dial on a telephone. "Maybe. We can see."

"Is it far?"

"Not too far. Maybe ride twenty minutes."

I thought that the way Pinky drove, a twenty minute ride could be from fifteen to thirty miles. He's lucky there aren't any police to nab him for speeding.

"You done eatin'?"

"Uh-huh. You said you'd tell us how you got the name Pinky."

"Well, I was moseying along one of duh beaches where duh sand is kinda pink. A boat come ashore vid two officers. They is from duh navy, duh US Navy. They is lookin' to hire someone to vatch duh water from a wood lighthouse they was puttin' up to confuse duh Nazi submarines. They promise me a jeep after duh war if'n I do it. So I say yes. Then young Navy man axed me questions. Next day give me dis ornaments to wear." Pinky pulled the dog tags out of his shirt to show us. "They tell me I's a member of duh Allies. Got my real name on 'em."

Millie asked, "What's your real name?"

"Herbert Osborne. See vy I like Pinky?"

"That's not so bad, but I do like Pinky better."

"The Navy men say if I see a submarine, I's s'posed to talk on duh radio and tell 'em where I see duh sub, even if nighttime. My call name be Pinky."

Miss Carla scolded, "Pinky, you tell these chirren duh truth." She looked like she would hit him with the big wooden spoon she took from her apron. She shook it at him.

"Oh, all right. Those Navy men said I make up a name to call myself. I is lookin' at my hands at duh time. They's black dis way, but pink dis way." He turned his hands over a couple of times and smiled. "Dat's how I git Pinky."

Miss Carla said, "Now dat's better. Millie an Rocky, don't let dat man tell you big stories. If what he say don' sound right, it's probably not." She stood up and walked toward the kitchen, "I have to go to duh market. Pinky, you vatch out for our guests. Make sure you come back here. I'll find rooms for all."

"Yessum. I do dat for sure."

Pinky looked at Millie and me. "Want to look-see at dat old broken-down lighthouse?"

I said, "Sure, let's check it out."

Chapter 24

WHERE'S MILLIE?

We followed Pinky to the jeep and climbed in, expecting a break-neck ride to the coastline to see what we thought was an ancient lighthouse that was ready to fall over. We drove slowly through the little town. Pinky seemed to wave to nearly everyone. I was amazed to see all the smiles and waves he got back. I was thinking that the ride we were on was like riding a float in a New Year's parade. The jeep was painted in many bright colors and Pinky's shirt seemed to be in camouflage so he became part of the jeep.

Shallows Town would be a fun place to ride bikes and investigate. We had been creeping down the street that became the highway, the engine vibrating the whole vehicle. After passing the last building, a small house with an old car parked at the side, Pinky's foot became a lead weight and suddenly the air was whipping Millie's hair over her shoulders and we hung onto each other for safety. Shallows Town was left in a cloud of sand.

I watched Millie's wristwatch to see how long we drove before sighting the old lighthouse. It took us seventeen minutes to get there. I wouldn't have thought it was an old light house, it was just a three-story wooden building with a railing around the roof. It was square with sloping walls. Pinky parked his jeep behind a sand dune about 100 yards away from the building. No one at the lighthouse would be able to see us.

"Okay, out you go."

Millie and I jumped out of the jeep and watched Pinky tilt back the seat and pull out a tan metal box about two feet long. It looked a little like a tool box I had seen in Mr. Morgan's garage. But the box wasn't full of tools, it had a telescope in it. I had seen one in a war movie once. It was for use in a trench, to see above the ground but not risk being wounded. It was painted the color of greenish-sand.

"We goin' to vatch dat lighthouse vidout be seen. Git down an' crawl aside me to duh top. Don't stick anythin' up high as duh scope."

We followed Pinky's orders and slithered beside him to the top of a dune. We watched him looking at the old lighthouse.

"Uh-huh. There a man on duh top. He got a gun—a rifle."

"Can I see?" Millie beat me to the question. Pinky rolled over, still holding the telescope, and Millie took a look, steadying the scope with both hands.

"I see him. Looks like he's asleep."

"Not asleep, gun move 'round."

Millie snaked away and I took her place. I moved the telescope around and could see the rear fender of a light-green car, parked behind the lighthouse. Then I focused on the man; he was sitting in a chair, smoking a cigarette. It looked like little white clouds were rising from his gun and drifting toward the water, but he wasn't shooting. I couldn't see his face, the railing was in the way.

"Do you think Millie's parents are in that old building?"

"Maybe. Vy don't we go for a little walk? Missy Millie, stay here with Kaleidoscope."

Millie gave Pinky a blank look and frowned—then she smiled. "You mean your jeep?"

"That's right. She called Kaleidoscope 'cause of all her colors. Ve gone for maybe ten or fifteen minutes."

"Okay." She looked at her watch.

We skidded down the dune and Pinky put his scope back in the box under the seat. We walked down to the beach and moved toward the old lighthouse, but we pretended to be looking for things in the sand near the water. We had only been gone from the jeep for about five minutes when we saw a speedboat coming toward the old building. We stopped and watched the boat come ashore. Two men got out and started walking toward the lighthouse.

"C'mon, ve go back." Pinky grabbed my arm and pulled. We started running and followed our footprints back to the jeep. I was out of breath when we got to Kaleidoscope, but Pinky wasn't even breathing hard. I couldn't see Millie. Was she sitting on the ground on the other side of the jeep?

"Millie! Where are you?" There was no answer. "Millie!" I listened but there wasn't a sound, no birds—nothing."

Pinky pulled his telescope out and turned toward the old building. He didn't try to conceal himself. He scanned the beach, gradually tilting the scope down to see the area leading to the wooden lighthouse.

"Dare she is! A man got 'er over 'is shoulder." He was quiet for a few seconds and then said, "Bad news. Ve must do somethin' quick. Jump in, ve gotta take a ride."

"Is she alive?"

"She's a kickin' an' a sluggin'. She a real fighter, dat one."

Pinky tried to start the jeep, but it was dead. He popped the hood and bent over the engine. About a minute later, he got in the jeep and started the motor. We roared backwards for about thirty yards and skidded to a stop. He shifted and we shot forward into a right turn. It was a bumpy ride to the beach. We weren't even on a road. I held one hand on the seat cushion and the other on the side of the jeep.

When we hit the beach and were racing toward the speedboat, Pinky yelled, "Hold duh steering wheel, jist vere it is!"

I scooted over next to him and grabbed the steering wheel with my left hand. I didn't know what Pinky was going to do, but I followed his orders. Whatever we were doing, Millie's health was in danger. All I had to do was hold us on course for a few seconds while Pinky pulled something from beneath his seat. His big fist hid what it was for a moment, but then he said, "Pull dat metal ring!"

He was holding a grenade in his right hand! I had never seen one up close, only in war movies and those were props. The jeep was slowing down as we closed in on the powerboat.

"Okay. Now you sit back." Pinky was driving with his left hand and raising his right hand like he was going to throw a baseball; it was the grenade. As we passed the boat, I watched the grenade leave Pinky's grip and sail into the speedboat. I heard a thunk as the little metal pineapple hit the inside of the boat. My head was thrown back as Pinky's foot hit the gas. I heard a clunk in the back of the jeep and then Kaleidoscope swerved toward the water. I turned to look at the speedboat. It exploded with a loud blast, like ten cherry bombs going off at the same time. The outboard engine was twirling in the air, headed out to deeper water. Bits and pieces of the boat were flying in all directions.

I laughed and turned to look at Pinky. He grinned, but then his expression turned to pain. I could see a small red area on the back of his shirt growing in size. Pinky had been shot!

"Is it bad?"

"Not sure—we need see Miss Carla."

"What can I do?"

He handed me a handkerchief and said, "Press against center of the blood."

We had gotten off the beach and headed toward the road that went back to Shallows Town. I worried that I might have to drive. I had never driven a car or a jeep before. What would we do if Pinky couldn't drive Kaleidoscope? I watched Pinky to see if he was having problems, but he seemed strong and able to drive without any problems. Then he dropped his right hand to his lap and steered with his left. When we hit the road, the jeep was going even faster than it had before when Millie and I were riding with Pinky.

A white pickup flashed by going in the opposite direction. The driver had sounded his horn, but I didn't know if it was a warning that we were going too fast or because he recognized Pinky. At the edge of town we slowed a bit, but people stepped away from the roadway when they heard the jeep coming. Cars were giving us plenty of room. We arrived at Miss Carla's and skidded, the brakes squealing, then we rolled off the road into the parking area and stopped. Pinky turned off the engine and handed me the keys. I jumped out and helped Pinky slide out of the driver's seat. He leaned on me a little, just to give himself some stability, and we made it to the front door.

"Miss Carla! Pinky needs your help! He's been shot!"

Pinky lurched forward and sank into one of the dining room chairs. He laid his head on the table. I still pressed on the wound, but the bleeding had nearly stopped.

Miss Carla came running with her kitchen medical kit. When she saw Pinky's blood-stained shirt, she said, "Oh, my! Vat happen? Who in God's universe would shoot Pinky?"

She cut off his shirt with her scissors and told me to get some hot water and a clean washcloth from the kitchen. When I got back, Miss Carla was asking Pinky some questions. His eyes were closed but he was talking just like always. The skin was puffed up about four inches down from the top of his right shoulder and three to four inches from his backbone. There was a small bloody hole where Miss Carla was spreading an orange solution with a tongue depressor wrapped in cotton. Pinky's back was covered with muscles—probably more than Mr. Morgan's and Dad's put together. He was a powerful man, but gentle.

She asked, "How you feel, Pinky?"

"Jist fine, ma'am. Can you pull out dat bullet? I s'pect it's gunna hurt some."

"I'm going to lessen duh pain. I'm goin' to inject some lidocaine around duh wound so it'll be numb while I search for dat bullet. It's goin' to hurt some, but it shouldn't be too bad. Bite on a folded up napkin so you won't break any teeth.

"That's okay, you jist find dat bullet an git it out. I be fine then."

I watched with great interest as a probe was inserted in the hole and moved around in Pinky's shoulder. "I sure do wish we had X-ray machine." It seemed like forever before Miss Carla struck the bullet, but it was only a few minutes. My shoulder hurt just watching, but I never got sick seeing the blood. As Carla probed, Pinky never said anything or made any faces from pain. The next part made me hurt even worse. Miss Carla pushed a long-nosed, curved pliers into the hole and pulled out the bullet. It clinked when she dropped it into a small, shallow, metal pan. "Got it!" Carla looked at me. "Now we fix dat hole."

"How did you learn to do that, Miss Carla?"

"I was nurse in England during duh war, Rocky. I saw lots of bullet holes. This one wasn't too bad. It sure helps to have lidocaine, though; we didn't have it back then."

She poured some powder into the hole and sewed it shut with some stitches. I ground my teeth together and made some faces when I watched her sewing the hole closed. It hurt to see that curved needle being poked through Pinky's skin.

"Pinky, you can sit up now. I'll cover dat hole with a bandage and get you a clean shirt. Come back tomorrow and I'll inspect dat wound. We don't want infected."

Pinky sat up and smiled at us. "Yes'um. I be back. Thank-you Miss Carla—you good doctor."

"You're very welcome. Just don't go around getting all shot up. I'm getting you somethin' to eat and drink. You need to replace all dat blood."

Miss Carla put all her instruments in the metal pan and disappeared into the kitchen. In a few minutes, she brought us some lunch, and had us tell her what had happened.

"So, where is Millie?"

Pinky was still eating, so I answered all her questions.

"We don't know. Last time we saw her, she was being taken into the old lighthouse. That's when we blew up the boat and Pinky got shot. I think the man on the roof shot him."

"Why did you blow up duh boat?"

"We thought if the men took the boat and any prisoners, we wouldn't be able to tell where they went. But they have a car and we can follow it and find it on the island."

Miss Carla nodded. "Well, dat make perfect sense."

Chapter 25

THE WW2 LIGHTHOUSE

I was surprised by what Pinky said. I thought we would be done for the day, but Pinky was thinking way ahead of me. "Let's burn down dat lighthouse."

"What?" I wasn't sure I heard him correctly. "Burn it down? Can you drive?"

"No problem, vet's go! We need find Missy Millie."

We had been on the road going north for about ten minutes when Pinky said, "What you got in dat bag?"

"Some clothes, a pocket knife, a slingshot, and some marbles."

Pinky grinned and commented, "You play marbles?"

"No, I shoot 'em."

"How far?"

"Maybe eighty to a hundred yards."

"Good shot?"

"Yes, sir."

I could see Pinky was thinking. He was quiet. He didn't ask any more questions. I wondered what was going on in his mind, but I didn't want to ask for fear of interrupting his thoughts. I watched for the spot where we had turned off to go to the old wooden lighthouse, but when we got there, we just kept on going. I looked at Pinky, but he was still concentrating on something. Maybe he forgot to turn. Should I tell him we missed the turnoff? No, he knows what he's doing, he was in the war. I started to imagine how we were going to burn down that old lighthouse and why.

We made a sharp turn to the right, almost on two wheels, and headed toward the ocean. We were making our own bumpy road. I was being thrown around, but I hung on really tight—like before when we were speeding to Miss Carla's. Pinky's wound hadn't made any difference in the way he drove Kaleidoscope. When I could see the water, Pinky slowed down and we turned right again and went up a small sand dune. At the top, I could barely see the top of the lighthouse for a second, and then we went into a low spot, slid in the sand and stopped.

Pinky motioned for me to get out. He reached under the seat and grabbed the telescope. Then he went to the rear of the jeep and opened a compartment that was held shut by a spring clip. I smiled when I saw what he pulled from the box; two emergency flares. He gave me the flares and motioned for me to follow him.

We kept our heads down and ran about fifty yards toward the lighthouse. Pinky sat down, turned the scope toward the wooden building, and gradually lifted the lenses.

"Hmm. Gun's still there. So's the car. Got your knife?"

"Uh-huh. You want it?"

"No. You use. Cut one-inch off one of dem flares."

"Which end?"

"Don't care. Jist cut it off and hand to me."

I half-cut and half-sawed through a flare and handed it to Pinky. He took a stick match from his pocket and screwed it into the center of the cut part of the flare and showed it to me.

"Make more like dis. Use up duh whole stick."

When we finished, we had eight little flares with matches as fuses. I was beginning to understand what Pinky was going to do. He needed a diversion so he could get close to the building without being seen by the shooter.

"Git out your slingshot an' give me duh other flare."

I got my slingshot from my backpack and Pinky handed me his little container of matches after taking out two for himself.

"Here's duh plan. I sneakin' close to dat buildin' and lightin' it on fire. After I leave here, count to a hundert, slow like this." He showed me how fast to count. "Then you start shootin' those little flares at duh lighthouse, but you gotta move 'round—shoot from different spots so's they can't tell where you is. Okay?"

"How fast should I shoot them?"

"Well, shoot an' move—shoot an' move. Try to hit duh car. Maybe we'll burn it up, too." He smiled and I smiled back. This was going to be fun.

"I'll sure try."

"You jist to duh best. Okay, I go now."

I forgot to ask Pinky how I was supposed to light the matches. The little box he had given me didn't have a scratch pad on it. I looked at the telescope laying on the ground and saw the focusing threads on the eyepieces, they should work. I had wasted some counts, but I started with twenty and continued. When I got to 100, I lit a match and lit a little flare on fire, loaded it in the pouch and pulled back the slingshot as far as I could and let the burning mini-flare fly in the direction of the lighthouse. I took a quick look to see where it had gone. It had landed about ten yards short of the wooden building.

I shot the next flare from a little closer, and it bounced near the car. I moved again and shot again, but I didn't try to see where the flare landed, I just kept shooting until all eight flares were gone. I moved to a new position and took a look at the building. I couldn't see Pinky, but the side of the building next to where the car was parked had started burning. Where was Pinky?

I focused the telescope on the car. I thought maybe Pinky would set it on fire if one of my flares didn't do the job. That's when I got a big surprise. Three men and two women were getting into the car; no, one woman and a girl, Millie. I recognized the woman, it was Millie's mom. Two of the men had hand guns and the third was Mr. Harris. One of the gunmen got in the driver's seat. It was the captain of the yacht! I had seen him before when I was listening to the conversations before Millie and I left the yacht. The other gunman must have been the man on the roof that shot Pinky. I watched as the car drove away and then I ran to the burning building. The flames weren't very big yet, just one wall was on fire near the ground.

I had always heard to never go into a burning building, but I had to find Pinky. He would die if he's in there. The door closest to where the car had been parked was open, so I went in and looked around. The fire was just burning through the first floor wall, but there wasn't much smoke yet, except near the ceiling. It reminded me of a low cloud hanging over the bay at Crafton in January when it was cold but there wasn't any wind.

I yelled as loud as I could, "Pinky! Are you in here?" I didn't hear anything but the crackle of the fire. "Pinky! Where are you?" I was worried now. If he was knocked out, I wouldn't be able to pull him out of the burning building, he was too heavy. Then I heard a woman's voice.

"Rocky! Is that you?"

It sounded like Mom. "Mom, where are you?" I moved into a short hallway and looked into a room on the right, opposite to the fire. I saw her tied to a chair and a post. I ran to her, pulled my knife from my pocket, dropped to my knees, and started cutting the ropes around her legs. When the ropes fell away, I went behind her and cut the ropes off her wrists and arms. I was glad my knife was really sharp.

She looked at me and said, "Who is Pinky?"

"He's my friend, Mom. Have you seen him? He's a big Negro man—very strong, but really nice."

"I think they took him upstairs. There was a fight and he must have been knocked out. I heard a thump on the floor up there."

I turned and looked for stairs to the second floor. Mom said, "The corner room—back to the left." It took me less than five seconds to get to the second floor and find Pinky. He was trying to sit up but his arms didn't seem to work very well. I think he was groggy from being hit in the head and his back was sore from his wound. His feet were tied together, but I freed him from the ropes and helped him stand.

"I hear another voice, Master Rocky."

"That's my mom. She's downstairs. Let's get out of here, the building is on fire. The smoke's getting thicker." I put my arm around Pinky's waist and he leaned against the wall as we started moving to the stairway. The stairs appeared steeper than they had looked from the first floor. There wasn't a handrail but there were marks where there must have been one in the past. Mom came up halfway and we worked our way down the steps while coughing.

As soon as we were outside, I pointed and we staggered toward the dune where the jeep was parked. Pinky couldn't drive, he was barely awake.

We sat down in the sand next to the jeep. "How did you get here, Rocky?"

"Didn't Millie tell you?"

"I haven't talked to Millie. She was with her parents in another room. The captain said they were going to the yacht so Elena could watch her family being killed. We have to get to the yacht with the police."

"Pinky is the only law on this part of the island right now, Mom, and he's not official. We'll have to get to the yacht ourselves. We have to try to help Elena."

Mom bit her lower lip and frowned, "Where can we get a gun and a boat—a fast one?"

"We have to get to Shallows Town. Pinky knows everyone there. We can borrow a boat, but I don't know about a gun. Maybe Pinky knows."

Pinky was listening to us and began moving his arms and legs and making fists. He moved his head around like he had a sore neck and then said, "Know a man—has fast boat, no gun. We go to Shallows Town, but you drive." He squinted and looked at Mom.

"Can you drive a jeep, Mom?"

"If it has a motor, I can drive it. Do you know the way to Shallows Town?"

"Sure." I pointed inland and said, "We drive inland to the road, make a left and go as fast as we can to the town. Then Pinky can tell us where to get a boat." I gave her Pinky's keys.

"Okay, let's go!" We ran to the jeep.

Mom handled that old jeep almost as well as Pinky did. She was a little surprised when she looked at the dash and didn't see a speedometer, but we all knew she was going over the speed limit anyway. The first minute or so, Mom looked a little stiff, but then she relaxed and she gave me a big smile. About ten minutes of zooming down the road put us at the edge of town. Pinky said to slow down and take the first turn to the left. I had thought we would be going into town, but instead, we went to the beach and made a right turn toward a building at the water's edge.

The building was attached to a floating dock that stuck out into the water about forty or fifty feet. When we got closer, I could see the building was floating. Mom followed Pinky's directions and we parked beside a white pickup. It looked like a Ford, similar to Dad's. I think it was the one that had passed us before.

Pinky climbed out of Kaleidoscope and said, "Come vid me."

Mom pulled the key out, stuck it in her shirt pocket, and stepped to the ground. She reached out for my hand and we went toward Pinky. We walked across some planks to a porch. He opened a door and we went into the building. I expected to see a boat or two, but there wasn't a boat under the roof; there was a seaplane. Pinky said, "Changed mind—plane much faster than boat." He gave us a big grin.

Mom was as surprised as I was. We both stood there with our mouths open.

"Mom, can you fly a plane?"

Chapter 26

RETURN TO THE YACHT

Mom shook her head. "No, Rocky. That's something I didn't learn at the FBI or CIA training facilities."

"But I can." I turned around to see who was standing behind us. It was a man with yellow hair, not blonde—bright yellow. I thought he was wearing a wig, but he introduced himself as Quincy Gattis, pilot of the Bahamian Eagle. He said Bahamian eagles have bright-yellow feathers. The nose of the seaplane was painted bright-yellow, the fuselage baby-blue.

Pinky said, "These people need to git to duh yacht anchored offshore near lighthouse Abaco-2. That's duh old relic from duh war."

Mom quickly told Mr. Gattis who we were and explained our problem. Pinky and Quincy stepped aside and talked so fast I couldn't understand what they were saying. They used some words I had never heard before, but most of it sounded like English. I was thinking Jerry would know more about their language than I would." Pinky looked at Mom and asked, "Vat you weigh?"

Mom frowned and replied, "About 130 pounds. Why?"

"Master Rocky?"

"I weigh about eight-five pounds." I was almost positive Mom didn't know my weight.

"Okay, dat's close enough. Here's vat ve's goin' to do."

He told us the plan Pinky and he had developed during their strange conversation. As he explained what they had planned, Mom and I both smiled, 'cause we would never have thought it would be possible. I wondered if all pilots were as clever as Quincy. I'm sure Dad would have figured out the same thing in our situation. I didn't know if he ever flew a seaplane, though.

Quincy gave a loud whistle and a woman, dressed in blue shorts and a yellow blouse, came half-way out of a small office door and said, "Vat can I git for you, Quin?"

"Two pontoon pillows, Vera. Hurry." Quincy told us, "The ride in the pontoons is a little bumpy. You'll put duh pillow 'round your head so you don't bump it. The pillow will also dim'nish some of duh noise."

Vera handed the pillows to Mom and me and whispered, "I's his wife."

Mom said, "Thank-you. I'm Sandra and this is Rocky."

Vera nodded, "Good fortune."

"Quick, folks. Pinky say we short on time."

Quincy helped Mom into the left pontoon and me into the right one. He showed us how to pop open the hatch so we could escape. "Ready, Pink?"

"I ready, boss." They both laughed. I could hear them talking, even though I was sealed inside the seaplane's right float.

I heard some noises and then could feel us moving slowly. I imagined we were drifting out of the covered hanger into open water. The engine started, coughed a little at first, and then sped up, faster and faster, until the engine sounded like it might tear off the front of the plane. The prop and engine whined like crazy and we started bumping across the water, the vibrations getting faster and the noise increasing. All of a sudden it was quiet, except for the engine noise. We were in the air. I grinned, thinking this was the coolest ride I had ever taken and it might never happen again. I hoped Mom was having as good a time as I was.

In less than five minutes, I felt like I was slowly going down in an elevator. I guessed we were going to land on the water. Quincy had told us it would be bumpy again, but much of the rough ride would vanish as he taxied slowly through the calm water. There was hardly any wind today and the ocean was mirror-like. There was a big thump when we hit the water. The plane slowed down and was drifting with the engine going very slowly. Then I could feel the plane turning and I was getting ready to pop the hatch. I could tell the plane was moving into position when he would gun the engine and move directly at the yacht. I was ready.

Two seconds after he gunned the engine, I popped the hatch and slid into the water. I had taken a big gulp of air as I left the float and went under the surface of the crystal clear water. I hoped the waves from the floats would hide us as Mom and I swam underwater. I could hear the engine speed up again. Quincy had said he was going to circle around the yacht and approach from the opposite side to divert attention from us. When the Bahamian Eagle reached the other side of the yacht, Pinky was going to slip out of the cockpit and drop into the water. Nobody on the boat would be able to see him because the fuselage would be in the way. We were supposed to meet at the stern. I had told Mom and Pinky we could get aboard there without being seen.

I could see the keel of the boat and then I saw Mom a little ahead of me. I was almost out of breath, but I had to force myself to take a few more strokes before breaking the surface. I had to make it to the hull where I couldn't be seen by anyone on deck. Five more strokes, four more, three, and I hit the side of the boat. I was jerked upward and my head broke the surface. I turned over, exhaled, and filled my lungs with fresh air. I couldn't remember anything feeling so good. Mom had reached the hull a few seconds before and was waiting for me. She had pulled me up a foot or two from below the surface.

I took several gulps of air and calmed down. "Where's Pinky?" I whispered and wiped the salt water from my eyes. Just as we looked around us, Pinky's head appeared next to the boat. It seemed all three of us had made it undetected. At least there weren't any voices coming from directly above us.

Then we heard Quincy yelling over the noise of the idling engine, "This is a protected area. You must not dump any waste in these waters. This is an official warning. Any violations will result in your vessel being seized by The Bahamian government." He was speaking like a British official.

Pinky smiled at us and Mom gave a thumbs up. We didn't hear any reply for a few seconds, then I heard a familiar voice. It was Elena. She was yelling, over the noise of the engine, so Quincy could hear her.

I looked at Pinky and said, "That's our friend, Elena."

"Vat she look like?"

Mom answered, "She's about my size, very pretty—short dark hair."

Pinky nodded and started up the side of the yacht. Mom was next and then I grabbed a rung and pulled. Water was draining from my backpack, but I didn't care, the noise from the plane's engine would cover the sound of the water draining off my back. When my head was over the deck, I saw Mom and Pinky motioning for me to join them. Pinky was waving for me to hurry up. I was doing the best I could. I could hear the seaplane taking off.

"We don't know where they are, or how many of them are guarding Elena." Mom was worried about the three of us against at least three of the kidnappers.

"I'll find out." I know where to go to listen and they won't be able to see me.

Mom said, "Are you sure?"

I smiled. "Did you ever see me when I listened to you during the trip down here from Crafton?"

"Okay, but be careful."

"Geez, Mom." I couldn't believe she said that. I dipped one shoulder and got the wet pack off my back. I held it out to Mom. "Can you hold my backpack? I need a couple of things from it."

Mom took the pack from me. It was still dripping wet. I opened it and pulled out my slingshot and a half-dozen marbles. I put five marbles in my pocket and one in my mouth, and then I sat on the deck to remove my shoes and socks. I gave a quick glance to Mom and Pinky and said, "I'll be right back."

Mom gave me a half-smile, half-frown and mouthed be careful. I smiled, nodded and started toward the emergency equipment room. Everything I knew about the yacht was related to the position of that small room. When I got there, I listened, but couldn't hear anything. I was glad I had taken off my shoes, because when I walked, they would have squished.

I thought to check the dining area first. It was easy to hide and listen there. As I moved closer to where I had listened before, I couldn't hear any talking, just somebody drumming their fingers. I figured one of the kidnappers was nervous, waiting for someone. Then it got quiet. I held my breath for a few seconds and then some soft tapping sounds started up. I had to get closer to see what was going on.

I crouched down and moved slowly until I saw someone's back. It was Elena. How could I tell her I was behind her? I moved a little sideways and saw a woman I had never seen before.

She was kind of pale and skinny, wore glasses, and held a handgun. She was tapping her foot on the deck.

That's when I got an idea. I was going to roll a marble across the floor. Elena would know I was behind her if I used a black one. We had talked about codes before and we made up ways to communicate without seeing or hearing the other person. Some of a rhyme we had was:

White from the right if want to fight,

Black from the back if you want to attack.

I had a white marble in my mouth, so I fished a black one from my pocket and stepped back into my hiding place. I knelt and rolled the marble slowly across the deck into the dining area, as if the boat had tilted and the marble just happened to roll across the floor.

"What's that?" I heard the skinny woman's voice.

Elena said, "Oh, some children were on board. They must have forgotten one of their marbles."

"Stupid American children—always playing games."

"Have you ever been in a hurricane and wondered what it would be like in the eye?"

"Shut up! No more talking!"

I had heard enough to know that Elena wanted me to shoot the woman in the eye. But how would I do it? If I stepped out to see her, she would see me and shoot me or Elena. I had to surprise her. I stood there thinking and then Elena said, "Can I untie my shoe? It's very painful."

"Oh, all right. No funny business."

Elena stood up and I crept up behind her, ready to shoot a marble. I pulled back on the rubber bands as far as I could and when Elena sat back down I let the marble go. The woman didn't have a chance to react. The marble crashed into her glasses and smacked into her right eye. She screamed, dropping the gun. Her hand went up to her eye. Stuff squirted out and was dripping off her fingers and dribbling from her cheek. Elena grabbed the gun and said, "Good shot, Rocky. Where in the heck did you come from?"

"The seaplane. Mom's here, too, and my friend Pinky. I'll get them."

I turned and went out the way I had come. When I got to the deck, I yelled, "Mom! It's all right. Elena has the gun."

Pinky and Mom were coming forward from the stern. Mom was running. I had never seen her move that fast. She grabbed me and squeezed. "Are you all right?"

"Sure, Mom. There's a lady with Elena in the dining room. She had a handgun, but I shot her in the face with a marble and she dropped the gun. She'll need a doctor, her eye is really bad."

Pinky and I followed Mom to Elena and the skinny woman. Elena had placed a towel over the woman's eye and put her broken glasses on the table. She was moaning, lying there on the deck at Elena's feet. I kind of felt sorry for her, but not that much. She would have shot us if I hadn't hit her eye. I figured she would be blind in her right eye, but there are lots of people with only one eye, like soldiers that got shot in the war, but I don't think many soldiers got shot in the eye with a marble.

Elena said, "Is the seaplane returning?"

"In 'bout fifteen minutes. Quincy told me. He goin' to check on us after he look at duh lighthouse fire. He report it to duh police."

Mom explained to Elena what had happened at the old lighthouse and introduced Pinky.

Pinky had a big smile when Mom explained how Quincy and The Bahamian Eagle got involved. Elena laughed when she heard about the yellow haired Quincy and his plane. She looked at me, smiled, and said, "There's no such bird called a Bahamian Eagle. It's imaginary."

I had thought so, but I wasn't sure. I knew that eagles usually lived around mountains and there weren't any mountains in The Bahamas, the average elevation of the islands is close to sea level. Millie told me that during our trip on the yacht.

Elena told us that two crew members were locked in the engine room. Mom and I went down and released them. They were happy to see Mom again, but they had never seen me before. The cook, a woman about as old as the skinny woman, but not at all skinny, went up to see if she could do anything for the injured woman. The cook's name was Fiona Norton. Her haircut was short, almost like a man's. The engine mechanic's name was Vern Richards. He was about the same height as Dad, but not as muscular. We shook hands and he went back to work.

Mom, Fiona, and I went back to the dining room. I could hear the engine noise of Quincy's plane and watched it land and taxi over to the yacht. Pinky grabbed the edge of the wing when Quincy shut off the engine. I could hear the two men talking and then Pinky came back to the dining room.

"Need a boat. Gotta take duh lady to Nassau hospital."

I wondered why they needed a boat. "Can't Quincy fly her there?"

Chapter 27

TRAP ON THE YACHT

"**Y**es, Master Rocky. Have to get duh lady from duh yacht to duh plane without swimmin'."

That was something I hadn't thought of. Salt water in her eye would be very painful.

"I know where the life rafts are. Want one of those?"

"That vill do duh trick."

Pinky followed me to the emergency supplies room and I showed him the inflatables. I figured one of the rafts weighed more than I did, but Pinky picked one up with his left hand and carried it to the outside deck. He read the instructions and pulled on a piece of rope. The package exploded into a raft about five-feet wide and eight-feet long. I jumped back, thinking it would push me off into the water. The hissing sound was over in a few seconds.

Pinky dropped the raft into the water and Quincy pulled it over so he could get in. Then he shoved off from the closest float and drifted over to the yacht. Elena had the skinny lady in handcuffs and was leading her to the edge of the deck above the raft. Pinky had her sit and he grabbed her hands and lowered her down to Quincy. After she was sitting in the rubber boat, Pinky lowered Elena to the raft. She was going to escort the woman under arrest to Nassau.

Quincy and Elena got the one-eyed lady in the plane, but it took several minutes. When they were ready to take off, Elena stepped on the pontoon closest to us and waved. "I'll be back as soon as I get her taken care of. Bye!"

We all waved and I shouted, "Hurry back!"

Mom was scanning the waters around the yacht to the beach. "We have to get that rubber raft out of sight. What do you think, Pinky?"

"I use Master Rocky's knife."

I took my scout knife from my pocket and tossed it to Pinky. He walked off the deck of the yacht and dropped into the water next to the raft. When he came up, he sliced the rubber lifeboat in two places and the air escaped with a sound that I imagined would come from a big whale. I relaxed my lips and blew air from my mouth making a similar sound.

"Please don't do that at home, Rocky. Susan will run around making that noise for a week." We both laughed.

We watched as Pinky began forcing the sinking raft under the water. After a couple minutes had passed, the rubber boat was on the bottom. We could see it, but no one would notice it as being a deflated life raft; it was just a dark area like a rock on the ocean bottom. Pinky came aboard and returned my knife. It was almost dry. He must have wiped it off. I shoved it into my left pocket.

Mom said we should plan for the kidnappers and the Harris family to arrive at the yacht. The kidnappers would still think Elena was being held by Corrine, the skinny lady. Mom had found out her name. Fortunately, Fiona and Corrine had the same hair color, but other than that, they didn't look at all alike, except for being about the same height.

We all gathered in the dining room. Mom had devised a plan right after Elena flew off with Corrine and Quincy. When the kidnappers arrived, they would probably want to know from Corrine if everything was all right before they came aboard. Fiona and I would be waiting on the bridge. She would stand with her back to the bridge window and wave the handgun so the kidnappers could see it. If they wanted her to say something, I would try to imitate Corrine's voice since I had heard her speak before I shot her in the eye. I knew I could imitate her groans accurately. Mom and I practiced a few words that I might say to the bad guys. I put my hand over my mouth so the words weren't very clear.

When they started coming aboard, the Harris family first, I would take the gun to Mom in the dining area. She would be in the galley with Vern, who had a wrench for a weapon and some twine to tie up the kidnappers. Pinky was to be our linebacker, just in case anyone tried to get away. Pinky had thought ahead and Mom agreed that we should put the boarding ladder over the side. That prevented Fiona from assisting with the boarding. Mom figured one of the kidnappers would come aboard and help the Harris family up the ladder.

Pinky was worried that both kidnappers had guns and they would escort the family members to the dining area together in a group of five. That would leave Mom's gun against two of theirs, not good odds, especially with the Harris family in the way. It was decided that I, using Corrine's voice, would ask the Captain to come to the bridge. I would be ready with my slingshot and Pinky would grab his gun and wrestle him to the deck.

Pinky thought it would work because the captain would expect to see Corrine guarding Elena. Fiona would have her back to the bridge doorway and I would be sitting so the captain could only see my bare legs and would think I was Elena. When Fiona turned around, the shocked captain would be looking at Fiona and I would let him have a marble in the face. I just had to be sure to hit him where it would hurt. Pinky would bear hug him and Fiona or I would grab his gun, hopefully off the floor.

After taking our positions, we had to wait about ten minutes before we saw a small boat coming toward the yacht. Pinky saw it first and alerted the rest of us. I took a quick peek from the bridge and then ducked out of sight.

When the boat came alongside, the captain yelled, "Corrine, is everything all right?"

I tried to sound like Corrine and said, "Yes, Captain, we're on the bridge. Would you come here?" Fiona didn't have to wave the gun so I took it and ran down to Mom.

I heard the captain bark out, "Go see what Corrine wants, Georgi!" I suddenly realized our plan was changing already, and the Harris family had just climbed onto the yacht. We had to carry out our plan anyway. I had to get back on the bridge before Georgi got there. I could hear him coming toward the stairway as I was going up two steps at a time. I would get to the bridge first, but I'd be out of breathe. I sat down, tried to relax, got my slingshot ready and listened to the thump of the footsteps on the treads. Georgi sounded like he was overweight and climbing stairs was not something he wanted to do. Maybe he had sore feet. I hoped Pinky was coming up behind him, barefooted and moving with hardly a sound.

"Corrine, what d'ya want? You sounded strange. Are you sick?"

Fiona put her finger to her lips so I wouldn't say anything. I was too scared anyway. I didn't make a sound. Then I saw him, a big guy with black hair and a five o'clock shadow, looking down at his feet as he came up to the bridge. He wore dark-green shorts and a loose, light-green, short-sleeve shirt with cigarettes in his chest pocket. His handgun was in his right hand at his side. He hadn't seen me yet, but would in a second or two.

Fiona turned around to face him. "Corrine isn't here, I'm here with this boy." She stepped aside, looked at me, and I let him have it right in the mouth. It sounded like the marble broke some of his teeth. It made a cracking sound as I saw it disappear into his open mouth. He had frowned when he saw Fiona and had started to say something just as the marble whacked him in the face. His head snapped back as if he was trying to avoid a bee flying at his face. Then Pinky grabbed him and threw him to the floor. There was a thump when Pinky fell on top of him and took the gun from his hand. Georgi just laid there, motionless. I think he was knocked out. That's when I saw blood oozing out of the corner of his partly open mouth. The marble must have broken off some teeth or knocked 'em clear out.

Pinky's belt, an old piece of rope, was used to tie Georgi's hands behind his back. Pinky stood up holding the gun. He said, "I help your mother, Master Rocky," and Pinky started back down the stairs. I probably should have stayed with Fiona, but I followed Pinky. My marbles had been hitting their targets so far, but I hoped I was done shooting. I had had enough of shooting people in the face, even if they were kidnappers.

We had just started down the stairs to the dining area when Pinky suddenly stopped and we listened to a man talking. I recognized the captain's voice. "Well, Mrs. Linfield, it looks like we have a standoff. You shoot me and I shoot the girl."

Pinky motioned with his hand that I should turn around and move back. I thought he was trying to get me out of the way of flying bullets, but that wasn't it. As soon as we got out of earshot, he knelt beside me and said, "How d'we git to duh far side of duh galley?"

"Follow me, I'll show you."

I led Pinky to the stern and we went below deck to the engine room.

"Got more marbles, Rocky?"

I wondered why Pinky wanted to know about my marbles. Did he know about Elena's and my code? "I've got four more in my pocket."

"Good. When we git to duh galley, roll some marbles across duh floor, slow like—two or three of 'em. Stay behind me."

I didn't know what Pinky was thinking, but I would do anything he wanted me to do to save Millie and her parents. I told him how to get to the galley and as he moved slowly through the ship, I wondered how he could move his big body so quietly. I tried to do what he did, but I could hear my clothes moving and hear my feet touching the deck. We were almost in the galley when I heard the captain say, "What are you going to do? I'm waiting. Put down that gun and we'll have a little talk."

Pinky and I moved closer and I could see the captain's back. We were about ten feet behind him. He was holding Millie with his left hand around her neck. She wasn't moving. I wondered if she was unconscious and he was holding her up, or she was just afraid to move. I couldn't see the captain's gun, but I imagined it was pointed at her head.

Pinky made a motion that I should roll the marbles. I got down on my knees, took two marbles from my pocket and rolled them across the deck. Then I heard Mom say, "It looks like you have a gun pointed at the back of your head, Captain. You know what a forty-five slug does to the brain? When my man pulls the trigger, your brains will come out your eye sockets, but you won't feel a thing. You'll be dead before you hit the deck."

Pinky moved forward and put the gun against the back of the captain's head. I had to smile at what Mom had said. It had sounded really scary.

"Let go of the girl and give me the gun." Mom's orders were very clear. I guess the captain took Mom's threat seriously. He didn't want to die, so he removed his hand from Millie's neck and gave Mom his handgun.

Millie, crying, ran to her mom and they hugged each other. Mr. Harris circled them with his arms and said, "Thank-you Sandra, Rocky, and this gentleman." Mr. Harris extended his hand toward Pinky. As they shook hands, Pinky introduced himself and began tying up the captain with an oily piece of rope Vern handed him.

Mom introduced Vern to the Harrises and after they talked for a minute, Vern went up to the bridge to help bring Georgi to the main deck. I went over to Millie and said, "I'm glad you're all right. Did the captain hurt your neck? You looked like you couldn't move."

"No, he was holding very tightly, but it wasn't too bad. I was afraid to move—I didn't want him to start shooting if I slipped out of his filthy hand."

Mom was in charge. She asked Pinky if he could pilot the yacht to Nassau.

"Yes'um, I kin do dat. We git there t'mara—'bout noon."

Mom frowned, shook her head, and said, "Pinky, I don't want you to stay up all night. We'll stay here tonight and leave in the morning. There are enough beds on the boat for everyone to get some sleep. We'll eat, get some rest, and make our way to Nassau tomorrow."

"Yes'um. We be there t'mara night."

"Thank-you, Pinky. All right, now that that is settled, we need to find a place for our two prisoners to stay—a secure location."

"I know where, but there's no lock on the door." Millie told Mom about the emergency equipment room where we had stayed for more than two days. Vern said he could install a temporary lock on the door, but it would have to be disabled after the prisoners were transferred, in order to satisfy marine requirements.

Chapter 28

NASSAU AND HOME

We had to stay in The Bahamas for five more days because of legal matters. The next Monday, Mom and Elena had to testify and so did Mr. and Mrs. Harris. Millie and I went to the judge's chambers with Pinky and waited. A man in uniform appeared and asked us to follow him, but he didn't explain why. We didn't know we had to testify. It turned out to be pretty simple. The judge, dressed in a black robe and wearing a white wig, asked us to swear to tell the truth. Pinky, Millie, and I said we would and he asked us some questions. Then he said we could leave. Pinky took us back to the judge's office. We waited for another thirty minutes, then Mr. and Mrs. Harris, Elena, and Mom came and got us. Mom said the trial was over and we were free to go home. Pinky took us souvenir shopping.

During those five days in Nassau, Pinky acted as our tour guide so we wouldn't get swindled at tourist traps. I was amazed that he knew so many people. Almost every place we visited, people shook hands with Pinky and they talked like they hadn't seen each other in years. I couldn't understand most of what they said; they talked fast and used their funny English that was common in The Bahamas. I thought I'd have to live there for quite a while to figure out their lingo. I imagined it was like cowboys living with Indians in the 1800s.

We didn't buy many souvenirs, but we looked at many things: beautiful shells and carvings, paintings that were very costly—a few cheap ones, and some stuffed birds. Mom bought a couple of trinkets for Granma and Suzy. I didn't see her get anything for Dad, but I wasn't watching her all the time. Millie and I looked around for ourselves in some of the shops, but we didn't want to use any of our money. I wanted to give all of it back to Granma.

"Millie, if you want to, go ahead and buy something. Don't you want to get something for Jerry?"

"Well, yes, but I don't want to use your money. I'll borrow a few dollars from my parents. I want to send Jerry a postcard of the beach at Nassau. Here, I want you to take the money." She gave me the thirty bucks I had given her before we got on the yacht. We hadn't had to spend any money on food. After eating at Miss Carla's, I think the CIA paid for all our meals. The Bahamian government paid for our rooms during the trial. Mom bought us some snacks as we wove our way through the markets.

After the trial, on our last full day on the islands, Miss Carla had us over for dinner. Quincy and his wife came to eat with us, too. Quincy told us about the lighthouse fire. It burned for several hours, but when he flew over it the first time, it looked like someone had made a big bonfire. He didn't see anybody there. It was another scrap from the war that was to be torn down and hauled away. It had done its part. I think Pinky was the only one that was sorry to see it go. It had been part of his war-time life.

Quincy volunteered to fly us to Miami. He said he had to go there anyway to pick up some engine parts for another island-hopper's airplane. It was only about an hour to Miami. We would leave in the morning.

After dinner, I followed Pinky outside and we watched the sun setting.

"I guess you be goin' dat way t'mara."

"I want to thank-you for all your help, Pinky."

"Ah, Master Linfield, I must tank you. You saved muh bones from bein' broiled alive. You and your mum pulled me from dat lighthouse fire. You a good young man. You good shot vid marbowls."

"You're welcome, Pinky." We watched the bottoms of the western clouds turning pink and the horizon becoming yellow-orange. The nearly full moon was low in the eastern sky. The sky was beautiful. "I have a question for you. Why do you let Miss Carla boss you around?"

Pinky started laughing and slapped his thigh. "You doan know?" He looked me in the eye and put his arm around my shoulders. "Miss Carla, she my mum."

"She doesn't look old enough to be your mom."

"She give birth when she sixteen. It be wery hard times back then. They come from So' Car'lina after WWI. She and my pappy dive for sponges until he gat hurt. He die in hospital. I never see him, but Miss Carla have much love for dat man. She not marry anymore."

I understood what Pinky had felt without a father, but he had a worse time than I did. Dad was only gone for about two years, Pinky's dad was gone forever.

"Miss Carla said she was in England during the war. You stayed here?"

"Sure do dat. I work at Nassau 'til Navy hire me for workin' on Abaco. They give me jeep and radio and I make call-name Pinky."

"They gave you Kaleidoscope?"

"No. They give me big jeep—take it back after war. Then I git Kaleidoscope after a time."

"You didn't get paid?"

"Oh, yes. I come by towsand dollar vid small jeep."

"How'd you spend the money? Did you have a girl friend?"

"She tell me she vant go to England. She take money, never come back. I learn big lesson. No more vimmen." He smiled at me and said, "Missy Millie your girl?"

"No. We're just friends. We're only ten years old. Maybe I'll get a girl when I'm older—maybe fifteen or sixteen. I should have some money by then—you know, to go on a date. Maybe take her to a movie."

"Good thinkin', Master Rocky. Be a pleasure to know you."

"Same here, Pinky. You're a good friend. I'll never forget you. Maybe I'll come to see you sometime."

"Ve better go in. Near time for sleepin'. Plenty sunlight t'mara. Miss Carla say I gatte go fishin'. She runnin' low on fishes."

Miss Carla and Pinky were able to find space for all of us to stay overnight before being taken to Quincy's for our flight to Miami. We had originally planned to stay in a hotel farther into Shallows Town, but Miss Carla insisted we stay at her place. After breakfast, an old beat-up school bus showed up. We said our goodbyes and the bus took us to Quincy's. Mom and I sat beside each other and enjoyed the smooth flight to Miami. Taking off and landing was sure different in the cabin than when we rode in the floats. It was much quieter and hardly bumpy at all in the cushioned seats.

We left Abaco at 10:30 and arrived in Miami about ten minutes after twelve o'clock noon. We ate at the airport and got aboard a big airliner for the trip to Washington, D.C. Mom said it was a DC-3 but not as big as the newer model DC-6. It took us the rest of the day to get to Boston. From Miami, we went to Atlanta, then to Washington, D.C. Elena had to report to the CIA, so she stayed in the capital. Then we flew to New York, where the Harrises lived. Mr. and Mrs. Harris had to take care of things at their home, so Millie was going to continue school at Crafton until Christmas break. Finally, after more than an hour in the air from New York, we landed in Boston. We were so tired, we stayed overnight near the airport.

We ate snacks on the planes, but we had a real dinner in Boston. Mom called Dad and he was going to pick us up in the morning. We would be out of school at least one more day. Millie, Mom, and I had been away from Crafton for twelve days. Millie and I had missed eight days of school. I hoped I wouldn't have too much homework to make up. Millie said we might have to go to school if we got home before lunch. We would both have some explaining to do to Jerry. Millie, Mom, and I were Dad's only passengers returning to Crafton. The only luggage we had was Mom's. Our backpacks didn't take up much space, they were almost empty except for dirty underwear. We had eaten all the cookies.

Dad arrived at the motel at 8:35 in the morning. We all gave him big hugs and Mom and Dad did some kissing. I was always a little embarrassed when they kissed out in public, but it didn't bother me much in Boston; we were in a city where nobody knew us. I don't know why it bothered me. I think kissing is a personal thing between two people that shouldn't be done in public. I'll ask Millie what she thinks—maybe Granma will know more about it.

It took most of the day to get to Crafton, so we didn't have to go to school. Millie and I talked a lot in the back seat. Most of our conversation was about The Bahamas and Pinky. Millie thanked me again for helping rescue her family. That's when I asked her about kissing.

"What do you think about kissing, Millie?"

"You want us to kiss?"

"No, not that. I just want to know if you get embarrassed when your parents kiss."

"Oh. I don't think I get embarrassed, usually I just look away. Is that embarrassment? I guess it depends on the kissing: if it's a quick greeting or a goodbye, I don't care, but if it's like their lips are stuck together and they're making some noises, that's different. That's when I look away or leave the room."

"But what if your parents kiss in public?"

"In public? I don't think I've ever seen them kiss in public, but I'm sure they did when they got married. Maybe we should ask your grandmother about kissing. She could tell us about it."

"That's what I was thinking. Do you want to kiss me? It would just be an experiment." I thought we should try it while we were in the back seat. Mom and Dad wouldn't see us.

"I don't think so. Maybe some other time—like under the mistletoe at Christmas."

"I don't think Eskimos kiss, they rub noses. I wonder if that came about from them getting sick after kissing—you know, exchanging germs."

"Maybe because of bad breath. For energy when it's so cold, they eat a lot of blubber from seals and whales."

I grinned. "I might try some blubber sometime—if I can put catsup on it."

Millie started laughing and Mom said, "What are you guys talking about?"

I answered, "Blubber," and everybody laughed.

Chapter 29

POISON

e arrived in Crafton at 3:48 p.m. Wednesday afternoon. We had stopped for lunch in Portland and when I found out about the Portland Head lighthouse, we paid it a visit. That took another hour, but I liked seeing a lighthouse that was different from ours in Crafton. The buildings at the lighthouse were much bigger than ours; the keeper's house was three stories high. A large family could live there. Millie and I climbed up to the gallery; it was marked sixty-two feet, but the top of the beacon was at least sixteen feet higher. Millie and I slept the rest of the way home.

Granma, Suzy, and Surprise were waiting for us. Surprise started barking and running around the car when we got to the parking lot. He jumped all over me when we got out of the car. Millie picked him up and carried him into the house. It was getting cold and we got in the house as fast as possible. We only had our light jackets that we took to The Bahamas. We shivered in the cold on the coast of Maine.

When I saw Granma, I gave her a hug and said, "I'm sorry I lied to you." I stuck my hand in my pocket and pulled out the fifty dollars she had loaned me. "Here's your money, Granma." I thought she would count it to see if it was all there, but she didn't, she just put it in her pocket.

"I forgive you, Rocky. If you hadn't gone with Millie, I don't know what would have happened. You and your marbles saved everyone. When

I talked to Sandra on the phone last night, she told me what you did to rescue her and the Harrises."

Millie jumped up from the floor and said, "I'm going to take a bath—I feel grungy all over."

"I'm next, Millie." I went up to my room, tossed my backpack on the floor next to my bed, and got clean clothes from my dresser. I sat down on my bed for about a minute thinking about how nice it was to be back home. Then I remembered I had to go to school tomorrow. I'll have to explain where I was for the past twelve days. I bet some of the kids will think I made it all up, but this time I'm not talking to a newspaper reporter. I'll tell Jerry what happened, but he's the only one that gets to hear Millie's and my story.

All of a sudden, Surprise barked and I nearly jumped out of my skin. He was on the top step of the stairs looking at me. I hadn't heard him come up the steps. Surprise had never been in the attic before, so I coaxed him to come all the way into my room. He went all around sniffing everything and then jumped up on the bed beside me. I gave him a hug and scratched his belly when he rolled over on his back.

"So, you're happy I'm home, huh?"

He barked again and looked at me. I wish dogs could talk, they could tell of all the things they do and the odors they smell. I know a dog's nose is much more sensitive than a human's. Maybe he would like blubber—or catsup. I wondered what Surprise's favorite food would be.

I heard Millie say she was through with the bathroom and I could have it. I took my slippers and pajamas downstairs and called Surprise to come down the steps. He wouldn't come down so I had to go up, grab him, and carry him down. I put the stairs up, went in the bathroom and got in the tub with the hot water running. Ivory soap and hot water got me clean in a few minutes, but the water felt so good I laid back and almost went to sleep.

My dreamy world was interrupted by Mom, "Rocky, hurry up. Other people want to use the bathroom."

"Okay, Mom. I'm almost done." I pulled the plug with my toes, turned on the hot water, adjusted it with some cold, rinsed the soapy water off, and dried with a big soft towel; the white one with two black stripes at each end, and got into my pajamas. I was out of the bathroom within two or three minutes of Mom telling me to finish with my bath. I really felt good.

When I got to the living room, Millie was already telling about our stowaway travel. I wish she had waited for me, but I hadn't missed much, only the first day in that emergency equipment room. I got to tell them about our use of the bathroom on the yacht. Suzy seemed to like the part when I told them I peed in a Coke bottle.

We finished our story in about thirty minutes, then we had some popcorn. We were having a good time talking about Pinky, the rides in Kaleidoscope, Quincy, the rides in his plane, and the things we saw in Nassau, when the phone rang. Granma answered it.

"Oh, no! Not Carla! Has Aaron been notified?"

When I heard the name Carla, I thought the call was about Miss Carla, but then I realized Granma didn't know Miss Carla. It had to be someone else.

"Who is it, Mom?" Mom asked Granma who was on the phone as she and Dad got up from the sofa and were moving toward the kitchen. Granma didn't sound right.

I heard the clunk of the phone being hung up and Granma stepped into the living room. "Mrs. Nesbitt has passed away. She died in her sleep last night. I've known Dorothy Carla since high school. I'm going to miss her."

That was sad news for Granma. Mrs. Nesbitt was Granma's best friend and next-door neighbor. Then I thought of Aaron, Lt. Nesbitt, Mrs. Nesbitt's son. Mrs. Nesbitt had told Granma that she was going to be helping Elena plan Aaron's and Elena's wedding. Now there would be a funeral, right before the wedding—planned for Thanksgiving. Maybe the wedding would be postponed until Christmas.

Granma sat down on the chair beside the kitchen door and looked at the floor. I watched Granma look up at Mom and Dad. "I think I'll go to bed. It's been a long day."

"Okay, Mom. I'll drive you home."

"No, dear, I'd like to stay here—if it's all right with you. I can sleep on the sofa."

"No, Mom, I don't want you to suffer a night's sleep on the sofa. Susan can sleep out here. You take her bed." Mom looked at Suzy and said, "You don't mind using the sofa for your bed tonight, do you?"

Suzy said, "Granma, you can use my bed, I'll use the sofa. It'll be like camping." She smiled at Mom and Granma and said, "But I want my pillow."

"Thank-you Susan, I'll get you some blankets." Mom went to the hall closet and came back with a blanket, a comforter, and a sheet to fold in the middle. Then she looked at Millie and me and said, "I think we should all go to bed. All that travelling has worn us out. You guys have to go to school tomorrow. I don't want you to be cranky in the morning. I'll write both of you a note for the principal."

I wondered what Mom was going to write to the principal. Probably something about taking us to The Bahamas because it might be the only time we'd ever make the trip. If she told the truth about the kidnapping and what I did with my slingshot, Mr. Howell would tell the school superintendent, Mr. Sayre. He might not let me go to school anymore. He might think I would be a danger to the other kids. But I would never take my slingshot to school.

Millie and I went to school as usual. Mom gave Millie a sealed envelope to give to Mr. Howell. We didn't know what she had written, but Mr. Howell read the note, didn't smile or anything, and said, "You'd better go to your classrooms. You've got some catching up to do."

We ate lunch with Jerry and apologized for not telling him what we were doing. He didn't mind as long as we told him our whole adventure. Millie started the story, but she wasn't eating, just talking, so I took over for a few minutes. Then Millie continued. We went back and forth several times. Jerry finished lunch first. He listened closely to us telling all or experiences, asking questions about the jeep, the hand grenade, and the seaplane. Millie gave him a colorful seashell she had bought in Nassau. She told me that it cost a whole dollar.

Friday night, Lt. Nesbitt and Elena came to dinner, but we didn't have room for them to stay with us. They had decided to stay in his mother's house until after the funeral. Besides helping to arrange for the funeral next week, Elena packed things from the house of sentimental value that Aaron wanted. The lieutenant and Granma talked a lot. When Granma came over during the week, she told us about Aaron being so sad about his mother not being able to enjoy times with her grandchildren. Aaron and Elena weren't even married yet.

Granma knew about funerals. She had gone through Granpa's funeral a few years ago, so she knew what had to be done. Funny thing, but I couldn't remember what was happening when he died. I guess I was too young to understand what was going on back then. I was Suzy's age.

On Wednesday the following week, Aaron and Elena came to dinner again at the lighthouse. That's when we all found out from Aaron that his mom had been poisoned with tasium cynide. I had never heard of it. At school the next day I asked Miss Hill what it was. She told me potassium cyanide was a poison, so I looked it up in the library.

Aaron had mentioned to Granma that the coroner told the police chief that Mrs. Nesbitt was poisoned, most likely from potassium cyanide. Mrs. Nesbitt's lips were blue so the police chief ordered an autopsy. The autopsy confirmed the poisoning. The police interviewed Granma and she told them that Dorothy usually drank a cup of tea with extra sugar before going to bed. When the sugar was investigated, the police found that almost half of the sugar was the poison. Fortunately, when Elena and Aaron were in the house, they didn't use any of the sugar; most of the time they ate at restaurants. They drank their coffee black, no sugar. That's the way the Navy men liked it.

During the week, Millie and I caught up with all our homework and when Friday rolled around we were both tired of school. Because of the autopsy, the funeral for Mrs. Nesbitt had been delayed until Saturday, one day later. After dinner, Mom and Dad took us to a western movie. It was *Carson City* with Randolph Scott. Suzy didn't like it and wanted to leave before it was over. Mom took her to the lobby and bought her some popcorn. On the way home, the rest of us told Mom what she had missed. She laughed and said, "Well, I guess I didn't miss much."

We were home by 9:30. Suzy went right to bed, but Millie and I talked about the funeral. We decided to stay home on Saturday. Mom and Dad said we could stay home alone as long as we stayed in the house and kept the door locked. Mom said she would put a sign on the library door telling people to come back tomorrow.

In the morning, I woke up smelling coffee and heard Mom's humming. Then I smelled my favorite breakfast: bacon, eggs, and pancakes. I pictured smothering the buttered pancakes with maple syrup. My mouth was watering before I could get my shoes on. I took a look outside from my attic windows. The sky was gray and a few rain drops were hitting the windows and running down the glass.

When I got downstairs, I pushed the steps up and looked in the living room. Millie and Suzy were watching a kids program on TV and drinking orange juice. Millie said they had gotten up when Mom did. I didn't hear the TV from my room, the sound was turned way down so not to wake Dad up. He had been very busy at the store since Millie and I went to The Bahamas. Kids were getting ready for Halloween and he had sold a lot of masks and costumes. Next Friday was Halloween. I hadn't thought about trick-or-treating until he mentioned selling the masks. I think Millie and I will take Suzy and get some candy from Granma's neighbors. Dad said that some of his customers had already begun shopping for Christmas gifts.

As we ate our pancakes, Mom asked, "Do any of you want to go to the service for Mrs. Nesbitt?" We all looked at each other and shook our heads. I didn't want to see and hear Granma crying and tears from the Lieutenant. I said, "I'd rather stay here and watch TV. It's all rainy outside." I didn't want to get dressed up, either, but I didn't want to say that. I could think of only one time I talked to Aaron's mother. She gave us some books to sell to Mr. Waicukauski when he was in charge of the library. That was three and a half months ago.

Chapter 30

HIDING

Mrs. Nesbitt's funeral was scheduled for 2:00 p.m. at the House of Our Lord Christ church on the other side of town. The church is almost in the country, about a quarter mile from Crafton, set apart from town by some farmland. The wife of the farmer had given the land to the church when they retired and moved to Florida. Mom told me where the church was. Mom and dad would be gone for about two and a half hours after 1:00 o'clock when they were leaving to pick up Granma. Mom said Elena and Arron were driving there by themselves. The funeral was expected to be over by 3:00, and they would be back home within a half-hour. Aaron and Elena would be having dinner with us and Granma, too.

When Mom and Dad left, they told us to stay inside and lock the door. That was the second time I had heard that. It was raining and we didn't want to go out anyway. Mom and Dad had their long coats on, covering their dark clothes. Dad beeped the horn when they drove away.

"What should we do, Rocky?" Suzy was sitting on her hands on the sofa with her legs kicking up and down.

"I don't know. Got any ideas?"

Millie said, "We could play Monopoly."

"Nah, Suzy can't count money. If we help her, and she loses, she'll say we cheated her. It's happened before."

"How about a puzzle? We could do it on the dining room table."

"Nah. We're going to have dinner on the table tonight. We'd have to put the puzzle back in the box."

"Do you have a card table? We could use that."

"Oh, yeah. Good thinkin', Millie. I'll get it out of the hall closet. You and Suz get a puzzle from your bedroom closet." There were about five puzzles on a shelf in the back of my old bedroom closet. I hoped they were still there.

I pulled the folded legs away from the top until I heard each one click into place and then flipped the table right-side up. Each of us got a chair from the dining room and we were set. Millie had picked out the puzzle: 500 pieces; an old west farm scene. That was strange—I had never seen it before. Maybe Dad had brought it home from the store. I hoped none of the pieces was missing.

We had been working on the straight edges of the puzzle for maybe ten or fifteen minutes when I heard a car stop in the parking lot. Looking out the front door, I saw a blue car, just like the one I had noticed following Dad's pickup truck the day he took Elena and Mom to the pier. The driver was just sitting there as if he was waiting for someone. But then the door opened and the guy got out.

I yelled, "Millie, Susan, lock yourselves in the bathroom! There's a big man coming to the house." I wanted to get my slingshot, but it was in the attic, so I grabbed a just-washed kitchen knife that was on the countertop. I waited at the doorway from the hall to the kitchen. If he broke in, I was in a perfect spot to stab him.

Millie and Susan had done what I told them. I heard the click of the lock on the bathroom door. But the front door was really on my mind. I heard footsteps coming across the porch, and then a rapping on the door. Then someone's bare knuckles were banging on the door frame.

I said, "Who is it? What do you want?" I tried to lower my voice, but it wasn't working.

"It's Ensign Thorndike, remember me?"

"Oh! I remember you. Just a minute, I'll open the door." I put the knife back on the kitchen counter and went to the door, pushed the curtain aside and looked out. I had to make sure it was Thorny. He was smiling and said, "Hi, Rocky. Please let me in. It's wet out here."

I could see the wet spots on his khaki overcoat and some raindrops running down his cheeks. It was Thorny, but his hair was longer than when I saw him last summer.

I yelled at Suzy, "Suzy, you can come out now. It's Ensign Thorndike."

I unlocked the door and Thorny stepped into the hall as he wiped raindrops from his face. Suzy came running down the hallway and jumped into Thorny's arms.

"Oh, Thorny! I've missed you so much!"

"It's good to see you, Susan. How are you guys? It's been a few months." Then he spotted Millie and said, "This young lady must be Miss Harris."

I introduced Millie to Thorny. Suzy was sitting on Thorny's right forearm, but he quickly switched her to his left side and shook hands with Millie. "You're as pretty as your sister."

"Thank-you, Ensign."

There was a moment of silence before Suz pulled on Thorny's shirt collar and said, "You're supposed to say you're welcome."

"Oh." He looked at Millie and said, "You're welcome." Thorny looked at Suzy and said, "Thank-you for reminding me, Susan."

Suz grinned and said, "You're welcome."

Thorny set Susan down, turned around, and locked the front door. When the lock clicked, Thorny parted the curtains and said, "Are you expecting anyone, Rocky?"

I shook my head. "No."

"Well, a dark-blue sedan just pulled into the driveway. Looks like two men inside."

"I think a dark-blue car followed Elena and Mom to the yacht when they were going to The Bahamas. It might be the same car. I didn't see the license plate, it was too far away."

"They're getting out and they're armed. Take the girls and get in the attic—pull up the steps and sit on the mattress. Hurry!"

I herded the girls up the steps into the attic. Millie went first and pulled on Suzy, I pushed. It only took us a few seconds to get up the steps. Then I heard, "Is there a gun in the house, Rocky?"

"Yes, in the locked drawer in the kitchen. I don't have a key, but there's a hammer in the bottom drawer at the left of the sink."

"Thanks. Stay in the attic until I tell you it's safe to come down."

Millie and Suzy had gotten on top of the bed and after I pulled up the steps, I got on the bed beside them. Then we heard a smashing sound. I think Thorny had broken open the top drawer where the gun was. Granma kept her loaded .38 there. She always had a full clip of bullets in the handle. I'll bet Thorny was a good shot, his arms were really muscular and I saw him with a .45 before. The .45 looked small in his big right hand.

We heard some pounding at the door and then a loud voice, "We want the girl. Give us the girl and we'll go away. We'll give you thirty seconds and then we're coming in."

"Which girl are you talking about?"

There was about a ten second silence and then we heard the voice again, "The Harris girl, not the little one."

Thorny said, "You'll have to take her from me. I'm armed. If you come in the house, you'll get shot."

"Yeah—what with, a slingshot?"

"Stay away or you'll regret it." I heard Thorny say something, but it wasn't loud enough for me to hear. I figured he was talking to himself or he was trying to call the police. Then I heard Thorny say, "Damn phone is dead."

Sometimes the phone doesn't work when it rains really hard, but this time I thought it was probably because the men had cut the wires. I heard some glass break, like something had broken one of the small windows out of the front door. A big crash followed. I think the men had kicked in the front door. Mom and Dad were going to be really mad. It was cold outside and we didn't have a replacement door.

A few seconds after the big noise, there was a gunshot, then a second one, and a sound like someone had fallen on the floor. I was hoping that it wasn't Thorny. Millie and Susan were looking at me, their eyes as big as sixty-watt light bulbs. We heard another gunshot, but it wasn't in the house, it was outside in the rain. I heard three more rapid shots, like— bang, bang, bang. Next, a car started and drove away, and I heard one more shot. A couple of seconds later there was crunching sound and a blaring car horn.

I went over to the window and rubbed the corner of the glass to make a spot so I could see out. When I looked out with one eye, I saw Thorny running toward the wrecked car. He reached under the hood and jerked something. The horn went quiet. Thorny leaned into the driver's side for a few moments and then came back towards the house.

"What's happening, Rocky?" Millie and Suzy were watching me look out the window.

"Thorny's all right. He's coming back from that blue car. It wrecked by the turnoff sign to the lighthouse. I think the car knocked the sign down, but nobody got out of the car. I think the driver's badly hurt—or dead."

We heard footsteps on the porch and then some sounds in the hallway. The furnace had come on so we couldn't hear much after that. I was guessing that Thorny was trying to close the front door. I heard some banging around. It sounded like Thorny was using a hammer and nails.

He was probably putting the door back together; it must have been smashed when one of the men broke in the house.

I was telling the girls what I thought the sounds were so they wouldn't be scared, at least for Suzy. I don't think Millie was scared. We pretty much think alike. She had heard everything I did, maybe a little more. Her hearing was a little better than mine. I found that out when we were on the yacht. I wondered if girls were better listeners than boys, or maybe it was something else.

"What time is it?" I looked at Millie and she laughed. I didn't understand until she pointed at the clock on the little table next to the head of my bed. I was sitting beside it. Then she told me, after I smiled.

"It's almost three o'clock." We both laughed.

"Thank-you."

Millie looked at me like I was a dummy and shook her head. Suzy poked Millie in the side with her finger. Millie looked at Suz as if to say 'Why'd you do that?', but then Millie reacted, "You're very welcome."

Suz said, "That's right," and nodded.

Chapter 31

A SURPRISE FOR MILLIE

We left the funeral at exactly 3:05 and headed home. I was thinking how nice it was going to be to change out of my good clothes and relax for a few minutes before Elena and Aaron came over for dinner. The rain had let up some, but there was still some wind and an occasional smattering of drops on the windshield.

"Marty, do you want to go home first?"

"Yes, I think we should get Surprise and take him to your house. He loves to be around the kids. I also want to change out of these shoes, they're pinching my feet. I need my slippers."

We turned at Pier Road and headed up the hill to the corner where I would turn to go to Marty's. That's when I heard the police siren. I had been in Crafton long enough to recognize the difference between the fire truck's warbling and the shriller whining of the police siren. For a moment, there was a second siren, different than the one from a police car. I frowned, but not for long. Sandra said, "That's the ambulance from the hospital."

"I wonder if there's been an accident on Lighthouse Road. Maybe some cars crashed. The rotten weather might have contributed to a wreck. We'll find out what happened on the way home."

Marty said, "The last accident on Lighthouse Road was when a truck struck a pedestrian—you weren't home then. That's when we met Elena."

195

It took about seven minutes for Marty to change her shoes, pick up Surprise, and lock her door. Another minute and we were near the approach road to the lighthouse and home. The ambulance, the firetruck, and a police car were parked at our turnoff. I drove slowly past the vehicles, pulled over, and rolled down my window. Police Chief, Joe Bynum, stepped up to the car and leaned down so we could talk.

"Hi, Chief. Anyone hurt in the accident?"

"Not an accident. The driver was shot and killed. There's another body over at your house." He pointed at our residence.

"What!?"

"No kidding. That young fella, over there—." He whistled and signaled for a man in a trench coat to come over to our car. I didn't recognize who it was, but Sandra did when he was right in front of the car. "—shot and killed both of them. He was protecting your kids."

"Lee, it's Ensign Thorndike. He's the Navy man that was shot when we were in Western Maine last summer. I wonder why he's here."

I got out of the car with the motor running. It was chilly and I wanted to keep the heater running for the women. I shook hands with the ensign and introduced myself.

"I've heard a lot about you, Commander, mostly from your son and wife. I heard about Lt. Nesbitt's mother passing away and decided to come to the funeral, but I was too late. I stopped at the lighthouse to say hello and was talking to the kids when these two thugs showed up. They wanted Millie."

"Susan has told me about you, Ensign. You're one of her favorites. Thank-you for being here and taking care of the kids."

Sandra leaned over to the driver's window and said, "Where are the children?"

"They're in the attic, Mrs. Linfield. I told them to stay up there until I said they could come down. I didn't want them to see the guy I shot in the hallway. He broke through the door and I had no choice. He didn't get a shot off. I shot the other one as he was trying to drive away."

"Has the stiff in the house been removed?" I wanted the body gone so the kids wouldn't see it, especially the girls.

"Yes, Sir. That one's in the ambulance. He's the guy that shot me at the lake. I talked to the guy in the car after he wrecked. He swore on his mother's grave that they didn't poison Mrs. Nesbitt. They were a cousin and an uncle of the man agent Harris killed several months ago at Mrs. Makler's. Apparently that's the last of the family that wanted revenge. The others were put in jail in The Bahamas."

"You did a great job, Ensign. Thank-you."

"No problem. Well, Sir, I had to demolish a drawer in your kitchen to get Mrs. Makler's gun. Rocky told me where it was. The front door will have to be replaced, also. The first guy I shot kicked it in." The ensign came over to the car window, bent down and looked in the back. "The police chief has your firearm, Mrs. Makler. It sure came in handy."

"I'm glad you could make use of it, Thorny. You did a fine job."

"Thanks. I couldn't let those idiots take Millie."

I asked the ensign to join us for dinner and he accepted the invitation. He wanted to visit with Aaron and Elena and express his condolences. He also wanted to talk with the children about the trip to The Bahamas and see if Susan still collected colored rocks.

When we got in the house, the claw hammer was still on the floor below the sink where Thorny had dropped it when he retrieved Marty's gun. The torn-off drawer front was in the waste basket beneath the sink. When Sandra came in the house, she stopped and looked at the demolished door, tapped on the wall in the hallway, and then called to the attic.

"Kids, you can come down now. We're all home, including Surprise."

I watched the stairs descend from the ceiling and stepped over to guide the girls down to the hallway and safety. I let Rocky come down without any aid. I'm sure he wanted it that way. For the first few minutes, it seemed like everyone was talking simultaneously. I was astonished that after such a short period of hubbub we all seemed to understand what had happened.

Marty, Sandra, and Millie went in the kitchen and surveyed the damage before they began to organize for dinner. I stuck my head in the kitchen and said, "I'll fix the drawer tomorrow. It's not as bad as it seems. I'm more concerned about the front door."

Marty told me she had an old front door in her garage. We could have it. So, I waited for Susan to quit talking to Thorny. When she was catching her breath, I asked him to help me retrieve the door from Marty's place. He seemed to be slightly relieved that I had rescued him from Susan.

"Susan, Thorny and I have to go to Granma's and get a door so I can replace our broken one. It's going to get cold tonight and we need to close the front door."

"Can I go with you?"

I was surprised by Susan's request. I thought for a moment and said, "Sure. Get your winter coat." I looked at Thorny, shook my head, and grinned. He smiled and got his coat from the hall closet. It was still light outside, but the sun was going down. When we arrived at Marty's house, I aimed the pickup headlights on her garage and Thorny raised the door. He scanned the walls, looked at me, and shook his head. There was only one place left to inspect. I leaned out the window and said, "Check out the ceiling."

He looked up, shielded his eyes from the headlights, gave me a thumbs up, and smiled. "I see it, but we'll need a ladder."

Marty's ladder was behind the garage. It took us about ten minutes to get the door down and into the back of my truck. The door was solid, still had hinges and knobs, and was fairly heavy. The four glass panels were opaque, covered with a thick layer of dirt. The whole door would have to be cleaned off, both sides were dusty. An application of soap and water, a fresh coat of paint, and some money would be saved until next spring. I just hoped the hinges fit the same locations as the ones that were on the damaged door.

When we got back to the lighthouse, Elena and Aaron were there after having changed from their mourning clothing at the Nesbitt home. Sandra told me they arrived a few minutes after we left to retrieve the door. Ensign Thorndike talked with the new arrivals for about a minute and then Aaron and Thorny helped me hang the door. It took us about twenty minutes to put the door in position and another ten to finish the cleanup. Fortunately, the hinge positions had matched perfectly. Dinner was served as soon as we washed our hands.

No mention of the recent shootout or the funeral were made during dinner, the conversation was, for the most part, about the upcoming holidays. Following dessert, which was strawberry shortcake, we adjourned to the living room. Sandra and Marty served the adults coffee and the kids had hot chocolate. Surprise ate some doggy-treats from the kids for his performances of sit, bark, and lie down.

We had been talking for about five minutes when the phone rang. Marty was closest, so she answered, "Hello, Linfield residence."

I didn't hear anything else for at least a minute, maybe longer, but I saw some of Marty's facial expressions as she listened. When her face suddenly blossomed into an enormous smile, I knew something of great importance had happened.

"Lieutenant, you need to take this call."

Aaron stood up, handed his nearly empty coffee cup to Elena, and said, "Who is it, Mrs. Makler?" His expression was one of puzzlement as he received the phone from Marty.

"It's Elena's father. He has a question for you."

Aaron stepped into the kitchen. A hush came over the living room. We all knew it wasn't polite to listen. Everybody looked around self-consciously, but didn't utter a word. I expected it was something about the upcoming marriage, something a father of the bride might want to know from the groom.

The next thing we heard was, "Sure, I'd like to sell the property. Elena and I already talked it over. We don't need houses in two different locations and we don't want to look after a rental." There was a short pause and then, "I'll call you back tomorrow with a price. If that is satisfactory, we have a deal. Thank-you Mr. Harris. Goodbye."

We all began talking again before we heard Aaron hang up the phone. I looked at Elena and she was moving her head from side to side and smiling as if to say, 'I can't believe you were all listening.'

Aaron rejoined us in the living room. "I guess you heard one part of my conversation."

We all smiled and laughed nervously. Sandra said, "I apologize for the group, we couldn't help ourselves."

"That's okay. You'll all know about it in a few seconds. Mr. and Mrs. Harris have purchased a furniture store in Crafton, Rifkin's Furnishings, and they need a residence. They want to buy my mother's house—next door to Marty's."

Millie stood up and exclaimed, "What? I'm going to live in Crafton right next door to Mrs. Makler? That is wonderful!" She was so excited, she rushed to Marty and kissed her on the cheek. Then she headed for Rocky. He wasn't prepared for Millie's kiss—none of us were, but she kissed him on the lips. I watched as Rocky's face turned beet-red. He looked around and noticed that we had all seen the act.

I expected Rocky would go to his room or hide somewhere after that kiss, but all he did was say, "Geez, Millie, did you have to do that in front of everybody?"

Chapter 32

Escape From Manchuria

Millie could talk of little else than about her parents moving to Crafton. According to Millie, living about half-way between Jerry and Rocky was going to be heaven on Earth and her parents becoming business owners meant she would probably be staying in Crafton until she would be leaving for college. The only college I had heard her mention, in the short time I had known her, was Harvard. I don't think Jerry and Rocky had thought that far ahead, they were planning to shoot grackles with their slingshots next summer, wash cars, and mow lawns.

Aaron sold his property to the Harris family for $6,375. Two days before Halloween, the next Saturday, Harris's furniture arrived from New York and they began moving in. Natalie and Steven Morgan, Marty, Sandra, and I carried things into the house after the movers emptied the truck onto the front yard. Rhonda told us where she wanted the various pieces of furniture. Mr. Harris, Leroy, was taking inventory at the furniture store.

We had two days of dry weather which helped the Harris family immensely. Steve and I both took a half-day off from work that Thursday. Friday, after school, Sandra helped Rhonda and Millie move Millie's things from the lighthouse to her new home. Her new bedroom was a little bit larger, about twenty percent, than her lighthouse room. She was also going to have a closet twice as large as in her temporary space. Rocky decided to stay in the attic until the weather turned really rotten. I knew he would want to move back downstairs when there was snow on the roof and a menacing wind-chill from the northeasters.

November 2 was the first day our family activities had returned to normal. I was able to close the store and get home by 5:30 p.m. Susan was at one end of the sofa wearing her pajamas. Her legs were wrapped up in a blanket with Surprise on top. Rocky had covered his legs with the other end of the blanket and was petting the dog. After the "Hi, Dad's," I joined Sandra in the kitchen. There was a cold beer sitting on the counter, which I assumed was for me. I picked it up and took a sip just before giving Sandra a kiss on the cheek.

"Hey! That's my beer!"

I pretended to bring it back up and return it to the stubby bottle.

"Don't you do that!"

"Just kidding. I wouldn't even do that to my own beer. What can I do to help?"

"Please set the table after you wash—and get the kids ready to eat. They've been playing with the dog."

After dinner, the dishes washed and put away, Rocky reminded me to finish telling my story of how I got out of Manchuria. We were sitting around the dining room table and I couldn't remember where I had left off so I asked, "Do any of you remember what I was telling you?"

Susy raised her hand and waved it as if she were in school. "I do, Daddy. You said a man hit you with a stick, but you couldn't hit him back."

"Oh, yes. Now I remember. Dr. Zhang was giving me instructions so we could communicate without talking. I asked him when we could start for the Russian border, but he wouldn't answer me at first. But after about a week of thinking, he told me we wouldn't be able to go for about six months. It would be too cold, I didn't have the right clothing, and there wasn't much to eat along the way until spring arrived. When we did go north and through mountainous terrain, we would have to live off the land."

Susan had moved her chair next to mine and I put my arm around her shoulders. She looked up at me and said, "Daddy, couldn't you buy some food at a grocery store?"

I didn't want to explain that there were no grocery stores like in the states, but it was easier to say, "We couldn't go into a town. That would raise suspicion about me. The military police might arrest Dr. Zhang and me for questioning. If we said something wrong, we would be in deep trouble."

Rocky was leaning back in his chair, staring ahead, frozen in thought. After a few seconds, he said, "Did Dr. Zhang have a gun?"

"Nope. Our only weapons were a kitchen knife and some sewing needles. Dr. Zhang had some medical knives and a bone saw, but those were for humans and were sterilized. The first thing we had to do was get me some clothes that fit and some shoes. I was about six inches taller than most of the Chinese people, so we had to make me some long pants. In the spring, we could cut up a blanket and make clothes from it. I couldn't walk very far without shoes, but I began toughening my feet by walking barefoot. The needles would come in handy for sewing chicken feathers into the winter clothing. That's when I started growing my beard—at least most of my face would be warm. Whiskers developed without any help, they just grew a little bit every day."

I skipped telling about using the clothing from old people that died during the winter months. However, there were only three deaths, and those were from pneumonia.

"During that first six months we made clothes and fur boots from animal hides, and constructed backpacks to carry our things as we travelled by foot into the northern country. We were going to travel over some mountain ranges and through forests. Dr. Zhang was an expert at trapping small animals, like rabbits, using snares."

"You didn't eat rabbits, did you? They're so cute and cuddly, Daddy."

"Well, Susan, if you're going hungry, rabbit stew keeps your energy up so you can walk and hike around and over mountains. We made warm gloves from their fur. We hunted bigger animals, too."

"What bigger animals, Dad?"

"There were several types of deer, wild pigs, bears, and moose. There were also Siberian tigers, mostly across the Russian border, but we didn't hunt them, they hunted us." I grinned but Sandra looked at me as if I were crazy saying that to the kids. "We found bodies of deer, a wolf, and some bears, with signs that they had been killed by other animals. We found a bear that had been shot but must have run a long distance before it died."

"Did you ever kill a moose?"

I shook my head and looked at Rocky. "We saw a couple of moose, but never a dead one. We couldn't have killed one. We would have had to have spears or a rifle. We thought they would be too difficult to hunt."

"How did you break your leg, dear?"

"Yes, Daddy. How did you?"

"Well, it was August and very warm. We had been travelling for a little more than six weeks, getting farther and farther from Dr. Zhang's home, but closer and closer to the Russian border. He had a map, but it was hand-drawn and not very accurate. The first month we tried to adjust to the humid weather. Dr. Zhang wilted after a few hours of walking. He wasn't used to walking far, especially when carrying a heavy backpack. You have to remember he was almost sixty years old. We looked like Sherpas carrying large packs on our backs. We could only travel three or four miles per day. The distance we had to cover to reach Vladivostok was about 500 miles, but we were forced to hike through forests and valleys, across streams, and over mountain ranges. I guess we travelled nearly 600 miles.

"We had a few brief encounters with people, but Dr. Zhang told them we were botanists, hunting for plants, like ginseng, whose roots are thought to have medicinal benefits. Early in our journey, an old woman said we were headed in the right direction. Ginseng was in abundance on the forest floor farther to the north, maybe a few weeks away."

I was trying to set the stage for the accident that resulted in my fracture. I wanted the kids and Sandra to understand the hardships of Dr. Zhang's and my journey. I paused for a moment, which gave Sandra an opportunity to say, "Time for some hot chocolate. Let's give Daddy a chance to think about what comes next."

The minute hand on the kitchen clock was creeping toward twelve. It was almost eight o'clock and I had another half hour of my story to tell. I was relieved that Sandra had given me a break. I had told her previously, that when I broke my leg, some of my recollections were a bit murky. The days ran together and sometimes I lost track of the passage of time. Fortunately, most of the time, Dr. Zhang was there for company. When we all had our drinks, marshmallows added, I continued with my narrative.

"Our slow travel made one week into three and the nighttime temperatures were beginning to drop. October was only a week away. The broadleaf trees were dropping their leaves, but we actually found ginseng. Dr. Zhang and I harvested some of the roots. He said they might come in handy. I thought he meant as medicine for us, but I was wrong; he wanted the roots for bartering. Dr. Zhang knew that we were going to have to build some shelters to allow us to make it through the frigid winter months. We would need tools and food.

"About the middle of October, we came across some lumberjacks and miners. They had constructed a sizable camp and were waiting for the government to make a road to their location. Dr. Zhang was able to make friends with several of the men by tending to their injuries. The government doctors were still miles away, waiting for a good road to reach the camp.

"Two of the loggers showed us how to build a cabin and gave us an ax and a hatchet. We stayed there for about eight days before moving on. They wished us good luck. They had figured out we were going to cross the mountains and go to the coast. Dr. Zhang swore to me that he had never told any of the men where we were going. I believed him."

"Were you in Russia yet, Dad?"

"Nope. We were about twenty miles from the border. I found out later that the road had stopped going north because the Chinese and the Russians were arguing about it. The Russians didn't want a road from the mountains into Russia from China. The Russians didn't believe the Chinese just wanted a road for lumber and minerals."

Rocky frowned and said, "What happened to those men?"

"We never found out, Rocky. I hope they left the area and moved south to find another job. The day Dr. Zhang and I left the camp, it started snowing in the mountains a little higher in elevation than where we were hiking. That night it got very cold. The next day, we started looking for a place to build a cabin big enough for two. There were plenty of small trees we could cut down, and we found a spot where there were a number of fallen trees and a rocky area just below where the big evergreen trees grew up to the top of the hills around us."

I stopped to see if the kids looked tired, but they were drawn into my story. I hoped they weren't going to have bad dreams after the next part.

"When we stopped hiking to eat, I remember it was about lunchtime. Dr. Zhang disappeared into the trees for about fifteen minutes. I thought he was going to the bathroom. When he came back, he told me to get my things and follow him, he had found a cave."

Rocky was on the edge of his chair. "Were bears hibernating in the cave?"

"We checked the cave and the area around it, but we didn't see any signs of bears that day. To fix the cave for our winter home, we used some of the downed trees and built a wall to cover the opening. We made a small door near the ground, just big enough to crawl through and we covered all the spaces between the logs with pine boughs and leaves. That's when I broke my leg. We were cutting boughs from live trees and I tripped and fell over a downed tree. My foot was caught and I fell backward. I knew the ax was behind me, so I turned to avoid it as I fell—Dr. Zhang and I both heard the bone break."

Susan's eyebrows rose almost to her hairline. "Did it hurt, Daddy?"

I wanted to laugh, but I was able to answer her question after a big grin. "It sure did. The pain was awful. I yelled and broke into a sweat. Dr. Zhang came running to my side and looked at the bend in my leg where there isn't supposed to be a bend. It looked like I had two knees in one leg. He said, 'We in trouble now.' He moved the tree limbs away from my foot and helped me move away from the log I tripped over. Then he said, 'Must move to cave. I will make leg straight.' Dr. Zhang tried to pull me across the leaves, twigs, and stones but he wasn't strong enough. He put some pine boughs behind me and said, 'Get on back.' I only had to turn from my side to my back to get on the boughs and then I helped him by walking on my elbows and rear end as he pulled on my collar."

Sandra reached out and took my hands in hers. "Boy, you were in a pickle." Susan laughed and repeated, as if a song, "You were in a pickle." I reached over, touched her nose, and said, "And you have a chocolate moustache." Rocky handed her his napkin.

"How did you get out of the pickle, Dad?"

"It seemed like forever before I was back in the cave. Dr. Zhang had to move me about twenty-five yards. He tried to make me comfortable and then picked up the hatchet and said, 'I be back.' I heard some chopping sounds and then I must have passed out—or gone to sleep. The next thing

I remember was Dr. Zhang tying up my leg to some branches. Then he said, 'This will be some hurt.'

"I nodded as if I was ready, but when he moved a branch, I almost screamed in pain. He had made a contraption to stretch my leg out to get the bones back in position. I think I passed out. Next, I heard him say, 'All over, leg straight.' He patted me on the chest and crawled through the door with the ax."

Rocky finished his drink and said, "Where did he go with the ax? What was he going to do?"

"I didn't know, but I didn't care, either. My leg hurt—so bad that I couldn't think of anything going on around me. After maybe an hour, Dr. Zhang came back with two long poles, a cluster of pine boughs, and a rock—about the size of my fist." I made a fist to show the kids how big the rock was.

"The poles were about six feet long, about the length of this table, and sharpened at one end. Dr. Zhang saw some bear tracks, where a bear had rubbed against a tree. He decided to make us some weapons in addition to the one he had in his pocket."

"Did he have a pistol from the miners?" I think Rocky could only think of a gun because we had an ax, a hatchet, and some sharp spears.

"No. He didn't have a gun, but he had a bag of black pepper. He told me we would put some in our hands and blow it into the face of a bear. The beast would probably run off if pepper went up its nose or got in its eyes. It wasn't long before we had an opportunity to test the pepper trick."

Chapter 33

GOODBYE TO RUSSIA

"Did a bear try to get you, Daddy?" Susan had gotten out of her chair and was standing, leaning against the table, elbows splayed wide, her hands cupped under her chin.

"A big black bear tried to get into our cave. It was snowing lightly and Dr. Zhang went out to get some more boughs from some nearby trees. I heard a yell and he came scrambling back inside our cave, dropping the boughs on the ground. He grabbed the hatchet and said, 'Big bear!' I sat up and he handed me one of the spears, but I didn't think I was going to be of any help; I couldn't move around much with a splint on my leg.

"We could hear the bear breathing as it approached our wall. Then it tried to open our door. We could see the big paw and claws starting to tear at the wall. Dr. Zhang waited until a paw stuck through the wall and he smacked it with the business end of our hatchet. I think the bear was getting mad; it started snorting and trying to rip open our wall. We waited for about a minute as it tore away some of our wall and stuck its snout through the opening. We were still not out of danger, so Dr. Zhang loaded up a handful of pepper and when that bear's nose came through the hole a second time, it got a cloud of pepper smack-dab in its face."

Susan started laughing and Rocky said, "Did the bear run away, Dad?"

"No, Rocky, it just backed off and rolled around in the snow trying to get the pepper out of its eyes with its paws. Dr. Zhang figured it was

209

time to go on offense, so he grabbed a spear with his left hand and the hatchet in his right and charged out of our cave. I don't think the bear could see anything. Dr. Zhang jabbed it right in the mouth and the spear stuck through the bear's neck. Now it had two problems, but Dr. Zhang wasn't finished. He hit that bear in the head with the hatchet, once with the flat part and then again with the sharp edge. The bear made a sound like the wind was knocked out of it. Dr. Zhang then killed that big old bear with the hatchet."

"That bear picked on the wrong people. Huh, Dad?"

"He sure did, but we were very fortunate that bear came to visit us. We made him into a very warm blanket to cover both of us. While Dr. Zhang skinned that big bear, I did what I could to help repair our wall. We got everything ready for another night in our cave. Dr. Zhang cooked some of the bear meat for dinner. It wasn't bad, but you know what, Rocky?"

Rocky frowned and said, "What, Dad?"

"We didn't have any catsup." I smiled and everybody laughed.

"What does bear meat taste like, dear?"

I wanted to say chicken, to lighten the mood, but I decided to tell the truth. "It's very tough and you have to chew it a long time to soften it up. It's greasy and fatter than beef, but Dr. Zhang told me, if you put it into stew and let it simmer, cool it, and remove the fat on top, it tastes much like hamburger. I don't know how else to describe it."

"How long did you stay in the cave, Dad?"

"We stayed there almost three months. I stayed inside most of that time except for crawling out to take care of business. After the first few days, my leg didn't hurt any more unless I twisted it slightly. That's when Dr. Zhang showed me what the rock was for."

"You didn't throw the rock at the bear, Daddy?"

"No, Susan. Dr. Zhang broke off a small chunk of thee rock with the hatchet. It was limestone and fairly soft. He used some harder rocks to grind it into a powder, mixed it with pine needles and ginseng, added water, and warmed the mixture. We could see bubbles coming off. He was making a solution with calcium in it to help my bone heal. Dr. Zhang was a very clever man. The solution tasted terrible, but I knew it would help, so I drank it, followed by lots of water from melted snow. That was my calcium soup. I had some every day.

"As soon as I could stand without pain, we went outside and set snares for small animals so we would have something to eat other than bear meat. To kill time, we used the animal fur to make mittens and stocking caps. He told me Chinese stories and legends and I told him stories about Paul Bunyan, Davy Crocket, and Wild Bill Cody. We also talked about the Second World War. He hated the Japanese. When a blizzard came, we spent Christmas and New Years in the cave staying warm. I wished I was back home with you guys, but I didn't say anything about it to Dr. Zhang. He didn't have anyone to go home to. During that storm, the temperature dropped far below zero, maybe twenty below, but we were pretty comfortable in our coats, mittens, stocking caps, and covered with the bear hide."

"What about a fire to keep warm, Dad?"

"We had small fires, mostly for cooking, but the wind had to be just right or we'd get smoked out of the cave. We had a lot of cold meals, but at the end of February, we decided to move on and crossed the border into Russia.

"It was difficult for me to walk in the snow. My leg was very weak and I didn't want to break it again. With homemade snowshoes, we made a couple of miles each day, but when we had to climb hills, I had to put a brace on my leg and hop through the forest. We saw signs of tigers, but never saw the actual animals.

"One night, after being in Russia a few days, some men came to our camp. I think it was about a week after we crossed the border. They were from a Russian team that was searching for tigers to mark so they could study how much territory the big cats needed. The men were afraid the tigers might be extinct before long if they weren't protected. We traded with them; they had rice and we had something they could sell, ginseng. They gave us a map with Russian and Chinese markings so Dr. Zhang could read it. That was very useful to us. Even with the map, it took us another month to get to the coast. My leg was getting stronger every day, but I still limped. I have to admit, I was afraid I might break it again if I used it normally. I think the limp became a habit; the muscles had been trained to limp."

Sandra said, "Anybody want a refill? There's more hot chocolate."

"More marshmallows, too?"

I think Susan has a thing for marshmallows. Rocky said, "Sure, Mom. I don't think I'll wet the bed. It hasn't happened in a long time."

Sandra filled our cups and dropped marshmallows in all our drinks. There was a chorus of thank-yous, and Sandra responded, "You're welcome," and curtsied. Susan grinned as she picked up her cup to take a drink.

I continued. "We slowly worked our way toward the coast. There was a small settlement called Barabash where we met a woman from Vladivostok. She was a Seventh Day Adventist from the United States, Mary Williams."

"You're kidding me." Sandra looked at me as if her doctor had just told her she was four months pregnant.

"I'm not kidding. Mary was there trying to spread the gospel where few westerners had ever been. She was handing out little Bibles and pamphlets with Jesus on the front. They were all written in Russian. She had a few things in Chinese, too. She looked Russian, so I made some hand signals to Dr. Zhang and he said, 'Where you born?'

"She answered, 'Russia. My parents moved to the states in the thirties when I was a teenager.'

"We decided not to tell her who I was until we could make sure who she was. After a week, we were in a small church talking—Dr. Zhang and Mary were talking, I was listening. The church was about the size of our library with about a dozen chairs of all different kinds, probably donations from the citizens of Barabash. Dr. Zhang said, 'Who the minister?'

"Mary said, 'I really don't know.' She turned away to look at the statue of Jesus behind the pulpit and I said, 'Mary, I have a question for you.'

"She hunched her shoulders, put her hands to her ears, and collapsed onto the nearest chair.

"I moved over to her, crouched down, put my hand on her shoulder, and said, 'Mary, are you all right?'

"'Oh, my God in Heaven, I thought God was speaking to me.'

"I laughed. 'I've never been mistaken for God before. That's new to me.'

"'But, I thought you couldn't speak.'

"'That's just an act Dr. Zhang and I cooked up so no one would know I was an American.'

"Then, I told her the entire story of how I got to Barabash with Dr. Zhang. I asked if she could help me get to an American base. Dr. Zhang grabbed my arm and said, 'I go, too.'

"Mary sat there in her heavily padded coat, took off her mittens and pulled a piece of paper from her pocket. We waited for her reply as she scanned over the writing on the paper. I took a look at the writing, but it was in Russian and I couldn't tell what she was reading. She lowered the paper to her lap, smiled, and said, 'I believe I can get you to Japan.'

"I told her that would be wonderful. We stayed in that little church for two days and then set out for the coast with Mary. Dr. Zhang and I both carried a small box of those little Bibles Mary was distributing. As we travelled, we handed out the Bibles. When we arrived at the coast, there was a boat waiting for us. Our boxes were empty."

Susan tapped on the table to get my attention, and said, "You and Dr. Zhang gave away all the Bibles?"

"We sure did, Susan. Mary did the talking and Dr. Zhang and I gave out the Bibles to anyone that would listen. The boat was a small fishing vessel, about the size of some of the private boats down at the pier. It took us to Vladivostok. We went aboard a passenger plane and flew to Tokyo. When we landed, the authorities didn't like it when Dr. Zhang and I didn't have papers, but Mary had contacted our embassy and they met with us. The next day we were on a flight to Anchorage. I reported to Elmendorf Air Force Base and after officials verified my identity, Dr. Zhang and I were on our way to Seattle.

"Dr. Zhang was able to contact relatives and stayed in Seattle. I flew to Chicago and then home to Boston. But that wasn't my home anymore, it was Crafton, Maine. Now you know what happened to me during those long months. Any questions?"

I looked at all the faces, Susan, Rocky, and Sandra, but apparently they couldn't think of what to ask. I'm sure the questions will come in the following days.

I said, "What time is it?"

Rocky slid off his chair and looked at the clock in the living room. "It's seventeen minutes after nine, Dad."

"Thanks, Rocky, but I was thinking of another time."

"You mean Military, Chinese, or Russian?"

"I know! I know!" Susan was grinning and shoving her chair against the table. "It's bedtime!"